P9-ELR-250

Goosebumps®

THE CAMPFIRE COLLECTION

THE CAMPFIRE COLLECTION

THE CURSE OF CAMP COLD LAKE

GHOST CAMP

WELCOME TO CAMP NIGHTMARE

R. L. STINE

SCHOLASTIC INC.

New York   Toronto   London   Auckland   Sydney
Mexico City   New Delhi   Hong Kong   Buenos Aires

The *Goosebumps* book series created by Parachute Press, Inc.

No part of this publication may be reproduced in whole or in part,
or stored in a retrieval system, or transmitted in any form or by any means,
electronic, mechanical, photocopying, recording, or otherwise, without
written permission of the publisher. For information regarding permission,
write to Scholastic Inc., Attention: Permissions Department,
557 Broadway, New York, NY 10012.

The Curse of Camp Cold Lake, ISBN 0-590-56893-0
Copyright © 1997 by Scholastic Inc.

Ghost Camp, ISBN 0-590-56882-5
Copyright © 1996 by Scholastic Inc.

Welcome to Camp Nightmare, ISBN 0-590-46619-4
Copyright © 1993 by Scholastic Inc.

Campfire Collection, ISBN 0-7607-4719-9
First Compilation copyright © 2003 by Scholastic Inc.

All rights reserved. Published by Scholastic Inc.
SCHOLASTIC, GOOSEBUMPS, and associated logos are trademarks
and/or registered trademarks of Scholastic Inc.

12 11 10 9 8 7 6 5 4 3 2   4 5 6 7 8/0

Printed in the U.S.A.

First Compilation printing, September 2003

THE CAMPFIRE COLLECTION

Contents

Goosebumps®

THE CURSE OF CAMP COLD LAKE

I got off to a bad start at Camp Cold Lake.

I was nervous when I arrived. And I guess I did some dumb things.

Well, I didn't *want* to go to a water sports camp.

I don't like to be outdoors. I *hate* the feeling of grass brushing against my ankles. I don't even like to touch trees. And I certainly don't like getting wet.

Sure, I like to go swimming once in a while. But not *every day*! What's the point of that?

I like to swim in a nice, clean pool. I took one look at the lake here — and I was *sick*. I knew there had to be horrible *things* swimming around in that water.

Ugly creatures, waiting below the surface. Thinking to themselves: "Sarah Maas, we're waiting for you. Sarah, we're going to rub our slimy bodies on your legs when you swim. And we're going to chew off your toes, one by one."

Yuck. Why do I have to swim in *slime*?

Of course, Aaron was so excited, he nearly exploded.

When we climbed off the camp bus, he was jumping up and down and talking a mile a minute. He was so crazed. I thought he was going to burst out of his clothes and go running into the lake!

My brother likes camp. He likes sports and the outdoors. He likes just about everything and everyone.

And everyone always likes Aaron. He's so enthusiastic. He's so much *fun*.

Hey — I like to have fun too. But how can you have fun when there are no malls, no movie theaters, no restaurants to get a slice of pizza or a bag of french fries?

How can you have fun up to your neck in a freezing cold lake every day? In a camp miles from any town? Surrounded on all sides by thick woods?

"This is going to be awesome!" Aaron declared. Dragging his duffel bag, he hurried off to find his cabin.

"Yeah. Awesome," I muttered glumly. The bright sun was already making me sweat.

Do I like to sweat? Of course not.

So why did I come to Camp Cold Lake? I can answer that in three words: Mom and Dad.

They said that a water sports camp would give me confidence. They said it would help make me more comfortable with the outdoors.

2

And they said it would give me a chance to make new friends.

Okay, I admit it. I don't make friends easily. I'm not like Aaron. I can't just walk up to someone and start talking and kidding around.

I'm a little shy. Maybe it's because I'm so much taller than everyone else. I'm a whole head taller than Aaron. And he's only a year younger than I am. He's eleven.

I'm tall and very skinny. Sometimes Dad calls me "Grasshopper."

Guess how much I like that.

About as much as I like swimming in a cold lake filled with hidden creatures.

"Be a good sport about it, Sarah," Mom said.

I rolled my eyes.

"Give camp a chance," Dad added. "You might surprise yourself and have a good time."

I rolled my eyes again.

"When you come home at the end of summer, you'll probably beg us to take you camping!" Dad joked.

I wanted to roll my eyes again — but they were getting tired from all that rolling.

I gave my parents a glum sigh. Quick hugs. Then I followed Aaron onto the camp bus.

He grinned the whole way to camp. He was really excited about learning how to water-ski. And he kept asking everyone if the camp had a high diving board over the lake.

Aaron made three or four good friends on the bus ride to camp.

I stared out the window, watching the endless blur of trees and farms. Thinking about my lucky friends who got to stay home and hang out at the mall.

Then here we were at Camp Cold Lake. Kids pulling their bags off the bus. Laughing and joking. Counselors in dark green T-shirts greeting everyone, pointing them in the right direction.

I began to cheer up a little bit.

Maybe I *will* make some new friends, I thought. Maybe I'll meet some kids who are a lot like me — and we'll have a great summer.

But then I stepped into my cabin. I saw my three bunk mates. I looked around.

And I let out a cry. "Oh, no! No way!"

2

I guess I shouldn't have freaked like that.

It made a very bad first impression.

But what was I supposed to do?

There were two bunk beds in the cabin. The three other girls had already chosen their beds. There was only one bed left — right in front of the window.

And the window had no screens.

Which meant that my bed would be *crawling* with bugs. I took one glance — and I knew I'd be swatting mosquitoes every night for the whole summer.

Besides, I can't sleep in a top bunk. I toss and turn a lot at night. If I slept on top, I'd fall on my head.

I had to sleep on the bottom. In the bed against the far wall, away from the open window.

"I — I can't do this!" I blurted out.

My three bunk mates turned to look at me. One had blond hair pulled back in a ponytail. Near her was a short, chubby girl with long brown hair. In the bottom bunk against the wall, an African-American girl with long cornrows stared across the cabin at me.

I guess they wanted to say hi and introduce themselves. But I didn't give them a chance.

"Someone has to trade beds with me!" I cried. I didn't mean to sound so shrill. But I was really upset.

Before they could answer, the cabin door swung open. A sandy-haired young guy in a dark green camp T-shirt poked his head in.

"I'm Richard," he said. "I'm the boss guy, the head dude. Everything okay in here?"

"No!" I cried.

I couldn't stop myself. I was just so nervous and unhappy. "I can't sleep in this bunk!" I told him. "I don't want to be near the window. And I need to sleep on the bottom."

I could see that the other girls were shocked by my outburst.

Richard turned to the girl who was sitting on the bottom bunk against the wall. "Briana, would you trade beds with —"

"Sarah," I told him.

"Would you trade bunks with Sarah?" Richard asked Briana.

She shook her head so hard, the beads in her cornrows rattled against each other. "I really don't want to," she said softly.

6

She pointed to the chubby girl with long brown hair, who sat on a camp trunk. "Meg and I were bunk mates last year," Briana told Richard. "And we kind of wanted to be together."

Meg nodded. She had a round, baby face. Squirrel cheeks out to here. And she wore blue and red braces on her teeth.

"I can't sleep in front of the window," I insisted. "I really can't. I hate bugs."

Richard stared hard at Briana. "How about it?"

Briana groaned. "Oh . . . all right." She made a face at me.

"Thanks," Richard said. I could see he was studying me.

He probably thinks I'm a real troublemaker, I thought.

Briana climbed off the bottom bunk. She dragged her duffel bag across the room to the bunk by the window. "It's all yours," she muttered.

She didn't say it in a friendly way.

I felt bad. My bunk mates hate me already, I thought.

Why do I always do that? Why do I always get nervous and start off on the wrong foot with people?

Now I've got to try really hard to make them my friends, I decided.

But a minute later, I did something horrible.

"Hey — thanks for trading bunks, Briana," I said. "That was really nice of you."

She nodded but didn't say anything. Meg pulled open her trunk and started shoving shorts and T-shirts into her dresser drawer.

The third girl smiled at me. "Hi. I'm Janice," she said. She had a raspy, hoarse voice. "Everyone calls me Jan."

Jan had a nice smile. She had her blond hair pulled back in a ponytail. She had dark blue eyes and red cheeks. She seemed to be blushing all the time.

"Were you here last summer?" I asked her.

She shook her head. "No. Briana and Meg were here. But this is my first summer. I went to tennis camp last year."

"I've never been to any kind of camp," I confessed. "I — I guess I'm a little nervous."

"Are you a good swimmer?" Briana asked.

I shrugged. "Pretty good, I guess. I don't swim much. I don't really like it."

Meg turned from her trunk. "You don't like to swim, and you came to a water sports camp?"

Briana and Jan laughed.

I could feel my face grow hot. I didn't want to tell them that my parents *made* me come to this camp. That just sounded too geeky. I didn't know *what* to say.

"I . . . uh . . . I like other things," I stammered.

"Oh — I *love* that swimsuit!" Briana declared. She pulled a bright yellow swimsuit from Meg's trunk and held it up in front of her. "This is excellent!"

Meg tugged it back. "Like it would really fit you!" she muttered, rolling her eyes. Her braces clicked when she talked.

Meg looked a little like a bowling ball next to tall, graceful Briana.

"Did you lose weight over the winter?" Briana asked her. "You look great. Really, Meg."

"I lost a little," Meg replied. She sighed. "But I didn't get any taller."

"I grew about a foot this year," I chimed in. "I'm the tallest girl in my school. Everyone stares at me when I walk through the halls."

"Boo hoo," Meg said sarcastically. "You've really got it tough. Would you rather be a shrimp like me?"

"Well . . . not really," I replied.

Ooops. I realized I'd said the wrong thing.

I saw a flash of hurt in Meg's eyes.

Why did I say that? I asked myself.

Why do I keep putting my foot in my mouth?

I picked up my backpack from where I had tossed it on the floor. I carried it to my bunk to unpack it.

"Hey — that's mine! Put it down!" Jan came rushing over to me.

I glanced down at the backpack. "No. It's mine," I insisted.

I started to unzip it — and it fell off the bed.

A whole bunch of things fell out and clattered across the cabin floor.

"Oh!" I cried out in surprise. The stuff *wasn't* mine.

I saw pill bottles. Medicine jars. And little plastic inhalers.

"Asthma medicine?" I cried.

Jan dropped to her knees and began gathering it all up. She glared up at me angrily. "Thanks a bunch, Sarah," she growled. "Thanks for letting the whole world know I have asthma. Why don't you stand up at the campfire tonight and announce it to the whole camp?"

"Sorry," I murmured weakly.

"I *told* you it was *my* backpack," Jan snapped.

Meg bent down and picked up an inhaler for Jan.

"Having asthma is nothing to be ashamed of," she told Jan.

"Maybe I like to keep some things to myself," Jan snapped. She shoved all the medicine into the pocket and grabbed the backpack away.

"Sorry," I said again. "Really."

All three girls glared at me. Briana shook her head. Meg *tsk-tsk*ed.

They hate me already, I thought.

I felt sick. Really sick.

They hate me, and it's only the first day. The first *hour*.

With a sigh, I slumped down on my bunk.

Can things get any worse? I wondered.

Guess the answer to that.

Later that night, we had our first campfire. It was built in a wide, flat clearing near the woods. Smooth logs were placed in a circle to be used as benches.

I dropped down on an empty log with my back to the trees. Flames from the big fire danced brightly against the gray evening sky.

The fire crackled and popped. It smelled so sweet. I took a deep breath.

Counselors tossed more sticks on the fire. Soon the flames rose up over their heads.

The night air was hot and dry. My cheeks burned from the heat tossed off by the fire.

I turned away and gazed into the woods. The dark trees shivered in a light breeze. In the gray light, I saw a squirrel dart between tall weeds.

I wondered what other animals lurked in the woods. I imagined there were bigger animals than squirrels in there. Bigger and more dangerous.

A loud *POP* from the fire made me jump.

It's creepy outside at night, I thought. Why can't they have the campfire indoors? In a fireplace or something.

I slapped a mosquito on my neck.

When I turned back to the fire, I saw Briana and Meg on another log bench. They were laughing about something. Talking to two girls I didn't know.

I saw Aaron on the other side of the flames. He was goofing with two other guys. They were wrestling around, trying to shove each other off the log.

I sighed. Aaron has already made a bunch of friends, I thought.

Everyone has made friends — but me.

Aaron saw me staring at him. He waved quickly, then turned back to his friends.

On the next log, three girls had their heads tossed back. They were loudly singing the camp song.

I listened carefully, trying to learn the words. But they had a giggling fit halfway through and didn't finish the song.

Two older girls sat down on the other end of my log. They looked about fifteen or sixteen. I turned to say hi to them. But they were busy talking.

One of them had a bag of Gummi Worms in her hand. She kept pulling them out of the bag one by one and slurping them slowly like spaghetti noodles.

Richard, the head counselor, stepped in front of the fire. He had a black baseball cap turned backwards on his head. His baggy shorts were torn and dirty from working on the fire.

He raised both hands over his head. "Are we all here?" he called out.

I could barely hear him. Everyone was still talking and laughing. Across the fire, I saw Aaron standing up, wiggling his whole body in a funny dance.

His friends were laughing their heads off. One of them slapped Aaron a high five.

"Can we get started?" Richard called out. "Can we start our welcoming campfire?"

A log cracked in the fire. Red embers shot up all around.

"Oh!" I let out a cry as a hand grabbed my shoulder.

"Who — ?" I spun around, startled. And stared up at Briana and Meg.

They leaned over me. In the darting firelight, I saw their frightened expressions.

"Sarah — run!" Briana whispered.

"Get up — quick!" Meg tugged my arm. "Run!"

"Why? What's wrong?" I sputtered.

5

I jumped shakily to my feet. "What's wrong?"

"Those boys," Meg whispered. She pointed across the fire. "They threw fireworks in the fire! It's going to explode!"

"Run!" both girls cried.

Meg gave me a shove to get me started.

I stumbled — and then lurched forward. As I ran, I shut my eyes tight, expecting the blast any second.

Could I get away in time? Were Meg and Briana escaping it too?

I stopped short when I heard the laughter.

Shrill, gleeful laughter.

"Huh?" Swallowing hard, I turned back.

And saw half the camp laughing at me.

Meg and Briana slapped each other a high five.

"No. Oh, noooo," I murmured. How could I fall for such a dumb trick?

How could they play such a mean joke on me?

15

They must have told everyone to watch. As I stood at the edge of the clearing by myself, I could feel all the eyes on me.

And I could hear kids laughing and making jokes.

I saw Jan laughing. And I saw Richard and some of the other counselors grinning and shaking their heads.

I know, I know. I should have laughed too. I should have made a joke of it.

I shouldn't have let it upset me.

But the whole day had been so terrible. I was so nervous. And so eager not to make any more mistakes.

I could feel my shoulders start to shake up and down. I could feel tears welling up in my eyes.

No! I ordered myself. You *cannot* cry! You cannot allow yourself to cry in front of the whole camp.

Sure, you feel like a total jerk, Sarah. But so what? It was just a joke. Just a dumb joke.

I felt a hand on my arm. I pulled away.

"Sarah —" Aaron stood beside me. His dark eyes were wide in the shadowy evening light.

"I'm okay," I snapped. "Go away."

"You're such a bad sport," he said softly. "Why can't you ever let things slide off you? It was just a joke. Why go nuts over a dumb joke?"

Do you know what I really hate?

I really hate it when Aaron is right.

I mean, he's my younger brother — right? What right does he have to be the sensible, calm member of the Maas family?

It really steams me when Aaron comes on like the *older* brother.

"Do I need your advice?" I snarled. "Take a hike." I gave him a shove toward the campfire.

He shrugged and hurried back to his friends.

I crept to the campfire. I didn't go to my old seat. It was too close to the fire — and too close to Briana and Meg.

I dropped down on the edge of a log near the woods, outside the glow of the fire. The darkness cooled me and helped to calm me down.

Richard had been talking for a while. I realized I hadn't heard a word he said.

He stood in front of the crackling fire. He had a deep, booming voice. But everyone leaned in to hear him better.

I gazed around the circle of campers. Their faces glowed orange in the bright firelight. Their eyes sparkled.

I wondered if anyone here would be my friend.

I knew I was feeling really sorry for myself. I wondered if any other new campers felt the way I did.

Richard's voice droned on in the back of my mind. He was saying something about the main lodge. Something about the meal schedule. Then he began talking about towels.

I started to pay attention when he introduced the head waterfront counselor. Her name was Liz.

Everyone clapped when she stood up beside Richard. One of the boys gave a loud wolf whistle.

"She's awesome!" another boy called out.

Everyone laughed.

Liz grinned too. She knew she looked really awesome. She wore tight denim cutoffs and a dark blue midriff top. She waved for everyone to get quiet.

"Are you all having a good time?" she called out.

Everyone cheered and clapped. Several boys whistled.

"Well, tomorrow will be your first day at the waterfront," Liz announced. "And before you go in the lake, there are lots of water rules we want you to know."

"Like, don't drink the water!" Richard chimed in. "Unless you're *very* thirsty!"

Some kids laughed. I didn't. The thought of drinking that disgusting, slimy water made me sick.

Liz didn't laugh, either. She frowned at Richard. "We need to take this seriously," she scolded.

"I *was* serious!" Richard joked.

Liz ignored him. "When you get back to your bunks, you will find a list of water rules on your bed," she continued, brushing back her long, frizzy red hair. "There are twenty rules on the list. And you need to know them all."

Huh? *Twenty* rules? I thought. How can there be twenty rules?

It will take all summer to learn twenty rules.

Liz held up a sheet of paper. "I'm going to go over the list with you now. If you have any questions, just call them out."

"Can we go swimming now?" a boy shouted, trying to be funny.

Lots of kids laughed.

But Liz didn't crack a smile. "That's rule number eight," she replied. "No night swimming, even if counselors are with you."

"Don't *ever* swim with counselors!" Richard joked. "They have germs!"

Richard is pretty funny, I thought. He seems like a good guy.

But Liz seems so *serious*.

The sheet of paper fluttered in the wind. She gripped it with both hands. Her red hair caught the glow of the fire.

"The most important rule at Camp Cold Lake is the Buddy System," Liz announced. "When you are in the lake, you must always have a buddy."

She glanced quickly at the campers seated around her. "Even if you are only wading in up to your ankles, you must have a swimming buddy with you," she said. "You may have a different buddy each time. Or you may choose a buddy for the whole summer. But you must *always* have a buddy."

19

She took a deep breath. "Are there any questions?"

"Will *you* be my buddy?" a boy shouted.

Everyone laughed. I laughed too. The kid's timing was perfect.

But once again, Liz didn't crack a smile. "As waterfront counselor, I will act as *everyone's* buddy," she replied seriously.

"Now, rule number two," she continued. "Never swim more than three boat lengths from one of our safety boats. Rule number three — no shouting or pretending to be in trouble in the water. No horseplay. No kidding around. Rule number four . . ."

She talked on and on, reading off all twenty rules.

I groaned. She talks to us like we're five year olds, I thought.

And there are so many water rules.

"Let me repeat one more time about the Buddy System . . . ," Liz was saying.

Gazing past the fire, I could see the dark lake. Smooth and black and silent.

The lake has tiny waves. No current. No dangerous tides.

So *why* are there so many rules? I wondered.

What are they scared of?

Liz talked for at least half an hour. Richard kept cracking jokes, trying to make her laugh. But she never even smiled.

She talked some more about every rule on the list. Then she told us to read the list carefully when we got back to our cabins.

"Have a safe summer, everyone!" she called out. "See you at the waterfront!"

Everyone cheered and whistled again as Liz stepped away from the fire. I yawned and stretched my hands over my head. That was really boring, I thought.

I've never heard of a place having so many rules.

I swatted another mosquito on my neck. I was starting to feel really itchy. That's what being outdoors does to me. It makes me itch like crazy.

The fire had died down. A blanket of purple embers glowed on the dark ground. The night air grew cool.

To end the campfire, Richard told everyone to stand and sing the camp song. "You new campers probably don't know the words," he said. "You're *lucky!*"

Everyone laughed. Then Richard began to sing, and everyone joined in.

I tried to follow along. But I couldn't catch all of the words. I picked up pieces of the song. . . .

"Wetter is better . . ."

"Get in the swim.
Show your vigor and vim . . ."

"Every son and daughter
should be in the water,
the cold, cold water
of Camp Cold Lake."

Yuck. I agreed with Richard about the words to the song. They were so lame!

Gazing across the fire, I saw Aaron singing his heart out. He seemed to know every word already.

How does he do it? I wondered, scratching my itchy legs. How does he manage to be so perfect? To fit in everywhere?

As the song ended, Richard raised his hands for quiet. "I have a few final announcements," he called out. "First of all, none of you can carry a tune! Second . . ."

I didn't hear the rest. I turned to find Briana and Meg standing beside me.

I took a step back. "What do you want?" I snapped.

"We want to apologize," Briana said.

Meg nodded. "Yeah. We're sorry we played that dumb joke on you."

Richard's voice droned on behind us. Briana put a hand on my shoulder. "We got off to a bad start," she said. "Let's start all over again. Okay, Sarah?"

"Yeah. Let's start fresh," Meg agreed.

A smile spread over my face. "Great," I said. "Excellent."

"Excellent!" Briana repeated, smiling too.

She slapped me on the back. "A fresh start!"

Richard was still making announcements. "Tomorrow at four-thirty, those interested in windsurfing . . ."

Aaron will probably try that, I thought. I watched Briana and Meg walk away.

A fresh start, I thought. I began to feel a lot happier.

The happy feeling lasted for about two seconds.

Then my back started to itch.

I turned to the fire and saw Briana and Meg staring back at me. They were both giggling.

Other kids had turned away from Richard and were watching me.

"Ohhhh." I groaned when I felt something warm wriggle against my back.

23

Something warm and dry, moving under my T-shirt.

"Ohhhh." It moved again.

I reached one hand back. And poked it under my shirt.

What is it? What did Briana put back there?

I grabbed the thing and pulled it out.

And started to scream.

7

The snake wriggled in my hand.

It looked like a long black shoelace. With eyes! And a mouth that kept snapping open and shut.

"Noooooo!" I totally lost it.

I let out a shrill scream. And I heaved the snake with all my might.

It sailed into the woods.

My back still itched like crazy. I could still feel it wriggling against my skin.

I reached back and tried to scratch with both hands.

Kids were laughing. Telling each other what Briana had done.

I didn't care. I just wanted to rub away the feeling of that snake against my skin.

My whole body tingled. I uttered an angry cry. "How *could* you?" I shrieked at Briana and Meg. "What is your *problem*?"

Aaron came hurrying over to be the grown-up again.

Just what I needed. Mr. Mature Kid Brother.

"Sarah, did it bite you?" he asked softly.

I shook my head. "I can still feel it!" I wailed. "Did you see it? It was three feet long!"

"Calm down," Aaron whispered. "Everyone is staring at you."

"Think I don't know it?" I snapped.

"Well, it was just a tiny snake," Aaron said. "Totally harmless. Try to get yourself together."

"I — I — I —" I sputtered. I was too upset, too angry to talk.

Aaron raised his eyes to Briana and Meg. "Why are those two girls picking on you?" he asked.

"I don't know!" I wailed. "Because . . . because they're *creeps*! That's why!"

"Well, try to calm down," Aaron repeated. "Look at you, Sarah. You're shaking all over."

"You'd shake too if you had a disgusting snake crawling up and down your skin!" I replied. "And I really don't need your advice, Aaron. I really don't —"

"Fine," he replied. He spun away and hurried back to his friends.

"I don't believe him," I muttered.

Dad is a doctor, and Aaron is just like him. He thinks he has to take care of everyone in the world.

Well, I can take care of myself. I don't need my little brother telling me to calm down every second.

26

Richard was still talking. But I didn't care. I stepped away from the campfire circle and started back to the cabin.

The path curved through a patch of woods, up the sloping hill where the cabins were perched. Away from the glow of the fire, I was surrounded by darkness.

I clicked on my flashlight and aimed the yellow circle of light at my feet. My sneakers crunched over dry leaves and twigs. The trees whispered above me.

How did I get off to such a bad start? I asked myself.

Why do Briana and Meg hate me so much?

Maybe they're just mean, I decided. Maybe they're total creeps. Maybe they're mean to everyone.

They think they're so hot because they were at camp last year.

Without realizing it, I had wandered off the path. "Hey —" I swung the flashlight around, searching for the way back.

The light swept over tilting trees, tall clumps of weeds, a fallen log.

Panic tightened my throat.

Where is the path? Where?

I took a few steps. My sneaker crunched over leaves.

And then my foot sank into something soft.

Quicksand!

8

No. Not quicksand.

There's no such thing as quicksand. I remembered that from some science book I read in fifth grade.

I lowered the flashlight.

"Ohhhh." Mud. Thick, gooey mud.

My sneaker sank deep into the ooze.

I pulled my leg up with a groan — and nearly toppled over backwards.

It's just mud, I told myself. It's disgusting — but it's no big deal.

But then I saw the spiders.

Dozens of them. The biggest spiders I ever saw.

There must have been a nest of them in the mud.

They were crawling over my shoe, crawling up the leg of my jeans.

"Ohhhh. Yuck!"

Dozens of spiders clung to me. I shook my

28

sneaker. Hard. Then I began batting at them with my free hand.

"I hate this caaaaaamp!" I screamed.

I beat some spiders away with the flashlight.

And then I had an idea.

I mean, why shouldn't I pay Briana and Meg back for what they did to me?

They embarrassed me in front of the whole camp. And I hardly did anything to them.

I emptied the batteries from the flashlight. I took a deep breath. Then I bent down — and scooped a bunch of spiders into the flashlight.

Yuck. I felt sick. I really did.

I mean, can you imagine — *me* handling spiders!

But I knew it would be worth it. Soon.

I filled the flashlight with the squirming, black creatures. Then I screwed on the top.

I stepped over a fallen tree trunk. Found the path. And carrying the flashlight carefully, I eagerly hurried to the cabin.

I stopped outside the door. The lights were on inside the cabin.

I peeked in through the open window. No. No sign of anyone.

I crept inside.

I pulled up the blanket on Briana's bed. Then I emptied half of the spiders onto her sheet. I carefully pulled the blanket over them and smoothed it out.

I was pouring the rest of the spiders into Meg's bed when I heard a shuffling noise behind me. Quickly, I pulled Meg's blanket back into place and spun around.

Jan stepped into the cabin. "What's up?" she asked in her hoarse, croaky voice.

"Nothing," I replied, hiding the flashlight behind my back.

Jan yawned. "It's Lights Out in ten minutes," she said.

I glanced at Briana's bunk. I'd left one corner of the blanket untucked. Briana won't notice, I decided.

I realized I was grinning. I quickly changed my expression. I didn't want Jan asking a lot of questions.

She turned and pulled a long white nightshirt from her dresser drawer. "What did you sign up for tomorrow?" she asked. "Free Swim?"

"No. Canoeing," I told her.

I wanted to be in a nice, dry canoe. Not flopping around in the dirty lake with fish and other slimy creatures.

"Hey. Me too," Jan said.

I started to ask if she would be my buddy. But Briana and Meg came strolling through the door.

They saw me — and burst out laughing.

"What was that wild dance you were doing at the campfire?" Briana teased.

"You looked as if you had a snake down your back or something!" Meg declared.

They laughed some more.

That's okay, I thought. Go ahead and laugh.

In a few minutes, when you climb under your covers, *I'll* be laughing.

I couldn't wait.

9

A few minutes later, Jan turned out the lights. I lay on the hard mattress, staring up at Meg's mattress above my head, grinning. Waiting . . .

Waiting . . .

Meg shifted her weight in the bunk above me.

I heard her gasp.

And then both Briana and Meg began to scream.

I laughed out loud. I couldn't hold it in.

"It bit me! It *bit* me!" Briana howled.

The lights flashed on.

"Help!" Meg cried. She leaped out of bed. Her bare feet hit the floor hard. It sounded like an elephant landing.

"It bit me!" Briana cried.

She and Meg were both on the floor now, dancing and wriggling. Slapping at their arms, their legs, their backs.

I bit my lip to make myself stop laughing.

"Spiders! Spiders all over!" Meg shrieked. "Ow!

It bit me too!" She pulled up the sleeve of her nightshirt. "Ow! That hurts!"

Jan stood at the light switch. I hadn't moved from my bed. I was enjoying it all too much. Watching them squirm and dance.

But Jan's words wiped the smile from my face.

"Sarah put the spiders there," she told Briana and Meg. "I saw her messing around at your bunks when I came in."

What a snitch. I guess she was still angry at me because I spilled her asthma medicine.

Well, that put an end to the fun.

I think Briana and Meg wanted to strangle me. They both had to go to the infirmary and wake up the camp nurse. They had to make sure the spider bites weren't poisonous.

How was I to know that these were the kind of spiders that bite?

It was just a joke, after all.

I tried to apologize when they came trudging back from the nurse. But they wouldn't speak to me. And neither would Jan.

Oh, well, I sighed. So they won't be my friends. I'll make other friends. . . .

The next morning in the mess hall, I ate breakfast alone. The room had two long tables that stretched from wall to wall. One for boys and one for girls.

I sat at the far end of the girls' table and spooned up my cornflakes in silence.

All the other girls were chattering away. At the other end of the table, Briana and Meg kept flashing me angry looks.

I saw Aaron at the boys' table. He and his friends were laughing and goofing on each other. Aaron balanced a pancake on his forehead. Another boy slapped it off.

At least *he's* having fun, I thought bitterly.

I had the sudden urge to go over and tell Aaron how unhappy I was. But I knew he would just tell me to lighten up.

So I sat at my lonely end of the table and choked down my cornflakes.

Did things get better when I arrived at the lake for canoeing?

Three guesses.

Kids were already pulling their canoes off the grassy shore, into the water. They all seemed to be paired up.

Liz walked over to me. Her white one-piece bathing suit glowed in the morning sunlight. She had her frizzy red hair tied behind her head.

She let a silver whistle fall from her mouth. "What's your name?" she asked, eyes on the lake.

"Sarah," I told her. "I signed up for canoeing, but —"

"You need a buddy," she said. "Find a buddy.

The canoes are over there." She pointed, then trotted away.

Canoes splashed into the water. The slap of the wooden paddles echoed around the shore.

I ran to the stack of canoes, searching for a buddy. But everyone had already chosen partners.

I was about to give up when I spotted Jan, pulling a canoe to the water. "Do you have a buddy?" I called.

She shook her head.

"Well, can I come with you?" I asked.

"I don't think so," she replied nastily. "Do you have any more spiders you want to set loose?"

"Jan, please —" I started.

"Are you two together?" Liz appeared behind us, startling us both.

"No. I —" Jan started.

"I *want* to be her buddy, but she doesn't want to," I said. I didn't mean to whine, but it came out that way.

Jan made an ugly face at me.

"Get your canoe in the water," Liz ordered. "You two are the last ones in."

Jan started to protest. Then she shrugged and sighed. "Okay, Sarah. Let's go."

We pulled on life preservers. Then I grabbed a paddle and one end of the canoe. We dragged it to the water.

The little boat bobbed against the shore. The

lake current was stronger than I thought. Low waves plopped steadily against the grassy shore.

Jan climbed in and took a seat in the front. "Thanks for embarrassing me in front of Liz," she muttered.

"I didn't mean —" I started.

"Okay. Push off," she commanded.

I tossed my paddle into the canoe. Then I leaned over and gave the boat a hard shove with both hands.

It slid smoothly away from the shore. Then I had to wade out to it and pull myself inside.

"Whoa!" As I struggled to hoist myself up, the canoe nearly tipped over.

"Watch it!" Jan snapped. "You're such a klutz, Sarah."

"Sorry," I murmured. I was so grateful to have a buddy, I didn't want any more trouble between us.

I pulled myself into the canoe and dropped down behind Jan.

The canoe bobbed up and down as we began to paddle. The rocking waters sparkled like silver under the bright morning sunshine.

It took us a while to find the right rhythm.

Neither of us spoke.

The slap of our paddles and the rush of water against the little canoe were the only sounds we made.

The lake gleamed in front of us like a giant,

round mirror. I could see several canoes up ahead. Jan and I were far behind them.

The rubber life preservers were hot and heavy. We pulled them off and dropped them to the canoe floor.

We paddled steadily, not too fast, not too slow.

I glanced back. The shore seemed miles away.

I felt a chill of fear. I'm not that strong a swimmer. I suddenly wondered if I could swim all the way to shore from out here.

"Hey!" As I stared back at the shore, the canoe suddenly started to rock.

"Whoooa!" I grabbed the sides.

I turned — and to my horror, saw Jan *standing up*!

"Jan — stop! What are you doing?" I shrieked. *"What are you doing?"*

The little boat rocked harder. I gripped the sides, struggling to steady it.

Jan took a step.

The canoe tilted. Water splashed over my feet.

"Jan — stop!" I cried again. "Sit down! What are you *doing*?"

She narrowed her eyes at me. "Bye, Sarah."

10

The boat tilted more as she raised one foot to the side. She pulled off the T-shirt she had over her swimsuit and tossed it to the canoe floor.

"No — please!" I begged. "Don't leave me out here. I'm not a good swimmer. What if the boat tips over? I don't think I can swim back from here!"

"You ruined my summer," she accused. "Now everyone knows I have asthma. So they won't let me go on the six-day canoe trip."

"But — but it was an accident —" I sputtered.

"And you're messing up everything for Briana and Meg too," Jan said angrily.

"No. Wait —" I started. "I apologized to them. I didn't mean —"

She shifted her weight.

Tilted the canoe the other way.

Then she shifted her weight again. Again.

Deliberately making the canoe rock.

Deliberately trying to frighten me.

"Don't tip it over, Jan. Please —" I pleaded.

She tilted it more. Made it rock so hard, I thought I'd tumble out.

"I'm really not a good swimmer," I repeated. "I really don't think I —"

She uttered a disgusted groan. Then she tossed back her hair. Raised her arms over her head. Bent her knees. Kicked off hard.

And dove into the lake.

"Noooo!" I let out a cry as the boat rocked violently. Jan's dive sent up a tall, foamy wave of water.

The canoe tilted . . . rocked . . .

. . . and flipped over!

I hit with a *smack*. Cold water rose up around me as I sank.

Frozen in shock.

I felt the canoe bounce above me on the surface.

Then I started to choke as water invaded my nose and mouth.

Sputtering and gagging, I thrashed my arms and legs.

Pushed myself . . . pushed . . . pushed myself to the surface.

And raised my head over the bobbing current.

Still sputtering, I sucked in a deep breath of fresh air. Then another.

Floating on the surface, I saw the canoe bobbing upside down on the water.

I struggled to catch my breath, to slow my racing heart.

Then I swam to the canoe. I grabbed on to it. Wrapped one arm around it. Held on for dear life.

Bobbing with the canoe, I squinted into the sunlight, searching for Jan.

"Jan? Jan?" I called to her.

"Jan? Where *are* you?"

I turned and searched in all directions.

A feeling of cold dread tightened my chest.

"Jan? Jan? Can you hear me?" I shouted.

11

I held on to the canoe with one hand and shielded my eyes with the other. "Jan? Jan?" I shouted her name as loudly as I could.

And then I spotted her.

I saw her blond hair glowing in the bright sunlight. And I saw her red swimsuit. Her arms moving steadily, smoothly. Her feet kicking up foamy waves.

She was making her way to shore.

She swam away and left me here, I realized.

I turned and searched for the other canoes. Squinting against the sun, I could see them far ahead of me. Too far away to hear my shouts.

Maybe I can turn the canoe over, I decided. Then I can climb in and paddle back to shore.

But where were the paddles?

I raised my eyes to the camp — and saw Jan talking to Liz. She was waving her arms frantically and pointing out to the water. Pointing to me.

A crowd of kids gathered around them. I could hear excited voices. Shouts and cries.

I saw Liz pull a canoe into the water.

She's coming to rescue me, I realized. Jan must have told her I couldn't swim all the way back.

I suddenly felt embarrassed. I knew all the kids onshore were watching me. I knew they were talking about what a wimp I must be.

But I didn't care. I just wanted to get back on dry land.

It didn't take Liz long to paddle out to me. When I pulled myself into the canoe, I started to thank her.

But she didn't let me get a word out. "Why did you do it, Sarah?" she demanded.

"Excuse me?" I gasped. "Do what?"

"Why did you tip the canoe over?" Liz asked.

I opened my mouth to protest — but only a squeak came out.

Liz frowned at me. "Jan says you deliberately tipped over the canoe. Don't you know how dangerous that is, Sarah?"

"But — but — but —!"

"I'm calling a special camp meeting because of this," Liz said. "Water safety is so important. The water safety rules must be followed at all times. Camp Cold Lake couldn't exist if campers didn't follow every rule."

"I wish it *didn't* exist," I muttered unhappily.

* * *

So Liz held a long meeting at the lodge. And everyone at camp had to be there.

She went over the rules of water safety again. Rule by rule.

And then she showed an endless slide show about the Buddy System.

I sat way on the side and stared down at the floor. But every time I raised my eyes, I saw Briana, Meg, and Jan glaring angrily at me.

Other campers kept staring at me too. I guess they all blamed me for this long, boring meeting. Jan probably told everyone in camp that I was the one who tipped over the canoe.

"I want you to memorize all twenty water safety rules," Liz was saying.

More campers stared angrily at me.

Everyone hates me, I thought, shaking my head sadly. And there is nothing I can do about it.

Then, suddenly, I had an idea.

12

"I'm going to run away," I told Aaron.

"Good-bye," he said calmly. "Good luck."

"No. Really!" I insisted. "I'm not kidding. I'm really going to run away from this camp."

"Send me a postcard," Aaron said.

I had dragged him away from the mess hall after dinner. I really needed to talk to him. I pulled him to the edge of the lake.

No one else was down here. Everyone was still at the mess hall in the lodge.

I glanced at the canoes, stacked in piles of three near the water. I pictured Jan's blond hair, her red swimsuit. I pictured her swimming away, leaving me in the middle of the lake.

And then lying to Liz. Getting me in trouble. . . .

I shook Aaron by the shoulders. "Why won't you take me seriously?" I cried through clenched teeth.

He laughed.

"You shouldn't shake a person after they've

just eaten the camp meat loaf." He let out a loud burp.

"You're so gross." I groaned.

He grinned. "It's a family tradition."

"Stop joking around. I mean it," I snapped. "I'm really unhappy, Aaron. I hate this camp. There is no phone here we can use. I can't call Mom and Dad. So I'm going to run away."

His expression changed. He saw that I was serious.

He skipped a flat stone across the water. I watched the ripples spread out, then disappear.

The lake reflected the gray evening sky. Every thing was gray. The ground, the sky, the water. Reflections of trees shimmered darkly in the gray water.

"Where are you going to run?" Aaron asked softly. I could see him quickly becoming the mature, "wiser" brother again. But I didn't care.

I had to tell him my plan. I couldn't leave camp without letting him know.

"Through the woods," I said. I pointed. "There is a town on the other side of the woods. When I get to the town, I'm going to call Mom and Dad and tell them to come get me."

"You can't!" Aaron protested.

I stuck my chin out. "Why not?"

"We're not allowed in the woods," he replied. "Richard said the woods were dangerous — remember?"

I shoved Aaron again. I was so tense, so angry, I didn't know what to do with my hands.

"I don't care what Richard said!" I bellowed. "I'm running away — remember?"

"Give the camp a chance, Sarah," Aaron urged. "We haven't even been here a whole week. Give the place a chance."

That's when I totally lost it.

"I *hate* it when you're so sensible!" I screamed.

I shoved him hard. With both hands.

His mouth flew open. He lost his balance — and toppled into the lake.

He landed on his back in the wet mud just past the shore.

"Ooof!" I heard the air shoot out of him.

"Sorry —" I started. "It was an accident, Aaron. I —"

He scrambled to his feet, pulling up greasy gunk and seaweed with him. Shaking his fists. Calling me all kinds of names.

I sighed. Now even my brother was furious at me.

What am I going to do? I asked myself. What *can* I do?

As I trudged back to the cabin, another plan began to form in my mind.

A really desperate plan.

A really *dangerous* plan.

"Tomorrow," I murmured to myself, "I'm going to show them all!"

13

I thought about my plan all the next morning. I was frightened — but I knew I had to go through with it.

Our group had Free Swim that afternoon. Of course, everyone had a buddy but me.

I dug my bare feet into the muddy shore and watched everyone pair up and head into the water. Puffy white clouds floated overhead, reflected in the nearly still water.

Tiny gnats jumped over the surface of the water. I stared at them, wondering why they didn't get wet.

"Sarah, it's swim time," Liz called. She hurried over to me. She wore a pink one-piece bathing suit under crisp white tennis shorts.

I adjusted my swimsuit top. My hands were trembling.

I really was scared by what I planned to do.

"Why aren't you swimming?" Liz demanded. She brushed a fly off my shoulder.

"I — I don't have a buddy," I stammered.

She glanced around, trying to find someone for me. But everyone was in the lake.

"Well . . ." Liz twisted her mouth fretfully. "Go ahead and swim by yourself. Stay close to the shore. And I'll keep an eye on you."

"Great. Thanks," I said. I smiled at her, then trotted enthusiastically to the edge of the water.

I didn't want her to guess that it wasn't going to be a normal swim for me. That I had something really terrible in mind. . . .

I stepped into the water.

Oooh. So cold.

A cloud rolled over the sun. The sky darkened, and the air grew colder.

My feet sank into the muddy bottom of the lake. Up ahead, I saw the gnats — hundreds of them — hopping on the water.

Yuck, I thought. Why do I have to swim with mud and gnats?

I took a deep breath and stepped out farther. When the cold water was nearly up to my waist, I lowered my body in and started to swim.

I swam a few long laps. I needed to get used to the water. And I needed to get my breathing steady.

A short distance away, Briana and some other girls were having some kind of relay race. They were laughing and cheering. Having a great time.

They won't be laughing in a few minutes, I told myself bitterly.

A tall spray of water rushed over me. I cried out.

Another wave smacked my face.

It took me a few seconds to realize that I was being splashed — by Aaron.

He rose up in front of me — and spit a stream of water into my face.

"Yuck! How can you put this water in your mouth?" I cried, totally grossed out.

He laughed and splashed away to join his buddy.

He won't be laughing in a few minutes, either, I told myself. He'll treat me differently after today.

Everyone will.

I suddenly felt guilty. I should have told Aaron what I planned to do. I didn't really want to scare him. I wanted to scare everyone else.

But I knew if I told my plan to practical, sensible Aaron, he would talk me out of it. Or go tell Liz so that she would stop me.

Well . . . no one is going to stop me, I vowed.

Have you guessed my desperate plan?

It was really quite simple.

I planned to drown myself.

Well . . . not really.

I planned to dive down to the lake bottom. Stay under. A long, long time.

And make everyone think that I had drowned.

I can hold my breath for a very long time. It's because I play the flute. I've really developed my lung power.

I can probably stay underwater for two or three minutes.

Long enough to scare everyone to death.

Everyone will panic. Even Briana, Meg, and Jan.

Everyone will feel sorry for how mean they were to me.

I'll get a new start. After my close call in the lake, everyone in camp will want to be nice to me.

Everyone will want to be my buddy.

So . . . here goes.

I took one last look at all the laughing, shouting swimmers.

Then I sucked in the biggest breath I had ever taken.

And plunged down, down to the bottom of the lake.

14

The lake was shallow for only a few feet. Then the lake bottom gave way in a steep drop.

I kicked hard, pushing myself away from the other swimmers. Then I pulled myself upright, lowering my feet.

Yes.

I dropped my hands to my sides and let myself sink.

Down, down.

I opened my eyes as I dropped to the lake bottom. I saw only green. Waves of pale light shimmered through the green.

I'm floating inside an emerald, I thought. Floating down, down in a sparkling green jewel.

I pictured the tiny emerald on the ring Mom wore every day. Her engagement ring. I thought about Mom and Dad, thought how sad they'd be if I really did drown.

We never should have sent Sarah to that water sports camp, they would say.

My feet hit the soft lake floor.

A bubble of air escaped my mouth. I pressed my lips tighter, holding the air inside.

I slowly floated up toward the surface.

I closed my eyes. I kept my whole body still to make it look as if I'd drowned.

I pictured the horror on Liz's face when she saw my body floating so still, floating under the water, my hair bobbing on the surface.

I almost laughed when I thought of Liz leaping into the lake to rescue me, having to get her crisp white tennis shorts wet.

I forced myself to remain still.

I shut my eyes even tighter. And thought about Briana, Meg, and Jan.

They'll feel so guilty. They'll never forgive themselves for the way they treated me.

After my close call, they'll see how mean they were. And they'll want to be best friends with me.

We'll all be best friends.

And we'll have a great summer together.

My chest began to feel tight. The back of my throat began to burn.

I opened my lips and let out a few more bubbles of air.

But my throat still burned, and so did my chest.

I floated facedown. I kept my legs stiff and let my arms hang loosely at my sides.

I listened for shouts of alarm.

Someone must have spotted me by now.

I listened for cries of help. For kids calling Liz.

But I heard only silence. The heavy silence you hear when you're underwater.

I let out another bubble of air.

My chest really hurt now. It felt about to explode.

I opened my eyes. Was anyone nearby? Was anyone coming to rescue me?

I saw only green.

Where is everyone? I wondered.

Liz must have spotted me by now. Why isn't she pulling me up out of the water?

I pictured her again in her white tennis shorts. I pictured her tanned arms and legs. I pictured her red hair.

Liz — where are you?

Liz — don't you see me drowning here? You said you'd keep an eye on me, remember?

I can't stay under much longer.

My chest is ready to explode. My whole body is tingling. Burning. My head feels about to pop open.

Can't anyone see me here?

A wave of dizziness swept over me.

I shut my eyes, but the dizziness didn't go away.

I pushed out the rest of the air in my lungs.

No air, I thought. No air left. . . .

My arms and legs ached.

My chest burned.

With my eyes closed, I saw bright yellow spots.

Dancing yellow lights. They grew brighter . . . brighter. They did a fast, furious dance all around me.

Around my burning, tingling body.

My chest . . . exploding . . . exploding . . .

I'm so cold, I realized. Suddenly, I feel so cold.

The dancing, darting yellow lights grew brighter. Bright as spotlights. Bright as flashbulbs, flashing in my eyes.

Flashing around my still, cold body.

I shuddered from the cold.

Shuddered again.

Cold, thick water filled my mouth.

I've stayed under too long, I realized.

No one is coming. No one is coming to save me.

Too long . . . too long.

I struggled to see. But the lights were too bright.

Can't see. Can't see.

I swallowed another mouthful of water.

Can't see. Can't breathe.

I can't stay under any longer. I can't wait any longer.

I struggled to raise my head out of the water. But it felt so heavy. It weighed a ton.

Can't stay down . . .

Can't breathe.

With a burst of strength, I moved my shoulders. Pulled them up.

Hoisted up my head.

So heavy ... so heavy. My hair filled with water. My hair so heavy. The water running down my face.

Over my eyes.

I turned to shore. Squinted through the bright, darting lights.

Squinted hard through the water running down my face.

Squinted ...

No one there.

I turned again. My eyes searched the water.

No one there. No one swimming. No one on the shore.

Where is everyone? I wondered. Shivering. Shuddering.

Where did everyone go?

15

I struggled to shore.

My feet were numb. I couldn't feel the muddy bottom as I staggered out of the water.

I rubbed my arms. I couldn't feel the touch of my hands. Couldn't feel the water pouring off me, running down my back.

Couldn't feel anything. Numb. Numb all over.

"Where is everyone?" I called.

But did I make a sound? Did I have a voice?

I couldn't hear myself.

I stepped onto the grass and shook myself. Like a dog trying to get dry.

Trying to shake some feeling into my cold, numb body.

"Where did you all go?"

Hugging myself, I stumbled forward. I stopped when I saw the canoes. All tacked upside down by the shore and tied up.

Weren't kids canoeing today? Weren't the canoes all out in the lake?

"Hey!" I shouted.

But why couldn't I hear my shout?

"Where *is* everyone?"

No one on the shore.

I spun around, nearly losing my balance. No one in the water.

No one. No one anywhere.

I stumbled past the life preservers and rubber rafts. Covered with a canvas tarp.

Isn't anyone going to use them? I wondered. Why are they covered up?

Why did everyone leave the lake so quickly?

Shivering, hugging myself, I made my way toward the lodge. I gasped when I noticed the trees.

Bare. All winter bare.

"Noooooooo!" a frightened wail escaped my throat. A silent wail.

Could anyone hear me?

When had the leaves fallen? Why had they fallen in the middle of summer?

I started to trot along the path to the lodge. Cold. So cold.

Something stung my shoulder. Something tingled my eyelids.

Snow?

Yes. Tiny white flakes drifted down, blown by a steady breeze. The bare trees rattled and creaked.

I brushed snowflakes from my wet hair.

Snow?

But I knew that was impossible.

All impossible.

"Heeeeeeey!" My shout echoed through the trees. Or did it?

Could anyone hear my frightened call?

"Helllllllllllp!" I shouted. "Somebody helllllllp me!"

Silence, except for the creaking tree limbs overhead.

I started to run again. My bare feet moved silently over the cold ground.

The cabins came into view as I made my way out of the trees. Their flat roofs were covered by a thin layer of snow.

The ground was as gray as the sky. The cabins were all dark, the shingled walls gray. Gray all around me.

A cold world of gray.

I pushed open the door of the first cabin I came to. "Hey — I need help!" I cried.

I stared into the empty room.

No one there. No camp trunks. No clothes scattered about.

I raised my eyes to the bunk beds against the wall. The blankets, the sheets — the mattresses — had all been taken away.

I guess this cabin isn't being used, I thought.

I backed out of the door. Turned and ran down the row of cabins. All dark and silent.

My cabin stood where the path curved up the

hill. With a sigh of relief, I ran up to it and pushed open the door.

"Briana? Meg?"

Empty. And dark.

The mattresses gone. The posters pulled down. No clothes. No bags or trunks.

No sign that anyone had ever lived in here.

"Where *are* you?" I shrieked.

And then, "Where am *I*?"

Where was my stuff? Where was my bed?

Uttering another terrified wail, I lurched out of the cabin.

Cold. So cold and numb. Running through the cold in my wet bathing suit.

I tore through the camp. Pulling open doors. Peering into bare, empty rooms. Calling. Calling for someone — anyone — to help me.

Into the main lodge. My cries echoing off the high, wooden rafters.

Or did they? Was I really making a sound?

Why couldn't I hear myself?

I burst into the mess hall. The long, wooden benches had been stacked on top of the tables. The kitchen stood dark and empty.

What has happened? I wondered, unable to stop my trembling.

Where did everyone go? Why did they all leave? How did they leave so quickly? How can it be snowing?

I stumbled back out into the gray cold. Wisps of gray fog floated low over the gray ground. I hugged my frozen body, trying to warm myself.

Terrified and confused, I wandered from building to building. I felt as if I were swimming again. Swimming in the thick gray mists. Swimming through endless layers of gray.

And then I stopped when I heard a voice.

A tiny voice. A girl's voice.

Singing.

She was singing in a high, frail voice.

"I'm not alone!" I cried.

I listened to her song. A sad song sung so softly.

And then I called out to her, "Where are you? I can't see you! Where are you?"

16

I followed the tiny voice to the lodge. I saw a girl perched on the wooden steps.

"Hey!" I called. "Hey! I was looking for someone! Can you help me?"

She kept singing, as if she didn't see me. As I walked closer, I realized she was singing the Camp Cold Lake song in her tiny, light voice.

She had long curls of white-blond hair that flowed down the sides of her face. A pretty face, delicate and pale. So incredibly pale.

She wore a sleeveless white T-shirt and white short shorts. Snowflakes fell all around us. I shivered. But she didn't seem to notice the cold.

She tilted her head from side to side as she sang. Her round blue eyes stared out at the sky. They reminded me of shiny blue marbles in her pale, pale face.

I stepped up in front of her. I brushed snowflakes from my forehead.

She didn't turn to me until her song was finished. Then she smiled. "Hi, Sarah." Her speaking voice was as soft as her singing.

"How — how do you know my name?" I stammered.

Her smile grew wider. "I've been waiting for you," she replied. "My name is Della."

"Della — I'm so cold," I blurted out.

She rose to her feet. Turned. And pulled something out from behind the steps.

A white bathrobe.

She held it up and slipped it around my trembling shoulders.

Her hands were so light. I could barely feel them.

She helped me tie the belt. Then she stepped back and smiled at me again. "I've been waiting for you, Sarah," she said. Her voice was a sigh, a whisper.

"Excuse me?" I cried. "Waiting —?"

She nodded. Her white-blond hair fluttered with every move of her head. "I can't leave without you, Sarah. I need a buddy."

I stared at her, trying to understand.

"Where *is* everyone?" I cried. "Where did everyone go? Why are you the only one here?" I brushed snowflakes from my eyebrows. "Della, how did it get to be winter?"

"You'll be my buddy — won't you, Sarah?" Her blue eyes burned into mine. Her hair glowed around her pale face.

I blinked. "I don't understand —" I started. "Please answer my questions."

"You'll be my buddy, won't you?" she repeated, pleading with those amazing eyes. "I've waited so long for a buddy, Sarah. So long."

"But, Della —"

She started to sing again.

I shoved my hands into the pockets of the robe. I shivered. I couldn't get warm. I couldn't stop shaking.

Why was she singing the Camp Cold Lake song so sadly?

Why wouldn't she answer my questions?

How did she know my name? And why did she say she'd been waiting for me?

"Della, please —" I begged.

Singing her strange, sad song, she floated up the wooden stairs to the lodge. Her hair shimmered, golden in the gray light. Swirls of fog curled around her as she moved.

"Oh!" I cried out when I realized I could see right through her.

"Della —?"

She floated over the stairs, tilting her head from side to side, singing in that breathy whisper of a voice.

"Della —?"

She stopped singing and smiled at me again. Snowflakes covered her blond hair. The fog still swirled around her.

I could see the dark shingles of the lodge through her body. I stared right through her.

"Sarah, you're my buddy now," she whispered. "I need a buddy. Everyone at Camp Cold Lake needs a buddy."

"But — but *you're dead!*" I blurted out.

Della is dead, I realized.

And I'm her buddy.

That means . . .

That means *that I'm dead too!*

17

Della floated over me. So light and pale. The wind fluttered her hair. It rose around her like a shimmering halo.

"You're dead," I murmured. "And I am too."

Saying the words sent a cold shudder down my body.

I began to realize the truth. I began to see what had happened.

Della had probably drowned here. Drowned in the lake.

That is why everyone at the camp is so crazy about water safety.

That explains the endless water safety lectures. And the long list of rules. And why the counselors insist on the Buddy System at all times.

Della drowned here.

And now I'm her buddy.

I'm her buddy — because I drowned too.

"Noooooooooo!" A long wail of horror, of disbelief, escaped my throat.

I threw my head back and wailed like an animal. Wailed out my sorrow.

Della floated over me, watching me. Waiting for me to stop. She knew what I was thinking. She knew I had figured everything out.

She waited patiently. How long had she been waiting there for me? Waiting for a buddy? Another *dead* buddy?

How long had she been waiting for another unlucky girl to drown?

"Noooo!" I moaned. "No, I won't do it, Della! I can't do it! I won't be your buddy! I won't!"

I spun around. So dizzy, I nearly dropped to my knees.

I started to run. The white robe flew open. It flapped beside me like wings as I ran away from her.

Ran barefoot over the snowy ground.

Ran through the swirls of fog. Through the gray.

"Come back, Sarah!" I heard Della call to me. "Come back! You have to be my buddy! I'm trapped here. Trapped as a ghost. I can't leave this camp — I can't get to the other world — without a buddy!"

But I didn't stop. I kept running through the camp. Past the cabins. Past the supply sheds at the edge of the woods.

I kept running from her calls. Running from her ghostly voice.

I don't want to be her buddy, I told myself. I don't want to be a *ghost*!

I blinked away snowflakes as I ran. Ran through the bare, creaking trees. Ran without looking back.

I stopped when I reached the lake shore. Stopped when I felt the cold water lap over my feet.

The cold, gray water.

I struggled to catch my breath. But my chest hurt. Felt about to explode.

Gasping, I turned — and saw Della floating through the trees. Floating toward me, her eyes glowing with blue fire.

"You can't leave without me, Sarah!" she called. "You can't leave, Sarah!"

I turned away from her. Turned back to the water.

My chest. My head.

Everything hurt so much.

I couldn't breathe.

My chest was going to burst.

I sank to the mud.

As the gray faded to black.

18

Pinpricks of white light danced above me.

I thought of fireflies, darting above the grass late at night.

The tiny lights grew brighter. Round, like flashlight beams.

Brighter still.

Until I was staring into a glowing ball of gold.

I blinked.

It took me a long while to realize that I was staring up at the sun.

I turned my head away.

I suddenly felt heavy. I could feel the ground beneath me. I could feel the weight of my body on the ground.

My body. My solid body, coming back to me.

I heard a groan. Someone moved above me.

I blinked several times. And squinted up at Liz.

Her face was red. Her mouth was twisted in a hard scowl.

"Ohhh." I groaned as she pressed both hands on my chest. Raised her hands. Pressed again.

I felt water slide from my open mouth.

I choked. Felt more water pour down my chin.

"She's coming around," Liz announced. She pressed hard on my chest again. "She's alive!" Liz cried.

Behind her, I could see bare legs. Swimsuits. Campers.

Yes. The other campers.

I groaned again. Liz continued to work over me.

I'm lying on my back, I realized. I'm on the lake shore. Liz is giving me CPR.

The other campers are standing around me. Watching. Watching Liz save my life.

"I'm — ALIVE!" The word burst from my throat.

I sat up. And gazed around.

Everyone is back! I realized. It's summer again. The leaves are back on the trees. The sun is beaming down.

And everyone is back. Including me!

Liz uttered a sigh and sank back on her knees. "Sarah, are you okay?" she asked breathlessly. She mopped sweat from her forehead with the back of her hand. "Are you okay?"

"I . . . I think so," I murmured.

I had a sour taste in my mouth. I still felt a little dizzy.

Behind Liz, some campers cheered and applauded.

"We thought you were gone for a moment." Liz sighed. "You stopped breathing. What a scare!"

Two counselors helped me to my feet. I tried to shake off my dizziness. "I'm okay!" I cried. "Thank you, Liz. You — you saved my life!"

I hugged Liz. Then I turned and hugged Aaron.

Briana and Meg were standing nearby. I startled them by hugging them too.

I was so happy to be alive! So happy to be away from that gray, gray winter. Away from that frightening ghost girl in the empty camp.

"Sarah — what happened?" Liz asked, placing a hand on my still-wet shoulder. She gently brushed back my hair.

"I'm not sure," I told her. "I'm really not sure."

Liz shuddered. "When you stopped breathing, I . . . I got so scared."

"I'm fine now," I told her with a smile. "Thanks to you."

"She did it for attention," I heard someone mutter.

I turned — and saw Jan whispering to another girl. "Now everyone has to say 'Poor Sarah,'" Jan whispered nastily. "Now everyone has to be nice to her."

I felt hurt. I opened my mouth to say something to Jan.

But I was so happy to be back, so happy to be *alive*, I just ignored it.

I rested a hand on Aaron's shoulder and let him walk me back to my cabin. "I'm going to enjoy the rest of camp," I told my brother. "I really am."

The nurse checked me out carefully. Then I rested all afternoon. I took a long nap.

When I woke up, I was starving. I realized I hadn't eaten all day.

I pulled on jeans and a camp sweatshirt and hurried to the campfire. As I trotted down the path toward the clearing by the woods, the aroma of hot dogs and hamburgers on the barbecue drifted out to me.

Richard greeted me at the campfire circle. "Sarah, you look great!" he exclaimed. "I heard about . . . what happened at the lake this after-noon."

"Well, I'm fine now," I told him. "I feel great."

"Hey — no more close calls," he scolded. "Or else you have to swim in the kiddie pool."

"I'll be careful," I promised.

"You'd better — because we don't *have* a kiddie pool!" he joked.

I laughed.

"Take a seat," he said, pointing to the circle of logs. "Take a seat, everyone!" he called out. "We're going to have a meeting before we eat!"

Most of the campers had already taken their places. I glanced around the circle quickly, searching for a place to sit.

"Sarah —?" A voice called to me.

"Sarah — over here."

I let out a shocked cry when I saw Della.

Della. By herself on a log back near the woods. Her blond hair shimmering around her pale face. The pink evening sunlight shining through her body.

Shining right through her.

"Noooo!" I moaned.

"Come over here, Sarah!" Della called. "Please — sit over here with me. Be my buddy!"

19

I raised my hands to my cheeks and let out a shrill scream.

"No! You're not here!" I wailed. "You're a ghost! You don't belong here! I'm alive now! I'm alive!"

I turned and saw Richard and Liz hurrying toward me.

Across the circle, Aaron jumped up and came running over. "Sarah — what's wrong? What *is* it?" he cried.

"Don't you see her?" I shrieked. I pointed to the log near the woods. "She's a ghost! But I'm alive!"

Liz wrapped her arms around me. "It's okay, Sarah," she whispered. "You're okay now."

"But — but she's *sitting* there!" I sputtered.

Everyone turned to the log.

"There's no one there," Richard said. He narrowed his eyes at me.

"You had a terrible shock," Liz said softly. "A

terrible shock. You're still not quite yourself, Sarah."

"But — but —" I stammered.

I saw Briana, Meg, and Jan huddled together, talking softly. Watching me.

What are they saying about me? I wondered.

"Do you want me to walk you back to your cabin?" Richard asked.

I shook my head. "No. I'm starving!"

Liz laughed. "Maybe *that's* your problem. You're so hungry, you're seeing things! Let's get you a hot dog — fast."

After a couple of hot dogs, I started to feel better. The campfire meeting began. I sat next to some girls from a different cabin.

As Richard talked, I gazed around the circle. Stared at the campers' faces, orange from the flickering campfire. Searching for Della.

Della the ghost . . .

Was she still here? Still watching me? Still waiting for me to be her buddy?

I sat forward tensely. My whole body stiff. My eyes straining to see her pale, pale face.

But she had vanished.

For now.

Liz took over the meeting. Most campers groaned when she started another lecture on water safety.

"We had a close call today," Liz said. "A frightening close call."

I knew everyone was staring at me. I could feel my face growing hot. I gazed into the yellow flames of the campfire.

When I raised my eyes, I saw Briana, Meg, and Jan on the next log, whispering together. About me?

"Our water safety rules are so important here at Camp Cold Lake," Liz was saying. "Some campers joke that having so many rules is the *curse* of Camp Cold Lake, because we talk about the rules so much."

She pressed her hands against her sides. Her eyes moved from camper to camper. "But as we saw this afternoon," she continued, "the Buddy System isn't a curse — it's a blessing."

A face rose up behind the darting flames of the fire.

I gasped.

Della!

No. A girl from another cabin, climbing up to get more food.

I sank back.

I have to get *away* from this camp, I decided. I can't have a good time here. Not if I always have to keep an eye out for Della.

Liz rattled on about the water rules.

Richard made a few announcements.

Everyone sang some camp songs.

When the campfire ended, I jumped up quickly and started along the path to my cabin. I had gone only a few steps when I heard fast footsteps behind me. And heard someone calling my name.

Was it the ghost?

I turned to see Aaron jogging up to me. "What was that screaming about?" he demanded. "Did you *really* think you saw a ghost?"

"Why should I tell you?" I snapped. I continued along the path, walking rapidly. "You'll only laugh at me."

"Try me," he replied, running to catch up. "I won't laugh. I promise."

"I saw a ghost girl," I told him. "I swear I did. She called to me. She wants me to be her buddy."

Aaron laughed. "No. Really," he said. "What did you *really* see? Be serious."

"I *am* serious!" I cried. "I have to get away from here, Aaron. I'm going to run away. Get to a phone. Call Mom and Dad. Tonight. I'm going to tell them to come get me."

"You can't!" Aaron replied. He grabbed my arm and forced me to stop walking. I could see kids staring at us as they walked past.

"Mom and Dad won't want to make more than one trip up here. So if you call them, they'll make *me* come home too," Aaron protested. "And I don't want to leave. I'm having a great time!"

"You don't understand," I told him. "I can't stay here. I can't —"

"Please, Sarah," he begged. "Try to stick it out. Give it a little more time. You're just a little messed up because of the lake this afternoon. But you'll be okay. Give it some time."

I didn't say yes, and I didn't say no.

I just told Aaron good-night and headed to my cabin.

I stopped outside the door. All the lights were on. I heard Briana, Meg, and Jan talking softly.

They stopped talking as soon as I stepped inside.

All three of them stared hard at me. Their expressions were tense. They moved quickly.

Moved toward me as I started across the room.

They formed a circle around me. Surrounded me.

"What *is* it?" I cried. "What are you going to do?"

20

"We want to apologize," Briana said.

"We've been kind of rough on you," Jan added in her scratchy voice. "We're really sorry."

"We've been talking about it," Briana said. "We —"

"We decided we've been really unfair," Meg interrupted. "We're sorry, Sarah."

"I — I'm sorry too," I stammered. I was so stunned by their apologies, I could barely speak.

"Let's start all over," Briana suggested. She grabbed my hand. "Nice to meet you, Sarah. My name is Briana."

"Excellent. A fresh start!" Jan declared.

"Thanks. I'm really glad," I told them. And I meant it.

Jan turned to Briana. "When did you do that to your nails?"

Briana grinned and raised both hands. Her fingernails were a shiny, bright purple. "It's a new color," she said. "I did it after our swim."

"What color is it?" Meg asked.

"Grape Juice, I think," Briana replied. "They all have such crazy names." She dug the bottle of nail polish from her pack and held it out to me. "Want to try it?"

"Well . . . *sure*," I replied.

All four of us stayed up far past Lights Out, making our fingernails purple.

Later, I lay in my bunk, drifting off to sleep. I had a smile on my face, thinking about my three bunk mates. My three *friends*.

They had really cheered me up.

But my smile faded when I heard a whispered voice float across the dark cabin. "Sarah . . . Sarah . . ."

I gasped.

And then the frail voice — soft as the wind — was so close . . . so close to my ear.

"Sarah. I thought you were my buddy, Sarah. Why did you leave me?"

"No — please —" I begged.

"Sarah, I waited so long for you," the ghostly voice whispered. "Come with me. Come with me, Sarah. . . ."

And then an icy hand gripped my shoulder.

21

"Ohhhhh!"

I bolted up in the bunk. And stared out at Briana's dark eyes.

She let go of my shoulder. "Sarah," she whispered. "You were whimpering in your sleep."

"Huh? What?" My voice quivered. My heart pounded. I realized I was drenched in sweat.

"You were whimpering in your sleep," Briana repeated. "Crying and moaning. I thought I'd better wake you."

"Uh . . . thanks," I choked out. "Must have been a bad dream, I guess."

Briana nodded and crept back to her bunk.

I didn't move. I sat there trembling, staring out across the dark cabin.

A bad dream?

I didn't think so. . . .

"You can skip the long-distance swim today if you want," Liz told me at breakfast the next morning. She leaned over my chair as I downed my cornflakes. I could smell the toothpaste on her breath.

"Well . . ." I hesitated. "How long is the swim?"

"We're swimming halfway across the lake," Liz replied. "Halfway out, then back. I'll be in a boat at the halfway point. It isn't really that far. But if you feel like skipping it today . . ."

I set down my spoon. I could see Meg and Briana watching me from across the table. Beside me, Jan was struggling to choke down a half-toasted, frozen waffle.

"Come on. Swim with us," Briana urged.

"I'll be your buddy," Jan said. "I'll swim with you, Sarah."

Our frightening canoe adventure flashed into my mind. Once again, I pictured that horrible moment when Jan jumped from the canoe. Tipping it over. Leaving me there.

But things were different now.

We were friends. All four of us were friends now. I had to forget about what happened with the canoe. I had to forget about our bad start.

"Okay," I agreed. "Thanks, Jan. I'll be your buddy." I turned back to Liz. "I'm ready to swim."

The morning sun still floated low in the sky. It kept fading behind broad, gray clouds. And each time the sun disappeared, the air became as cold as the water.

The lake was so cold in the early morning!

As I waded in, I suddenly realized why it was named "Cold Lake."

We all stepped carefully into the water, shivering and complaining. The water lapped over my ankles, stinging them. I stopped with a gasp and waited to get used to the cold.

I raised my eyes at the sound of a motorboat and saw Liz chugging to her place in the middle of the lake. When she reached the spot, she cut the engine. Then she picked up an electric megaphone.

"Warm up first, everyone!" she instructed us.

We all laughed. "Warm up? How are we supposed to warm up? It's freezing!"

Two girls near the shore began splashing each other.

"Stop it! Whoooa! It's *collld!*" one of them shrieked.

Taking another few steps over the soft lake bottom, I adjusted the top of my blue swimsuit. "We need wet suits," I told Jan.

She nodded, then waded out until the water lapped at her waist. "Come on, Sarah. Stick together." She motioned for me to follow.

I took a deep breath — and plunged into the water.

A shock of cold swept over my body. But I dove under the water and swam out a few strokes. Then I raised my head and turned back to Jan.

"Show off," she muttered. She dipped her hands in the water, still struggling to get used to the cold.

I laughed. "It's refreshing!" I exclaimed, brushing my wet hair back. "Come on — just push off. It isn't that bad."

Jan lowered herself into the water. Most of the swimmers were in the water now, moving in circles, floating on their backs, treading water.

"Line up, everyone!" Liz instructed from her boat. Her voice through the megaphone echoed off the trees behind us. "Line up. Two at a time. Let's go!"

It took a while for everyone to get in place. Jan and I were second in line.

I watched the first two girls begin to swim. One of them moved with smooth, steady strokes. The other one splashed and thrashed.

Everyone cheered them on.

Jan and I gave them about a two-minute head start. Then we began to swim.

I tried to copy the first girl's rhythmic stroke. I didn't want to look like a klutz. I knew all the other swimmers were watching. But let's get real. I'm not exactly headed for the Olympics.

Jan pulled ahead easily. As we swam, she kept turning back to make sure I was keeping up with her.

The turnaround spot was just past Liz's motorboat. I kept my eyes on it as I followed Jan through the water. It seemed *very* far away!

Jan picked up speed. My arms started aching about halfway to the boat.

I'm in bad shape, I told myself. I've really got to start working out or something.

Liz's boat bobbed gently up ahead of us. Liz was shouting something into the megaphone. But the splash of the water kept me from making out the words.

Up ahead of me, Jan picked up the pace.

"Hey — slow down!" I called. But there was no way she could hear me.

Ignoring the aching in my arms, I struggled to catch up to her. I kicked my legs harder, splashing up water behind me.

The sun dipped once again behind a high cloud. The sky darkened, and the water seemed to chill.

Liz's boat rocked in the water, just up ahead. I kept my eyes on Jan. Watched her steady kicks. Her hair bobbing on the lake surface like some kind of sea creature.

When Jan turns back, I'll turn back, I decided.

I swam a little faster. *Let's turn*, I pleaded silently. Jan, we're here. We're even with Liz's motorboat. I'm ready to turn back now.

But to my surprise, Jan kept stroking, kept swimming straight ahead. Her head ducked under the water. Her arms moved easily, gracefully, pulling her farther ahead of me.

"Jan —?"

My arms ached. My chest started to burn.

84

"Hey, Jan — can we turn now?"

She swam steadily ahead.

With a burst of energy, I pulled myself forward. "Jan, wait —" I called. "We're supposed to head back!"

She stopped stroking.

Did she hear me?

Breathing hard, my chest burning, I swam up to her.

She turned to face me.

"Jan —?" I gasped.

No. Not Jan.

It wasn't Jan. *It was Della!*

Her blue eyes sparkled as a gleeful smile spread over her pale, pale face.

"Keep swimming, Sarah," she whispered. "We're going to swim farther. And farther. You're my buddy now."

22

She grabbed my arm.

I tried to tug away. My wet arm slid in her grasp.

But her grip tightened around my wrist. And she held on. Pulling me. Pulling me with her.

"Owww!"

She was strong. So strong for such a frail-looking girl.

Such a frail-looking *ghost* . . .

"Let go!" I shrieked.

I struggled, slapping the water. Kicking. Squirming and twisting.

"Della — I won't come with you!"

I jerked my body around, spun hard — and broke free.

And dropped beneath the surface. Lifting both arms, I rose up, coughing and sputtering.

Where was she?

Where?

Was she right behind me? Ready to pull me with her, pull me out so far I couldn't swim back?

I spun away. The water rocked and tilted.

The clouds overhead appeared to roar past.

"Sarah . . . Sarah . . .?" Was she calling to me?

Why couldn't I see her now?

I turned again. My eyes stopped on the boat.

Yes. The boat.

Ignoring my racing heartbeats, my aching arms, I plunged forward.

The boat . . . got to reach the boat before she grabs me again.

Swimming furiously, kicking with my last bit of strength, I dove for the boat. Stretching my arms out . . . stretching . . .

And grabbed the side with both hands. Choking and gasping.

Grabbed the side of the boat and tried to pull myself in.

"Liz — help me." The words escaped my throat in a hoarse whisper.

"Liz — help me in."

The sun burst out from behind the clouds. I stared up into blinding golden light.

"Liz — please . . ."

Hands reached down for me. She bent to pull me into the motorboat.

Leaned forward. Pulling me up.

Blinking against the bright sunlight, I raised my eyes to her face.

No!

Not Liz's face. Not Liz!

Della!

Della — pulling me into the boat.

"What's wrong, Sarah?" she whispered. Pulling me. Pulling me up to her.

"Sarah, you're okay. You're perfectly okay."

23

"Let go!" I wailed.

I tore myself from her grip.

And tried to blink away the sun.

And stared up at Liz.

Not Della. Liz. Her face twisted in concern.

"Sarah, you're okay," she repeated.

"But —" I stared up at her. Waiting for her face to change again. Waiting for her to become Della again.

Had I only imagined Della's face? Had the streaming sunlight tricked my eyes?

With a sigh, I let her help me into the boat.

I slumped to my knees. The boat rocked up and down. Liz narrowed her eyes at me. "What happened out there?" she asked.

Before I could answer, I heard splashing outside the boat.

Della?

I froze.

No. Jan pulled herself up on the side. She

brushed her wet hair off her face. "Sarah — didn't you hear me calling you?" she demanded.

"Jan. I didn't see you. I thought that —" My voice caught in my throat.

"Why did you swim away from me?" Jan asked. "I'm your buddy — remember?"

Liz drove me to shore. I changed my clothes and went to see Richard. I found him in his head counselor's office, a little room about the size of a closet in the back of the main lodge.

He was resting his feet on top of his tiny desk. He twirled a toothpick in his mouth.

"Hey, Sarah — how's it going?" He flashed me a friendly smile and motioned for me to take a seat in the folding chair across from his desk.

I could see his eyes studying me.

"I hear you had another little problem in the lake," he said softly. He moved the toothpick to the other side of his mouth. "What's going on?"

I took a deep breath.

Should I tell him there is a ghost girl who has been following me everywhere? Who wants me to be her buddy?

He'd just think I'm nuts, I decided.

"You had a bad shock yesterday," Richard said. "We really thought that you drowned."

He lowered his feet and leaned over the desk toward me. "Maybe you went back in the water too soon," he said. "Too soon after the shock."

"Maybe," I murmured.

And then I blurted out the question that was really on my mind. "Richard, tell me about the girl who drowned here."

His mouth dropped open. "Huh?" The toothpick fell onto his lap.

"I know that a girl drowned in the lake," I insisted. "Can you tell me about her?"

Richard shook his head. "No girl ever drowned at Camp Cold Lake," he said. "Never."

I knew he was lying.

I had proof, after all. I had seen Della. And talked with her.

"Richard, please —" I begged. "I really need to know. Tell me about her."

He frowned. "Why don't you believe me, Sarah? I'm telling the truth. No campers have ever drowned at this camp. No boys. No girls."

I heard a soft sigh behind me.

I glanced back at the open doorway — and saw Della standing there.

I jumped to my feet. And pointed. "Richard!" I cried. "The girl who drowned! She's standing right there! Don't you see her?"

Richard raised his eyes to the doorway. "Yes," he replied softly. "I see her."

24

"Huh?" I gasped and grabbed the edge of his desk. "You see her?" I cried. "You really do?"

Richard nodded. He had a solemn expression on his face. "If it makes you feel better, Sarah, I'll say that I see her."

"But you don't *really* see her?" I demanded.

He scratched his sandy-colored hair. "No. I don't see anything."

I turned back to the doorway. Della grinned at me.

"Sit down. Please," Richard instructed. "You know, sometimes our mind plays tricks on us. Especially when we've been through a really bad scare."

I didn't sit down. I stood in front of his desk and stared hard at Della. Stared right through her.

"She's not in my mind! She's right there!" I shouted. "She's standing right there, Richard. Her name is Della. She drowned at this camp. And now she's trying to drown me too!"

"Sarah — please calm down," Richard said gently. He climbed around his desk and put a hand on my shoulder. Then he led me to the door.

I was standing face-to-face with Della.

She stuck out her tongue at me.

"See? There's no one there," Richard said.

"But — but —" I sputtered.

"Why don't you stay away from the lake for a few days," he suggested. "You know. Just hang out and relax."

Della mouthed his words as he spoke.

I turned away from her.

She giggled.

"Don't go to the lake?" I asked Richard.

He nodded. "Take a few days and rest up. You'll feel much better."

I knew I wouldn't feel better. I knew I'd still have Della following me everywhere, trying to make me her buddy.

I sighed. "That won't help," I told him.

"Then I have a different idea," he said. "Pick a sport you haven't tried, Sarah. Pick something really hard. Like water-skiing."

"I don't get it," I replied. "Why should I do that?"

"Because you will have to think so hard about what you're doing, you won't have time to worry about ghosts."

I rolled my eyes. "Yeah. Right."

"I'm *trying* to help you," he said sharply.

"Well . . . thanks," I replied. I didn't know what else to say. "I guess I'll go to lunch now."

I trudged out of the tiny office. And took a deep breath. The air was much cooler out in the main lodge.

I turned the corner and headed toward the mess hall in the front of the building. As I turned another corner, I heard Della's frail voice behind me.

"You can't get away, Sarah. You're my buddy. There's no need to run. You'll *always* be my buddy."

The soft words — so close to my ear — sent shivers down my back.

Something inside me snapped.

I couldn't hold in my fury.

"SHUT UP!" I shrieked. "SHUT UP! SHUT UP! SHUT UP — AND LEAVE ME ALONE!"

I spun around to see if she had heard me.

And gasped in horror.

25

Briana stood behind me.

Her mouth dropped open in shock. "Okay, okay. I'll go away," she said, backing up. "You don't have to be so nasty, Sarah. I was just coming to see how you were doing."

Wow. I felt so bad.

Briana thought I was talking to her.

"I — I —" I stammered.

"I thought you wanted to be friends," Briana snapped. "I didn't even say a word to you. And you bit my head off!"

"I wasn't talking to you!" I finally choked out. "I was talking to *her*!"

I pointed to Della, who leaned against the wall behind us. Della waved to me and giggled.

Sun from the open lodge window lit up Della's blond hair from behind. I could see the window right through her body.

"I was talking to her!" I repeated.

Briana raised her eyes to the window.

And the *strangest* expression spread over her face.

The next morning, I gulped down some gooey scrambled eggs for breakfast. Then I made my way to the boat dock.

Don't ask why I decided to try water-skiing.

I really don't have an answer.

I suppose I did it for Aaron. The night before, he begged me once again not to call Mom and Dad.

Aaron really didn't want to go home. He said he was having the best summer of his life.

Sure, I thought. It's *easy* for you to have a good summer. You don't have a ghost following you around.

"Please try to stay a while longer," Aaron begged.

I won't go to the lake, I decided. I'll hang around the cabin and read or something.

But in the morning, I realized that was a bad plan.

I'd be too scared to stay by myself in the cabin while everyone else was at the lake. I would have no way to protect myself against Della.

Yes, I know I wasn't thinking clearly.

I was so stressed out, I could barely think at all!

I should have stayed as far away from the water as possible.

But I really didn't want to be alone. So I followed

Richard's advice. And went to the boat dock. And told Liz I wanted to try water-skiing.

"That's great, Sarah!" Liz cried, flashing me a pleased smile. "Have you ever done it before? It's easier than it looks."

I told her I'd never tried it.

She pulled a yellow inflated life vest and a pair of skis from the equipment shed.

Then she gave me a short lesson. Showed me how to lean back and how to bend my knees.

A short while later, I was in the water waiting for the motorboat to come around. Meg was using the boat now, skiing behind it, sliding over the water. Her orange bathing suit glowed in the morning sunlight.

The hum of the boat echoed over the water. The lake bobbed and rippled in the boat's wake.

Meg let out a cry and let go of the towrope as the boat sped near the dock. She splashed into the water, then quickly pulled off her skis. Then she came walking to shore.

"My turn next," I said softly. I felt a knot in my stomach.

Meg flashed me a thumbs-up.

I struggled with the skis, but finally got them in place. Then I pulled up the towrope, gripping it tightly in both hands.

The boat motor sputtered and coughed. The boat rocked up ahead of me in the rippling blue water.

I steadied myself. Lowered myself the way Liz had shown me. And took a deep breath.

"Ready!" I called.

The motor sputtered — and then roared.

The boat pulled away so fast, the towrope nearly flew out of my hands.

"Whoooooooaaaa!" I opened my mouth in a long cry as the rope pulled me up.

Yes! The skis bounced over the surface. I bent my knees and gripped the towrope tightly.

I'm doing it! I realized. I'm water-skiing!

The boat picked up speed. We headed in a straight line over the sparkling water. The cold spray swept over my face, my hair.

I started to lose my balance. Tugged myself back up. Held on — and kept going.

"Yessss!" I cried out loud. What an awesome feeling!

But then the driver of the boat turned her head.

And I recognized Della's evil grin.

As she worked the controls, Della's white-blond hair flew up like wings around her pale face. Her blue eyes sparkled like the water.

Her grin grew wider as she saw the horror on my face.

"Turn around! Turn back! Please!" I begged.

She made the boat swerve hard.

I nearly toppled over. I gripped the towrope.

My skis slapped the surface. Pain shot up to my knees. The cold spray washed over me.

I gasped. Struggled to breathe.

Della threw back her head and laughed. The sound was drowned out by the roar of the motor.

I could see the sky through her body. The sunlight poured right through her.

"Turn around!" I screamed. "Stop! Where are you taking me? *Where?*"

26

Della didn't answer. She turned away from me, her hair flying wildly behind her head.

The boat bounced over the water, sending up tall waves of foam and spray.

The waves splashed over me. Chilling me. Blinding me.

Gripped in panic, it took me a long time to realize that I had an easy escape.

I let go of the towrope.

My hands shot up. The tow bar snapped against the water.

I skidded for a few seconds, my arms thrashing wildly. And then I toppled over and sank.

The life vest pulled me back up. I bounced on the surface, gasping, spitting out water. My heart pounded.

I felt so dizzy. The bright sunlight seemed to surround me. Which way was up? Which way to the shore?

I spun around and saw the motorboat in the distance.

"You didn't get me *this* time!" I called to Della.

But then I froze as the boat began to turn. Della swerved the boat, kicking up a tall wave of white water.

Swerved it back around. Until it pointed to me.

I gasped as I heard the motor roar.

I bobbed helplessly in the water.

The boat picked up speed, skipping over the rippling surface.

She's coming for me, I thought. She's coming to make me her buddy forever.

I'm trapped out here.

She's coming to run me over.

27

I treaded water, watching in horror as the boat sped toward me.

I've got to dive under it, I realized. The only way to escape is *down*.

I took a deep breath. Every muscle tensed. I knew I had to time my dive perfectly.

The boat roared closer. I could see Della crouched over the motor. Guiding the boat.

Aiming it.

I took another deep breath. And then I realized I couldn't dive.

The life vest — it was holding me up. No way I could plunge beneath the surface.

With a cry, I grabbed the front of the vest with both hands.

And tugged.

I can't do this! I realized. *I can't get this thing off in time!*

The water rocked harder as the boat sped nearer. The whole lake seemed to tilt and spin.

The boat — it's going to tear me to pieces! I thought.

I pulled at the vest. Pushed it.

Please — please — slide over my head!

No time. No time.

I can't dive!

The motor's roar drowned out my scream.

With a frantic tug, I pulled the life vest up. Over my shoulders.

Too late.

The front of the boat bounced over me.

Then the whirring motor blades sliced off my head.

28

I waited for the pain.

I waited for the darkness.

The water swirled around me. Blue, then green.

Choking on a mouthful of water, I thrashed up to the surface. Struggling to breathe, I let the waves rock me back and forth.

"The life vest!" I choked out.

I held half of the vest in each hand.

The motor blades had sliced the life vest in two.

I tossed the two pieces away. And started to laugh.

"I'm alive!" I cried out loud. "I'm still alive!"

I turned and saw the boat speeding across the lake. Did Della think she had won?

I didn't care. I spun around. Found the shore. And started to swim.

My close call gave me new energy. The strong, rocking current helped push me back to the camp.

I heard girls calling to me as I stumbled onto the grass. And I saw Liz jogging quickly over.

"Sarah —" she called. "Sarah — wait!"

I ignored her. I ignored them all.

I started to run.

I knew what I had to do. I had to get away from Camp Cold Lake. I had to get away as fast as I could.

I wasn't safe here. Not as long as Della wanted me for her buddy. Not as long as Della wanted me to drown too.

I knew no one would believe me. They all said they wanted to help. But no one could really help me — not against a ghost!

I burst into the cabin and tore off my wet swimsuit. Tossing it to the floor, I frantically pulled on shorts and a T-shirt.

I swept my wet hair back with both hands. Tugged on socks and my sneakers.

"Got to get away. Got to get away," I chanted to myself.

What to do? Where to go?

I'll run through the woods to the town on the other side, I decided. I'll call Mom and Dad. I'll tell them I'm hiding in town. I'll tell them to pick me up there.

I stopped at the cabin doorway.

Should I tell Aaron?

No. No way, I decided.

He'll only try to stop me.

I'll get a message to Aaron from town, I decided. I'll tell him where I am. But not until I'm safe. Not until I'm far away from this place.

I poked my head out of the cabin and searched around, making sure the coast was clear. Then I stepped outside and made my way around to the back.

And ran into Briana.

She narrowed her eyes at me, studying my face. "You're going?" she asked quietly.

I nodded. "Yes. I'm going."

Once again, Briana's expression changed. The light in her eyes seemed to fade.

"Good luck," she whispered.

29

Why is *she* acting so weird? I wondered.

I didn't have time to think about it. I gave Briana a wave. Then I ran past her and headed into the woods.

I glanced back as I followed a path between the trees. And saw Briana still standing there behind the cabin. Watching me.

Taking a deep breath, I turned and hurried along the path.

The trees overhead cut off a lot of the sunlight. It grew darker and cooler as I ran.

A hedge of sharp burrs and brambles scraped my bare arms and legs as I tried to edge past. I wished I had worn jeans and a sweatshirt. Something that covered me better.

My sneakers slipped over a thick blanket of dead leaves. I had to skip over fallen tree limbs and clumps of thorny weeds.

Tree roots rose up over the path. Tall, dry reeds leaned over me, as if reaching to grab me.

The narrow path divided in two. I paused — breathing hard — trying to decide which path to take.

Would they both lead me to town?

I held my breath when I heard a voice. Singing. A bird?

No. A soft voice. A girl's voice.

"Oh, no," I moaned. Raising my eyes to the sound, I saw Della, perched on a low tree limb. She tilted her head from side to side as she sang. Her blue eyes sparkled, gazing down at me.

"You — you followed me!" I stammered. "How did you know that I —" My voice caught in my throat.

She giggled. "You're my buddy," she replied. "We have to stick together."

"No! No way!" I screamed up at her. "You lose, Della. I'm not going to be your buddy. Because I'm never going to the lake again. I'm never going to drown like you!"

Della's smile faded. "Drown?" She shook her head. "Sarah, what made you think that? You're very confused. I didn't drown."

"Huh?" My mouth dropped open. I stared up at her in shock.

"Close your mouth, Sarah. A fly will fly into it." Della tilted back her head and laughed.

Then she shook her head again. "How could *anyone* drown at Camp Cold Lake?" she demanded. "They give a lecture about water safety every five minutes! No one ever drowned at Camp Cold Lake!"

"You didn't drown?" I cried. "Then how did you die?"

She rested her hands on the tree limb and leaned forward, peering down at me. I could see through her body, see the leaves shaking in the breeze.

"It's a simple story," Della said with a sigh. "One night I got tired of listening to the water safety lecture at the campfire. So I sneaked off into these woods."

She swept her hair back with a toss of her head. "I made one major mistake," she continued. "I didn't know the woods are filled with deadly poisonous snakes."

I gasped. "These woods? Snakes?"

Della nodded. "It's nearly impossible to cross through these woods without getting bitten," she sighed. "I died of a snakebite, Sarah."

"But — but —" I sputtered. "But you were always at the lake," I choked out. "Why did I always see you at the lake?"

"Don't you get it?" she replied. "That was my plan. I made you afraid of the lake, Sarah. I made you *terrified* of the lake. Because I knew you'd try to escape through the woods. I knew you'd run into the woods and die like me — and be my buddy."

"No —!" I protested. "I won't. I —"

"Sarah, look!" Della pointed toward the ground.

I gazed down — and watched a fat black snake curl around my leg.

30

"Buddies forever," Della sang cheerfully. "Buddies forever."

I stood frozen, gaping down in horror. Watching the fat snake wind itself around me. Feeling its warm, dry body scrape over my bare skin.

"Nooooo." A low moan escaped my throat as the snake arched its head.

"It won't hurt that much," Della said brightly. "It's like a bee sting, Sarah. That's all."

The snake let out a loud hiss. It snapped open its jaws.

I felt its body tighten like a warm rope around my leg.

"Buddies forever," Della sang. "Buddies forever . . ."

"No! Sarah is *not* your buddy!" a voice rang out.

I tried to turn toward the voice. But I couldn't move. I felt the snake tighten its hold on my leg.

"Briana!" I cried. "What are *you* doing here?"

111

She hurried out from behind a clump of tall reeds.

With one quick motion, she grabbed the snake in one hand. Slid it off my leg. And tossed it into the trees.

Briana raised her eyes to Della. "Sarah can't be your buddy, because she's *my* buddy!" Briana shouted.

Della's eyes grew wide. She cried out in surprise. She gripped the tree branch to keep from falling.

"You!" she exclaimed. "What are *you* doing here?"

"Yes, it's me!" Briana shouted up to her. "I'm back, Della."

"But — but how did you . . ." Della's voice trailed off.

"You tried to do the same thing to me last year," Briana said. "You tried all summer to make *me* your buddy. You terrified me — didn't you, Della?"

Briana uttered an angry cry. "You didn't think I'd come back. But I did. I came back to camp this summer . . . to protect the next girl!"

"Nooo!" Della wailed.

I finally understood. I stepped up to the tree beside Briana. "Briana is my buddy!" I declared. "And I'm coming back next summer to warn the *next* girl!"

112

"No! No! Nooooo!" Della raged. "You can't do that! I've waited so long! So lonnnng!"

She let go of the tree limb and shook her fists at Briana and me.

Lost her balance.

Her hands flew up as she started to fall.

She grabbed for the limb. Missed.

And dropped silently to the ground.

Then she was gone.

Vanished.

With a weary sigh, I climbed to my feet. I shook my head. "Is she gone for good?" I murmured.

Briana shrugged. "I don't know. I hope so."

I turned to Briana. "You — you saved my life!" I cried. "Thank you for following me. Thank you for saving me!"

With a happy cry, I stepped up to her. "Thank you! Thank you!"

I wrapped my arms around her to hug her.

And my hands went right through her body.

I gasped. I grabbed her shoulder. But I couldn't feel a thing.

I jumped back in shock.

Briana narrowed her eyes at me. "Della killed me last summer, Sarah," she said softly. "On the last day. But I didn't want to be her buddy. I just never liked her."

She floated forward, raised herself off the ground, hovered over me.

"But I need a buddy," she whispered. "Everyone has to have a buddy. You'll be my buddy — won't you, Sarah?"

I saw the hissing snake in her hand.

But I couldn't move.

"You'll be my buddy — won't you?" Briana repeated. "You'll be my buddy forever."

Goosebumps®

GHOST CAMP

"You know I get bus sick, Harry," Alex groaned.

"Alex, give me a break." I shoved my brother against the window. "We're almost there. Don't start thinking about getting bus sick now!"

The bus rumbled over the narrow road. I held onto the seat in front of me. I gazed out the window.

Nothing but pine trees. They whirred past in a blur of green. Sunlight bounced off the dusty glass of the window.

We're almost to Camp Spirit Moon, I thought happily.

I couldn't wait to get off the bus. My brother, Alex, and I were the only passengers. It was kind of creepy.

The driver was hidden in front of a green curtain. I had glimpsed him as Alex and I climbed on board. He had a nice smile, a great suntan, curly blond hair, and a silver earring in one ear.

"Welcome, dudes!" he greeted us.

Once the long bus ride began, we didn't see him or hear from him again. Creepy.

Luckily, Alex and I get along okay. He's a year younger than me. He's eleven. But he's as tall as I am. Some people call us the Altman twins, even though we're not twins.

We both have straight black hair, dark brown eyes, and serious faces. Our parents are always telling us to cheer up — even when we're in really good moods!

"I feel a little bus sick, Harry," Alex complained.

I turned away from the window. Alex suddenly looked very yellow. His chin trembled. A bad sign.

"Alex, pretend you're not on a bus," I told him. "Pretend you're in a car."

"But I get carsick, too," he groaned.

"Forget the car," I said. Bad idea. Alex can get carsick when Mom backs down the driveway!

It's really a bad-news habit of his. His face turns a sick yellow. He starts to shake. And then it gets kind of messy.

"You've got to hold on," I told him. "We'll be at camp soon. And then you'll be fine."

He swallowed hard.

The bus bounced over a deep hole in the road. Alex and I bounced with it.

"I really feel sick," Alex moaned.

"I know!" I cried. "Sing a song. That always

cures you. Sing a song, Alex. Sing it really loud. No one will hear. We're the only ones on the bus."

Alex loves to sing. He has a beautiful voice.

The music teacher at school says that Alex has perfect pitch. I'm not sure what that means. But I know it's a good thing.

Alex is serious about his singing. He's in the chorus at school. Dad says he's going to find a voice teacher for Alex this fall.

I stared at my brother as the bus bounced again. His face was about as yellow as a banana skin. Not a good sign.

"Go ahead — sing," I urged him.

Alex's chin trembled. He cleared his throat. Then he began to sing a Beatles song we both really like.

His voice bounced every time the bus bumped. But he started to look better as soon as he started to sing.

Pretty smart idea, Harry, I congratulated myself.

I watched the pine trees whir past in the sunlight and listened to Alex's song. He really does have an awesome voice.

Am I jealous?

Maybe a little.

But he can't hit a tennis ball the way I can. And I can beat him in a swim race every time. So it evens out.

Alex stopped singing. He shook his head unhappily. "I wish Mom and Dad signed me up for the music camp." He sighed.

"Alex, the summer is half over," I reminded him. "How many times do we have to go over this? Mom and Dad waited too long. It was too late."

"I know," Alex said, frowning. "But I wish — "

"Camp Spirit Moon was the only camp we could get into this late in the summer," I said. "Hey, look — !"

I spotted two deer outside the window, a tall one and a little baby one. They were just standing there, staring at the bus as it sped by.

"Yeah. Cool. Deer," Alex muttered. He rolled his eyes.

"Hey — lighten up," I told him. My brother is so moody. Sometimes I just want to shake him. "Camp Spirit Moon may be the coolest camp on earth," I said.

"Or it may be a dump," Alex replied. He picked at some stuffing that poked up from a hole in the bus seat.

"The music camp is so great." He sighed. "They put on *two* musicals each summer. That would have been so awesome!"

"Alex, forget about it," I told him. "Let's enjoy Camp Spirit Moon. We only have a few weeks."

The bus suddenly screeched to a stop.

Startled, I bounced forward, then back. I

turned to the window, expecting to see a camp out there. But all I could see were pine trees. And more pine trees.

"Camp Spirit Moon! Everybody out!" the driver called.

Everybody? It was just Alex and me!

The driver poked his blond head out from behind the curtain. He grinned at us. "How was the ride, dudes?" he asked.

"Great," I replied, stepping into the aisle. Alex didn't say anything.

The driver climbed out. We followed him around to the side of the bus. Bright sunlight made the tall grass sparkle all around us.

He leaned into a compartment and pulled out our bags and sleeping bags. He set everything down on the grass.

"Uh . . . where's the camp?" Alex asked.

I shielded my eyes with my hand and searched around. The narrow road curved through a forest of pine trees as far as I could see.

"Right through there, dudes," the driver said. He pointed to a dirt path that cut through the trees. "It's a real short walk. You can't miss it."

The driver shut the baggage compartment. He climbed back onto the bus. "Have a great time!" he called.

The door shut. The bus roared away.

Alex and I squinted through the bright sunlight at the dirt path. I swung my duffel bag over my shoulder. Then I tucked my sleeping bag under one arm.

"Shouldn't the camp send someone out here to greet us?" Alex asked.

I shrugged. "You heard the driver. He said it's a very short walk."

"But still," Alex argued. "Shouldn't they send a counselor to meet us out here on the road?"

"It's not the first day of camp," I reminded him. "It's the middle of the summer. Stop complaining about everything, Alex. Pick up your stuff, and let's get going. It's hot out here!"

Sometimes I just have to be the big brother and order him around. Otherwise, we won't get anywhere!

He picked up his stuff, and I led the way to the path. Our sneakers crunched over the dry red dirt as we made our way through the trees.

The driver hadn't lied. We'd walked only two or three minutes when we came to a small, grassy clearing. A wooden sign with red painted letters proclaimed CAMP SPIRIT MOON. An arrow pointed to the right.

"See? We're here!" I declared cheerfully.

We followed a short path up a low, sloping hill. Two brown rabbits scurried past, nearly in front of our feet. Red and yellow wildflowers swayed along the side of the hill.

When we reached the top, we could see the camp.

"It looks like a real camp!" I exclaimed.

I could see rows of little white cabins stretching in front of a round blue lake. Several canoes were tied to a wooden dock that stuck out into the lake.

A large stone building stood off to the side. Probably the mess hall or the meeting lodge. A round dirt area near the woods had benches around it. For campfires, I guessed.

"Hey, Harry — they have a baseball diamond *and* a soccer field," Alex said, pointing.

"Excellent!" I cried.

I saw a row of round red-and-white targets at the edge of the trees. "Wow! They have archery, too," I told Alex. I love archery. I'm pretty good at it.

I shifted the heavy duffel bag on my shoulder. We started down the hill to the camp.

We both stopped halfway down the hill. And stared at each other.

"Do you notice anything weird?" Alex asked.

I nodded. "Yeah. I do."

I noticed something *very* weird. Something that made my throat tighten and my stomach suddenly feel heavy with dread.

The camp was empty.

No one there.

2

"Where *is* everyone?" I asked, moving my eyes from cabin to cabin. No one in sight.

I squinted at the lake behind the cabins. Two small, dark birds glided low over the sparkling water. No one swimming there.

I turned to the woods that surrounded the camp. The afternoon sun had begun to lower itself over the pine trees. No sign of any campers in the woods.

"Maybe we're in the wrong place," Alex said softly.

"Huh? Wrong place?" I pointed to the sign. "How can we be in the wrong place? It says Camp Spirit Moon — doesn't it?"

"Maybe they all went on a field trip or some-thing," Alex suggested.

I rolled my eyes. "Don't you know anything about camp?" I snapped. "You don't go on field trips. There's nowhere to go!"

"You don't have to *shout*!" Alex whined.

"Then stop saying such stupid things!" I replied angrily. "We're all alone in the woods in an empty camp. We've got to think clearly."

"Maybe they're all in that big stone building over there," Alex suggested. "Let's go check it out."

I didn't see any signs of life there. Nothing moved. The whole camp was as still as a photograph.

"Yeah. Come on," I told Alex. "We might as well check it out."

We were still about halfway down the hill, following the path through the tangles of pine trees — when a loud cry made us both stop and gasp in surprise.

"Yo! Hey! Wait up!"

A red-haired boy, in white tennis shorts and a white T-shirt, appeared beside us. I guessed he was sixteen or seventeen.

"Hey — where did you come from?" I cried. He really startled me. One second Alex and I were alone. The next second this red-haired guy was standing there, grinning at us.

He pointed to the woods. "I was gathering firewood," he explained. "I lost track of the time."

"Are you a counselor?" I asked.

He wiped sweat off his forehead with the front of his T-shirt. "Yes. My name is Chris. You're Harry and you're Alex — right?"

Alex and I nodded.

"I'm sorry I'm late," Chris apologized. "You weren't worried, were you?"

"Of course not," I replied quickly.

"Harry was a little scared. But I wasn't," Alex said. Sometimes Alex can really be a pain.

"Where is everyone?" I asked Chris. "We didn't see any campers, or counselors, or anyone."

"They all left," Chris replied. He shook his head sadly. When he turned back to Alex and me, I saw the frightened expression on his face.

"The three of us — we're all alone out here," he said in a trembling voice.

3

"Huh? They *left*?" Alex cried shrilly. "But — but — where did they go?"

"We *can't* be all alone!" I cried. "The woods — "

A smile spread over Chris's freckled face. Then he burst out laughing. "Sorry, guys. I can't keep a straight face." He put his arms around our shoulders and led us toward the camp. "I'm just joking."

"Excuse me? That was a joke?" I demanded. I was feeling very confused.

"It's a Camp Spirit Moon joke," Chris explained, still grinning. "We play it on all the new campers. Everyone hides in the woods when the new campers arrive at camp. Then a counselor tells them that the campers all ran away. That they're all alone."

"Ha-ha. Very funny joke," I said sarcastically.

"You always try to *scare* the new campers?" Alex asked.

Chris nodded. "Yeah. It's a Camp Spirit Moon

tradition. We have a lot of great traditions here. You'll see. Tonight at the campfire — "

He stopped when a big black-haired man — also dressed in white — came lumbering across the grass toward us. "Yo!" the man called in a booming, deep voice.

"This is Uncle Marv," Chris whispered. "He runs the camp."

"Yo!" Uncle Marv repeated as he stepped up to us. "Harry, what's up?" He slapped me a high five that nearly knocked me into the trees.

Uncle Marv grinned down at Alex and me. He was so *huge* — he reminded me of a big grizzly bear at the zoo back home.

He had long, greasy black hair that fell wildly over his face. Tiny, round blue eyes — like marbles — under bushy black eyebrows.

His arms bulged out from under his T-shirt. Powerful arms like a wrestler's. His neck was as wide as a tree trunk!

He reached down and shook Alex's hand. I heard a loud *crunch* and saw Alex gasp in pain.

"Good firm handshake, son," Uncle Marv told Alex. He turned to me. "Did Chris play our little 'Alone in the Woods' joke on you guys?" His voice boomed so loud, I wanted to cover my ears.

Does Uncle Marv ever whisper? I wondered.

"Yeah. He fooled us," I confessed. "I really thought there was no one here."

Uncle Marv's tiny blue eyes sparkled. "It's one

of our oldest traditions," he said, grinning. What a grin! It looked to me as if he had at least *six rows* of teeth!

"Before I take you to your cabin, I want to teach you the Camp Spirit Moon greeting," Uncle Marv said. "Chris and I will show it to you."

They stood facing each other.

"Yohhhhhhhh, Spirits!" Uncle Marv bellowed.

"Yohhhhhhhh, Spirits!" Chris boomed back.

Then they gave each other a left-handed salute, placing the hand on the nose, then swinging it straight out in the air.

"That's how Camp Spirit Moon campers greet each other," Uncle Marv told us. He pushed Alex and me together. "You two try it."

I don't know about you, but this kind of thing embarrasses me. I don't like funny greetings and salutes. It makes me feel like a jerk.

But I had just arrived at camp. And I didn't want Uncle Marv to think I was a bad sport. So I stood in front of my brother. "Yohhhhhhhh, Spirits!" I shouted. And I gave Alex a sharp nose salute.

"Yohhhhhhhh, Spirits!" Alex showed a lot more enthusiasm than I did. He likes this kind of thing. He flashed me a sharp salute.

Uncle Marv tossed back his head in a loud, bellowing laugh. "Very good, guys! I think you're both going to be great Camp Spirit Moon campers."

He winked at Chris. "Of course, the campfire tonight is the *real* test."

Chris nodded, grinning.

"The campfire tonight?" I asked. "A test?"

Uncle Marv patted my shoulder. "Don't worry about it, Harry."

Something about the way he said that made me worry a *lot*.

"All new campers come to a Welcoming Campfire," Chris explained. "It's a chance to learn our Camp Spirit Moon traditions."

"Don't tell them any more about it," Uncle Marv told Chris sharply. "We want them to be surprised — don't we?"

"Surprised — ?" I choked out.

Why did I suddenly have such a bad feeling? Why did my throat tighten up again? Why did I have a fluttering feeling in my chest?

"Do we sing camp songs at the Welcoming Campfire?" Alex asked. "I'm really into singing. I take voice lessons back home and — "

"Don't worry. You'll sing. Plenty," Uncle Marv interrupted in a low, almost menacing voice.

I caught the cold look in his tiny eyes — cold as blue ice. And I felt a shiver roll down my back.

He's trying to scare us, I thought. It's all a joke. He's having fun with us. He always tries to scare new campers. It's a Camp Spirit Moon tradition.

"I think you boys will enjoy the campfire tonight," Uncle Marv boomed. "If you survive it!"

He and Chris shared a laugh.

"Catch you later," Chris said. He gave Alex and me a nose salute and vanished into the woods.

"This will be your bunk," Uncle Marv announced. He pulled open the screen door of a tiny white cabin. "Whoa!" He nearly pulled the door off its hinges.

Alex and I dragged our duffels and sleeping bags into the cabin. I saw bunk beds against three of the walls. Narrow wooden chests of drawers. Cubbyholes for storing things.

The walls were white. A light dangling from the ceiling cast a bright glow. The afternoon sun sent orange rays through a small window above one of the bunk beds.

Not bad, I thought.

"That bunk is free," Uncle Marv told us, pointing to the bed against the window. "You can decide who gets the top and who gets the bottom."

"I need the bottom," Alex said quickly. "I toss and turn a lot at night."

"And he sings in his sleep," I told Uncle Marv. "Do you believe it? Alex is so into singing, he doesn't even stop when he's sleeping!"

"You will have to try out for the talent show," Uncle Marv told Alex. And then he repeated in a low voice, "If you survive tonight." He laughed.

Why did he keep saying that?

He's kidding, I reminded myself. Uncle Marv is just *kidding*.

"The boys' cabins are on the left," Uncle Marv told us. "And the girls' cabins are on the right. We all use the lodge and mess hall. It's that big stone building near the woods."

"Should we unpack now?" Alex asked.

Uncle Marv pushed back his greasy black hair. "Yes. Use any cubbies that are empty. You'd better hurry, guys. The rest of the campers will be back from the woods soon with firewood. It will be time for our campfire."

He gave us a "Yohhhhhhhh, Spirits!" and a sharp nose salute.

Then he turned and lumbered away. The screen door slammed hard behind him.

"Fun guy," I muttered.

"He's kind of scary," Alex admitted.

"He's just joking," I said. "All summer camps try to terrify the new campers. I think." I dragged my duffel bag over to the bed.

"But it's all in fun. There's nothing to be scared about, Alex," I told my brother. "Nothing at all."

I tossed my sleeping bag into the corner. Then I started toward the low dresser to see if I could find an empty drawer.

"Whoa — !" I cried out as my sneaker stuck on something.

I peered down.

A blue puddle.

My sneaker had landed in a sticky blue puddle.

"Hey — " I tugged my sneaker out. The blue

liquid was thick. It stuck to the bottom and sides of my shoe.

I glanced around the room.

And saw more blue puddles. A sticky blue puddle in front of every bed.

"What's going *on* here? What *is* this stuff?" I cried.

4

Alex had his bag open and was pulling stuff out and spreading it on the bottom bed. "What's your problem, Harry?" he called without turning around.

"It's some kind of blue slime," I replied. "Check it out. There are puddles all over the floor."

"Big deal," Alex muttered. He turned and glanced at the blue liquid stuck to my sneaker. "It's probably a camp tradition," he joked.

I didn't think it was funny. "Yuck!" I exclaimed. I reached down and poked my finger into the tiny, round puddle.

So cold!

The blue slime felt freezing cold.

Startled, I pulled my hand away. The cold swept up my arm. I shook my hand hard. Then I rubbed it, trying to warm it.

"Weird," I muttered.

Of course, everything got a lot weirder. In a hurry.

"Campfire time!"

Uncle Marv's cry through the screen door shook our cabin.

Alex and I spun to face the door. It had taken us forever to unpack our stuff. To my surprise, the sun had lowered. The sky outside the door was evening gray.

"Everyone is waiting," Uncle Marv announced. A gleeful smile spread over his face. His tiny eyes practically disappeared in the smile. "We all *love* the Welcoming Campfire."

Alex and I followed him outside. I took a deep breath. The air smelled fresh and piney.

"Wow!" Alex cried out.

The campfire was already blazing. Orange and yellow flames leaped up to the gray sky.

We followed Uncle Marv to the round clearing where the fire had been built. And saw the other campers and counselors for the first time.

They sat around the fire, all facing us. Watching us.

"They're all dressed alike!" I exclaimed.

"The camp uniform," Uncle Marv said. "I'll get you and Alex your camp uniforms tonight after the campfire."

As Alex and I neared the circle, the campers and counselors rose to their feet. A deafening "YOHHHHHHHHHH, SPIRITS!" shook the trees. Then a hundred left-handed nose salutes greeted us.

Alex and I returned the greeting.

Chris, the red-haired counselor, appeared beside us. "Welcome, guys," he said. "We're going to roast hot dogs on the fire before the campfire activities begin. So grab a stick and a hot dog, and join in."

The other kids were lining up in front of a long food table. I saw a huge platter of raw hot dogs in the center of the table.

As I hurried to get in line, several kids said hi to me.

"You're in my cabin," a tall boy with curly blond hair said. "It's the best cabin!"

"Cabin number seven rules!" a girl shouted.

"This is an awesome camp," the kid in front of me turned to say. "You're going to have a great time, Harry."

They seemed to be really nice kids. Up ahead, a boy and a girl were having a playful shoving match, trying to knock each other out of line. Other kids began cheering them on.

The fire crackled behind me. The orange light from its flames danced over everyone's white shorts and shirts.

I felt a little weird, not being dressed in white.

I was wearing an olive-green T-shirt and faded denim cutoffs. I wondered if Alex felt weird, too.

I turned and searched for him in the line. He was behind me, talking excitedly to a short blond boy. I felt glad that Alex had found a friend so fast.

Two counselors handed out the hot dogs. I suddenly realized I was *starving*. Mom had packed sandwiches for Alex and me to eat on the bus. But we were too excited and nervous to eat them.

I took the hot dog and turned to the crackling fire. Several kids were already huddled around the fire, poking their hot dogs on long sticks into the flames.

Where do I get a stick? I asked myself, glancing around.

"The sticks are over there," a girl's voice called from behind me — as if she had read my mind.

I turned and saw a girl about my age, dressed in white, of course. She was very pretty, with dark eyes and shiny black hair, pulled back in a ponytail that fell down her back. Her skin was so pale, her dark eyes appeared to glow.

She smiled at me. "New kids never know where to find the sticks," she said. She led the way to a pile of sticks leaning against a tall pine tree. She picked up two of them and handed one to me.

"Your name is Harry, right?" she asked. She had a deep, husky voice for a girl. Like she was whispering all the time.

"Yeah. Harry Altman," I told her.

I suddenly felt very shy. I don't know why. I turned away from her and shoved the hot dog onto the end of the stick.

"My name is Lucy," she said, making her way to the circle of kids around the fire.

I followed her. The kids' faces were all flickering orange and yellow in the firelight. The aroma of roasting hot dogs made me feel even hungrier.

Four girls were huddled together, laughing about something. I saw a boy eating his roasted hot dog right off the stick.

"Gross," Lucy said, making a disgusted face. "Let's go over here."

She led me to the other side of the campfire. Something popped in the fire. It sounded like a firecracker exploding. We both jumped. Lucy laughed.

We sat down on the grass, raised the long sticks, and poked our hot dogs into the flames. The fire was roaring now. I could feel its heat on my face.

"I like mine really black," Lucy said. She turned her stick and pushed it deeper into the flames. "I just love that burnt taste. How about you?"

I opened my mouth to answer her — but my

hot dog fell off the stick. "Oh no!" I cried. I watched it fall into the sizzling, red-hot blanket of flames.

I turned to Lucy. And to my surprise — to my *horror* — she leaned forward.

Stuck her hand deep into the fire.

Grabbed my hot dog from the burning embers and lifted it out.

5

I jumped to my feet. "Your hand!" I shrieked.

Yellow flames leaped over her hand and up her arm.

She handed me the hot dog. "Here," she said calmly.

"But your hand!" I cried again, gaping in horror.

The flames slowly burned low on her skin. She glanced down at her hand. Confused. As if she didn't know why I was in such a panic.

"Oh! Hey — !" she finally cried. Her dark eyes grew wide. "Ow! That was hot!" she exclaimed.

She shook her hand hard. Shook it until the flames went out.

Then she laughed. "At least I rescued your poor hot dog. Hope you like yours burned!"

"But — but — but — " I sputtered. I stared at her hand and arm. The flames had spread all over her skin. But I couldn't see any burns. Not a mark.

"The buns are over there," she said. "You want some potato chips?"

I kept staring at her hand. "Should we find the nurse?" I asked.

She rubbed her arm and wrist. "No. I'm fine. Really." She wiggled her fingers. "See?"

"But the fire — "

"Come on, Harry." She pulled me back to the food table. "It's almost time for the campfire activities to start."

I ran into Alex at the food table. He was still hanging out with the short blond boy.

"I made a friend already," Alex told me. He had a mouthful of potato chips. "His name is Elvis. Do you believe it? Elvis McGraw. He's in our cabin."

"Cool," I muttered. I was still thinking about the flames rolling up and down Lucy's arm.

"This is a great camp," Alex declared. "Elvis and I are going to try out for the talent show *and* the musical."

"Cool," I repeated.

I grabbed a hot dog bun and tossed some potato chips on my plate. Then I searched for Lucy. I saw her talking to a group of girls by the fire.

"Yohhhhhhhh, Spirits!" a deep voice bellowed. No way anyone could mistake that cry. It had to be Uncle Marv.

"Places around the council fire, everyone!" he ordered. "Hurry — places, everyone!"

Holding plates and cans of soda, everyone scurried to form a circle around the fire. The girls all sat together and the boys all sat together. I guessed each cabin had its own place.

Uncle Marv led Alex and me to a spot in the middle.

"Yohhhhhhhh, Spirits!" he cried again, so loud the fire trembled!

Everyone repeated the cry and gave the salute.

"We'll begin by singing our camp song," Uncle Marv announced.

Everyone stood up. Uncle Marv started singing, and everyone joined in.

I tried to sing along. But of course I didn't know the words. Or the tune.

The song kept repeating the line, "We have the spirit — and the spirit has us."

I didn't really understand it. But I thought it was pretty cool.

It was a long song. It had a lot of verses. And it always came back to: "We have the spirit — and the spirit has us."

Alex was singing at the top of his lungs. What a show-off! He didn't know the words, either. But he was faking it. And singing as loud as he could.

Alex is so crazy about his beautiful singing voice and his perfect pitch. He has to show it off whenever he can.

I gazed past my brother. His new friend, Elvis,

had his head tossed back and his mouth wide open. He was singing at the top of his lungs, too.

I think Alex and Elvis were having some kind of contest. Seeing who could sing the leaves off the trees!

The only problem? Elvis was a *terrible* singer!

He had a high, whiny voice. And his notes were all coming out sour.

As my dad would say, "He couldn't carry a tune in a wheelbarrow!"

I wanted to cover my ears. But I was trying to sing along, too.

It wasn't easy with the two of them beside me. Alex sang so loud, I could see the veins in his neck pulsing. Elvis tried to drown him out with his sour, off-key wails.

My face felt hot.

At first, I thought it was the heat from the blazing campfire. But then I realized I was blushing.

I felt so embarrassed by Alex. Showing off like that on his first night at camp.

Uncle Marv wasn't watching. He had wandered over to the girls' side of the fire, singing as he walked.

I slipped back, away from the fire.

I felt too embarrassed to stay there. I'll sneak back into place as soon as the song is over, I decided.

I just couldn't sit there and watch my brother act like a total jerk.

The camp song continued. "We have the spirit — and the spirit has us," everyone sang.

Doesn't the song ever end? I wondered. I backed away, into the trees. It felt a lot cooler as soon as I moved away from the fire.

Even back here, I could hear Alex singing his heart out.

I've got to talk to him, I told myself. I've got to tell him it isn't cool to show off like that.

"Ohh!" I let out a sharp cry as I felt a tap on my shoulder.

Someone grabbed me from behind.

"Hey — !" I spun around to face the trees. Squinted into the darkness.

"Lucy! What are *you* doing back here?" I gasped.

"Help me, Harry," she pleaded in a whisper. "You've got to help me."

6

A chill ran down my back. "Lucy — what's wrong?" I whispered.

She opened her mouth to reply. But Uncle Marv's booming voice interrupted.

"Hey, you two!" the camp director shouted. "Harry! Lucy! No sneaking off into the woods!"

The campers all burst out laughing. I could feel my face turning hot again. I'm one of those kids who blushes very easily. I hate it — but what can I do?

Everyone stared at Lucy and me as we made our way back to the fire. Alex and Elvis were slapping high fives and laughing at us.

Uncle Marv kept his eyes on me as I trudged back. "I'm glad you make friends so easily, Harry," he boomed. And all the campers started laughing at Lucy and me again.

I felt so embarrassed, I wanted to shrivel up and disappear.

But I was also worried about Lucy.

Had she followed me to the woods? Why?

Why did she ask me to help her?

I sat down between Lucy and Elvis. "Lucy — what's wrong?" I whispered.

She just shook her head. She didn't look at me.

"Now I'm going to tell the two ghost stories," Uncle Marv announced.

To my surprise, some kids gasped. Everyone suddenly became silent.

The crackling of the fire seemed to get louder. Behind the pop and crack of the darting flames, I heard the steady whisper of wind through the pine trees.

I felt a chill on the back of my neck.

Just a cool breeze, I told myself.

Why did everyone suddenly look so solemn? So frightened?

"The two ghost stories of Camp Spirit Moon have been told from generation to generation," Uncle Marv began. "They are tales that will be told for all time, for as long as dark legends are told."

Across the fire, I saw a couple of kids shiver.

Everyone stared into the fire. Their faces were set. Grim. Frightened.

It's only a ghost story, I told myself. Why is everyone acting so weird?

The campers must have heard these ghost stories already this summer. So why do they look so terrified?

146

I snickered.

How can *anyone* be afraid of a silly camp ghost story?

I turned to Lucy. "What's up with these kids?" I asked.

She narrowed her dark eyes at me. "Aren't you afraid of ghosts?" she whispered.

"Ghosts?" I snickered again. "Alex and I don't believe in ghosts," I told her. "And ghost stories never scare us. Never!"

She leaned close to me. And whispered in my ear: "You might change your mind — after to-night."

7

The flames flickered, crackling up to the dark, starry sky. Uncle Marv leaned into the orange firelight. His tiny, round eyes sparkled.

The woods suddenly became quiet. Even the wind stopped whispering.

The air felt cold on my back. I scooted closer to the campfire. I saw others move closer, too. No one talked. All eyes were on Uncle Marv's smiling face.

Then, in a low voice, he told the first ghost story. . . .

A group of campers went into the woods for an overnight. They carried tents and sleeping bags. They walked single file along a narrow dirt path that twisted through the trees.

Their counselor's name was John. He led them deeper and deeper into the woods.

Dark clouds floated overhead. When the clouds covered the full moon, the darkness swept over the campers. They walked close together, trying to see the curving path.

Sometimes the clouds moved away, and the moonlight poured down on them. The trees glowed, silvery and cold, like ghosts standing in the forest.

They sang songs at first. But as they moved deeper into the woods, their voices became tiny and shrill, muffled by the trees.

They stopped singing and listened to the scrape of their footsteps and the soft rustlings of night animals scampering through the weeds.

"When are we going to stop and set up camp?" a girl asked John.

"We have to go deeper into the woods," John replied.

They kept walking. The air became colder. The trees bent and shivered around them in a swirling breeze.

"Can we set up camp now, John?" a boy asked.

"No. Deeper," John replied. "Deeper into the forest."

The path ended. The campers had to make their way through the trees, around thorny bushes, over a deep carpet of crackling dead leaves.

Owls hooted overhead. The campers heard the flutter of bat wings. Creatures scratched and slithered around their feet.

"We're really tired, John," a boy complained. "Can we stop and set up the tents?"

"Deeper into the woods," John insisted. "An overnight is no fun unless you are deep, deep in the woods."

So they kept walking. Listening to the low hoots and moans of the night animals. Watching the old trees bend and sway all around them.

Finally they stepped out into a smooth, wide clearing.

"Can we set up camp now, John?" the campers begged.

"Yes," John agreed. "We are deep in the woods now. This is the perfect place."

The campers dropped all the bags and supplies in the middle of the clearing. Silvery moonlight spilled all around them, making the smooth ground shimmer.

They pulled out the tents and started to unfold them.

But a strange sound made them all stop their work.

Ka-thump ka-thump.

"What was that?" a camper cried.

John shook his head. "Probably just the wind."

They went back to the tents. They pushed tent poles into the soft, smooth ground. They started to unfold the tents.

But the strange sound made them stop again.

Ka-thump ka-thump.

A chill of fear swept over the campers.

"What *is* that sound?" they asked.

"Maybe it's some kind of animal," John replied.

Ka-thump ka-thump.

"But it sounds so close!" a boy cried.

"It's coming from right above us," another boy said. "Or maybe beneath us!"

"It's just a noise," John told them. "Don't worry about it."

So they set up the tents. And they spread sleeping bags inside the tents.

Ka-thump ka-thump.

They tried to ignore the sound. But it was so close. So close.

And such a strange — but familiar — sound.

What could it be? the campers wondered. What on earth makes a sound like that?

Ka-thump ka-thump.

The campers couldn't sleep. The noise was too loud, too frightening — too near.

Ka-thump ka-thump.

They burrowed deep into their sleeping bags. They zipped themselves in tight. They covered their ears.

Ka-thump ka-thump.

It didn't help. They couldn't escape the sound.

"John, we can't sleep," they complained.

"I can't sleep, either," John replied.

Ka-thump ka-thump.

"What should we do?" the campers asked the counselor.

John didn't get a chance to answer.

151

They heard another *Ka-thump ka-thump*.

And then a deep voice growled: *"WHY ARE YOU STANDING ON MY HEART?"*

The ground shook.

The campers suddenly realized what the frightening sound was. And as the ground rose up, they realized — too late — they had camped on the smooth skin of a hideous monster.

"I guess we went *too deep* into the woods!" John cried.

His last words.

Ka-thump ka-thump.

The monster's heartbeat.

And then its huge, hairy head lifted up. Its mouth pulled open. And it swallowed John and the campers without even chewing.

And as they slid down the monster's throat, the sound of the heartbeat grew louder and louder.

Ka-thump ka-thump. Ka-thump ka-thump. Ka-THUMP!

Uncle Marv shouted the last *Ka-thump* at the top of his lungs.

Some campers screamed. Some gazed at Uncle Marv in silence, their faces tight with fear. Beside me, Lucy hugged herself, biting her bottom lip.

Uncle Marv smiled, his face flickering in the dancing orange flames.

Laughing, I turned to Elvis. "That's a funny story!" I exclaimed.

Elvis narrowed his eyes at me. "Huh? Funny?"

"Yeah. It's a very funny story," I repeated.

Elvis stared hard at me. "But it's *true*!" he said softly.

I laughed. "Yeah. For sure," I said, rolling my eyes.

I expected Elvis to laugh. But he didn't. The firelight flickered in his pale blue eyes as he stared at me. Then he turned to talk to my brother.

A chill ran down my back. Why was he acting so weird?

Did he really think I'd believe a crazy story like that was true?

I'm twelve years old. I stopped believing in things like the Easter Bunny and the Tooth Fairy a long time ago.

I turned to Lucy. She was still hugging herself, staring intently into the fire.

"Do you believe him?" I asked, motioning to Elvis. "Is he weird or what?"

Lucy stared straight ahead. She seemed so deep in thought, I don't think she heard me.

Finally she raised her head. She blinked. "What?"

154

"My brother's new friend," I said, pointing to Elvis again. "He said that Uncle Marv's story was true."

Lucy nodded, but didn't reply.

"I thought it was a funny story," I said.

She picked up a twig and tossed it on the fire. I waited for her to say something. But she seemed lost in thought again.

The flames of the campfire had died down. Sparkling red embers and chunks of burning wood spread over the ground. Chris and another counselor carried fresh logs into the meeting circle.

I watched them rebuild the fire. They piled armfuls of twigs and sticks onto the burning embers. When the sticks burst into flames, the two counselors lowered logs over them.

Then they stepped back, and Uncle Marv took his place in front of the fire. He stood with his hands in the pockets of his white shorts. The full moon floated behind his head, making his long black hair shine.

He smiled. "And now I will tell the second traditional story of Camp Spirit Moon," he announced.

Once again, the circle of campers grew silent. I leaned back, trying to get my brother's attention. But Alex was staring across the fire at Uncle Marv.

Alex probably thought the first ghost story was

kind of dumb, I knew. He hates ghost stories even more than I do. He thinks they're silly baby stuff. And so do I.

So what was Elvis's problem?

Was he goofing? Just teasing me? Or was he trying to scare me?

Uncle Marv's booming voice interrupted my thoughts. "This is a story we tell every year at Camp Spirit Moon," he said. "It's the story of the Ghost Camp."

He lowered his deep voice nearly to a whisper, so that we all had to lean closer to hear him. And in hushed tones, he told us the story of the Ghost Camp.

The story takes place at a camp very much like Camp Spirit Moon. On a warm summer night, the campers and counselors met around a blazing council fire.

They roasted hot dogs and toasted marshmallows. They sang the camp songs. One of the counselors played a guitar, and he led them in singing song after song.

When they were tired of singing, the counselors took turns telling ghost stories. And telling the legends of the camp, legends that had been passed on from camper to camper for nearly a hundred years.

The evening grew late. The campfire had died

low. The moon floated high in the sky, a pale full moon.

The camp director stepped forward to end the council meeting.

Suddenly, darkness swept over the circle of campers.

They all looked up — and saw that the moon had been covered by a heavy blanket of black clouds.

And swirls of fog came drifting over the camp. A cold, wet fog. Cloudy gray at first. Then darkening.

And thickening.

Until the fog swept over the camp, billowing like black smoke.

Tumbling and swirling, the cold wet fog rolled over the dying campfire. Rolled over the campers and counselors. Over the cabins and the lake and the trees.

A choking fog, so thick and dark the campers couldn't see each other. Couldn't see the fire. Or the ground. Or the moon in the sky.

The fog lingered for a short while, swirling and tossing, low over the ground. Wet, so wet and silent.

It moved on just as silently.

Like smoke blown away.

The moonlight shone through. The grass sparkled as if a heavy dew had settled.

The fire was out. Dark purple embers sizzled over the ground.

The fog swirled away. Swept over the trees. And vanished.

And the campers sat around the dead campfire. Their eyes blank. Their arms limp at their sides.

Not moving. Not moving. Not moving.

Because they were no longer alive.

The fog had left a ghost camp in its wake.

The campers, the counselors, the camp director — they were all ghosts now.

All spirits. All ghosts. Every last one of them.

They climbed to their feet. And returned to their bunks.

They knew the ghost camp was their home now — *forever!*

With a smile, Uncle Marv stepped back from the fire.

I glanced around the circle. The faces were so solemn. No one smiled or laughed.

It's a pretty good story, I thought. Kind of scary.

But it doesn't have much of an ending.

I turned to see what Alex thought.

And gasped when I saw the terrified expression on his face. "Alex — what?" I cried, my voice cutting through the silence of the circle. "What's wrong?"

He didn't reply. His eyes were raised to the sky. He pointed up.

I gazed up too — and let out a cry of horror.

As a black, swirling fog came sweeping over the camp.

9

My mouth dropped open as I watched the fog roll closer. It darkened the ground as it moved steadily toward us.

Darkened the trees. Darkened the sky.

This is *crazy*, I told myself.

This is *impossible*!

I scooted next to Alex. "It's just a coincidence," I told him.

He didn't seem to hear me. He jumped to his feet. His whole body trembled.

I stood up beside him. "It's only fog," I said, trying to sound calm. "It gets foggy out here in the woods all the time."

"Really?" Alex asked in a tiny voice.

The black smoky fog swirled over us.

"Of course," I replied. "Hey — we don't believe in ghosts, remember? We don't think ghost stories are scary."

"But — but — " Alex stuttered. "Why is everyone staring at us?" he finally choked out.

I turned and squinted through the thick fog.

Alex was right. All around the circle, the other campers had their eyes on Alex and me. Their faces appeared to dim behind the curtain of dark mist.

"I — I don't know why they're watching us," I whispered to my brother.

Fog billowed around us. I shivered. It felt cold against my skin.

"Harry — I don't like this," Alex whispered.

The fog was so thick now, I could barely see him, even though he stood close beside me.

"I know we don't believe in ghosts," Alex said. "But I don't like this. It — it's too creepy."

From the other side of the circle, Uncle Marv's voice broke the silence. "It's a beautiful fog tonight," he said. "Let's all stand up and sing the Camp Spirit Moon song."

Alex and I were already standing. The other campers and counselors obediently climbed to their feet.

Their pale faces shimmered in and out of the fog.

I rubbed my arms. Cold and wet. I dried my face with the front of my T-shirt.

The fog grew even heavier and darker as Uncle Marv began to sing. Everyone joined in. Beside me, Alex began to sing, quieter this time.

Our voices were muffled by the heavy mist. Even Uncle Marv's booming voice sounded smaller and far away.

I tried to sing too. But I didn't know the words. And my own voice came out choked and small.

As I stared into the swirling fog, the voices faded. Everyone sang, but the sound sank into the fog.

The voices vanished. All of them. All except for Alex's.

He seemed to be the only one still singing, his voice pure and soft beside me in the dark mist.

And then Alex stopped singing, too.

The fog swept on. The darkness lifted.

Silvery moonlight washed down on us once again.

Alex and I gazed around in surprise.

No one else remained.

Alex and I were all alone. All alone in front of the dying fire.

10

I blinked. And blinked again.

I don't know what I expected. Did I think they would all appear again?

Alex and I gazed across the circle in stunned silence.

They had vanished with the fog. The campers. The counselors. Uncle Marv.

A chill ran down my back. My skin still felt damp and cold from the heavy mist.

"Wh-where — ?" Alex choked out.

I swallowed hard.

A burned log crumbled into the purple embers. The soft thud startled me.

I jumped.

And then I started to laugh.

Alex squinted at me, studying me. "Harry — ?"

"Don't you see?" I told him. "It's a joke."

He squinted at me harder. "Huh?"

"It's a camp joke," I explained. "It's a joke they probably always play on new campers here."

Alex twisted up his whole face. He was thinking about it. But I don't think he believed me.

"They all ran off into the woods," I told him. "They hid behind the fog and ran away. They were all in on the joke. I'll bet they do it to every new kid."

"But — the fog — " Alex choked out.

"I'll bet the fog was a fake!" I exclaimed. "They probably have some kind of smoke machine. To help them with the joke."

Alex rubbed his chin. I could still see the fear in his eyes.

"They probably do this all the time," I assured him. "Uncle Marv tells the story. Then somebody turns on the smoke machine. The black smoke rolls over the campfire circle. And everyone runs and hides."

Alex turned and stared into the woods. "I don't see anyone hiding back there," he said softly. "I don't see anyone watching us."

"I'll bet they're all back at the cabins," I told him. "I'll bet they're waiting for us. Waiting to see the looks on our faces."

"Waiting to laugh at us for falling for their dumb joke," Alex added.

"Let's go!" I cried. I slapped him on the shoulder. Then I started running across the wet grass toward the row of cabins.

Alex ran close behind. The moon sent a silvery path across the grass in front of us.

164

Sure enough — as we came near the cabins, the campers all came running out. They were laughing and hooting. Slapping each other high fives.

Enjoying their joke. A joke they play on new campers when the fog rolls in, they told us.

I saw Lucy laughing along with a bunch of girls.

Elvis grabbed Alex and wrestled him playfully to the ground.

Everyone teased us and told us how scared we looked.

"We weren't scared even for a second," I lied. "Alex and I figured it out before the fog cleared."

That made everyone start laughing and cheering all over again.

"*Owoooooooh!*"

Some of the kids cupped their hands around their mouths and made ghost howls.

"*Owoooooooh!*"

That led to more laughing and joking.

I didn't mind the teasing. Not a bit.

I felt so relieved. My heart was still pounding like crazy. And my knees felt kind of weak.

But I felt so happy that it was all a joke.

Every summer camp has its jokes, I told myself. And this is a pretty good one.

But it didn't fool me. Not for long, anyway.

"Lights Out in five minutes," Uncle Marv's booming command stopped the fun. "Lights Out, campers!"

The kids all turned and scurried to their bunks.

I stared down the row of cabins, suddenly confused. Which one was ours?

"This way, Harry," Alex said. He tugged me toward the third cabin down the path. Alex has a better memory than I do for things like that.

Elvis and two other guys were already in the cabin when Alex and I came in. They were getting changed for bed. The other guys introduced themselves. Sam and Joey.

I made my way to the bunk bed and started to undress.

"*Owoooooooh!*" A ghostly howl made me jump.

I spun around and saw Joey grinning at me.

Everyone laughed. Me, too.

I like camp jokes, I thought. They're mean. But they're kind of fun.

I felt something soft and gooey under my bare foot. Yuck! I glanced down.

And saw that I had stepped in a fresh puddle of blue slime.

The cabin lights went out. But before they did, I saw blue puddles — fresh blue puddles — all over the floor.

The cold blue stuff stuck to the bottom of my foot. I stumbled through the dark cabin and found a towel to wipe it off.

What *are* these blue puddles? I asked myself as I climbed up to my top bunk.

I glimpsed Joey and Sam in the bunk against the wall.

I gasped.

They stared back at me, their eyes shining like flashlights!

What is going on here? I wondered.

What are the sticky blue puddles all over the floor?

And why do Sam and Joey's eyes glow like that in the dark?

I turned my face to the wall. I tried not to think about anything.

I had almost drifted to sleep — when I felt a cold, slimy hand sliding down my arm.

"Huh?"

I shot straight up. Still feeling the cold, wet touch on my skin.

I stared at my brother. "Alex — you scared me to death!" I whispered. "What do you want?"

He stood on his mattress, his dark eyes staring at me. "I can't sleep," he moaned.

"Keep trying," I told him sharply. "Why are your hands so cold?"

"I don't know," he replied. "It's cold in here, I guess."

"You'll get used to it," I said. "You always have trouble sleeping in new places."

I yawned. I waited for him to drop back onto the bottom bunk. But he didn't move.

"Harry, you don't believe in ghosts — do you?" he whispered.

"Of course not," I told him. "Don't let a couple of silly stories creep you out."

"Yeah. Right," he agreed. "Good night."

I said good night. He disappeared back to his bed. I heard him tossing around down there. He had a very squeaky mattress.

Poor guy, I thought. That dumb Ghost Camp joke with the fog really messed him up.

He'll be fine in the morning, I decided.

I turned and gazed across the dark cabin toward Joey and Sam's bunk. Were their eyes still glowing so strangely?

No.

Darkness there.

I started to turn away — then stopped.

And stared hard.

"Oh no!" I murmured out loud.

In the dim light, I could see Joey. Stretched out. Asleep.

Floating two feet above his mattress!

12

I scrambled to climb out of bed. My legs tangled in the blanket, and I nearly fell on my head!

"Hey — what's up?" I heard Alex whisper below me.

I ignored him. I swung myself around, and leaped to the floor.

"Ow!" I landed hard, twisting my ankle.

Pain shot up my leg. But I ignored it and hobbled to the door. I remembered the light switch was somewhere over there.

I had to turn on the light.

I had to see for sure that I was right. That Joey slept floating in the air above his bed.

"Harry — what's wrong?" Alex called after me.

"What's up? What time is it?" I heard Elvis groan sleepily from the bunk against the other wall.

I pulled myself across the cabin. My hand fumbled against the wall until I found the light switch.

I pushed it up.

The overhead light flashed on, flooding the tiny cabin in white light.

I raised my eyes to Joey's bunk.

He lifted his head from the pillow and squinted down at me. "Harry — what's your problem?" he asked. He was sprawled on his stomach, on top of his blanket.

Not floating in the air. Not floating.

Resting his head in his hands, yawning and staring down at me.

"Turn off the light!" Sam barked. "If Uncle Marv catches us with the light on . . ."

"But — but — " I sputtered.

"Turn it *off*!" Elvis and Sam both insisted.

I clicked off the light.

"Sorry," I muttered. "I thought I saw something."

I felt like a jerk. Why did I think I saw Joey floating in the air?

I must be as creeped out as Alex, I decided. Now I'm *seeing* things!

I scolded myself and told myself to calm down.

You're just nervous because it's your first day in a new camp, I decided.

I started slowly across the cabin to my bed. Halfway there, I stepped in a cold, sticky puddle of goo.

The next morning, Alex and I found our white Camp Spirit Moon uniforms — white shorts and

171

T-shirts — waiting for us at the foot of our beds.

Now we won't stand out like sore thumbs, I thought happily.

Now we can really be part of Camp Spirit Moon.

I quickly forgot about my fears from the night before. I couldn't wait for the camp day to get started.

That afternoon, Alex tried out for the Camp Spirit Moon talent show.

I had to be at the soccer field. A bunch of us were supposed to practice putting up tents. We were getting ready for an overnight in the woods.

But I stopped in front of the outdoor stage at the side of the lodge to listen to Alex sing.

A counselor named Veronica, with long, copper-colored hair all the way down her back, was in charge of the tryouts. I leaned against a tree and watched.

A lot of kids were trying out. I saw two guitar players, a boy with a harmonica, a tap dancer, and two baton twirlers.

Veronica played a small upright piano at the front of the stage. She called Alex up and asked him what song he wanted to sing.

He picked a Beatles song he likes. My brother doesn't listen to any new groups. He likes the Beatles and the Beach Boys — all the groups from the sixties.

He's the only eleven-year-old I know who

listens to the oldies station. I feel kind of sorry for him. It's like he was born in the wrong time or something.

Veronica played a few notes on the piano, and Alex started to sing.

What a voice!

The other kids had all been laughing and talking and messing around. But after Alex sang for a few seconds, they got real quiet. They huddled close to the stage and listened.

He really sounded like a pro! I mean, he could probably sing with a band and make a CD.

Even Veronica was amazed. I could see her lips form the word "Wow!" as she played the piano for Alex.

When Alex finished singing, the kids all clapped and cheered. Elvis slapped Alex a high five as he hopped off the small stage.

Veronica called Elvis up next. He told her he wanted to sing an Elvis song, since he was named after Elvis Presley.

He cleared his throat and started to sing a song called "Heartbreak Hotel."

Well . . . it really *was* a heartbreak — because Elvis couldn't sing a single note on key!

Veronica tried to play along with him. But I could see that she was having trouble. I think she probably wanted to stop playing the piano and cover her ears!

Elvis had a high, scratchy voice. And the notes

came out really sour. Sour enough to make your whole face pucker up.

The kids around the stage started grumbling and walking away.

Elvis had his eyes shut. He was so wrapped up in his song, he didn't even see them!

Doesn't he know how bad he is? I wondered. Why does he want to enter a talent show when he sounds like a squealing dog?

Elvis started to repeat the chorus. I decided I had to get away from there before my eardrums popped.

I flashed Alex a thumbs-up and hurried to the soccer field.

Sam, Joey, and a bunch of other kids were already unfolding tents, getting ready for tent-raising practice. Chris, the counselor, was in charge.

He waved to me. "Harry — unroll that tent over there," he instructed. "Let's see how fast you can put it up."

I picked up the tent. It was bundled tightly, no bigger than a backpack. I turned it over in my hands. I'd never set up a tent before. I wasn't even sure how to unwrap it.

Chris saw me puzzling over it and walked over. "It's easy," he said.

He pulled two straps, and the nylon tent started to unfold. "See? Here are the poles. Just stretch it out and prop it up."

He handed the bundle back to me.

"Yeah. Easy," I repeated.

"What's that noise?" Joey asked, looking up from his tent.

I listened hard. "It's Elvis singing," I told them.

The sour notes floated over the soccer field from the stage.

Sam shook his head. "It sounds like an animal caught in a trap," he said.

We all laughed.

Joey and Sam took off their sneakers and went barefoot. I took mine off, too. The warm grass felt good under my feet.

I unfolded the tent and spread it out on the grass. I piled the tent poles to the side.

The sun felt hot on the back of my neck. I slapped a mosquito on my arm.

I heard a shout and glanced up to see Sam and Joey wrestling around. They weren't fighting. They were just goofing.

They both picked up tent poles and started dueling with them, having a wild sword fight. They were laughing and having fun.

But then Sam tripped over a tent.

He lost his balance. Stumbled forward. Fell hard.

I let out a scream as the tent pole went right through his foot.

13

My stomach lurched. I felt sick.

The pointed pole had pierced the top of Sam's foot, nailing his foot to the ground.

Joey gaped, openmouthed, his eyes wide with surprise.

With a gasp, I searched for Chris. I knew Sam needed help.

Where had Chris wandered off to?

"Sam — " I choked out. "I'll get help. I'll — "

But Sam didn't cry out. He didn't react at all. Didn't even grimace.

He calmly reached down with both hands — and pulled the pole from his foot.

I let out a groan. *My* foot ached! In sympathy, I guess.

Sam tossed the pole aside.

I stared down at his foot. No cut. No blood.

It wasn't bleeding!

"Sam!" I cried. "Your foot. It's not bleeding!"

He turned and shrugged. "It missed my toes," he explained.

He dropped onto his knees and started propping up the tent.

I swallowed hard, waiting for my stomach to stop churning.

Missed his toes? I thought. Missed his *toes*?

I saw the pole sink right into his foot!

Or was I seeing things again?

For the rest of the afternoon, I tried not to think about it. I worked on the tent. Once I got it spread out, it was easy to set up.

Chris had us fold and unfold them a few times. Then we had a race to see who could set up a tent the fastest.

I won easily.

Sam said it was beginner's luck.

Chris said I was definitely ready for the overnight.

"Where do we go for the overnight?" I asked.

"Deep, deep into the woods," Chris replied. He winked at Sam and Joey.

I felt a chill, thinking about Uncle Marv's ghost story.

I shook the chill away. *No way* I was going to let myself get scared by a silly camp story.

We had instructional swim at the waterfront. The lake was clear and cold. I'm up to Junior

Lifesaver. Joey and I took turns rescuing each other.

I didn't think about Sam driving the pole through his foot. I forced it from my mind.

After the swim, I returned to the bunk to get changed for dinner. There were fresh puddles of blue goo on the cabin floor.

Nobody made a big deal about them. I didn't want to, either. So I tried hard not to think about them.

Alex came in, very excited. "I'm going to be the first act in the talent show!" he announced. "And Veronica liked my singing so much, she wants me to star in the camp musical."

"Way to go!" I cried. I slapped him a high five. Then I asked, "What about Elvis?"

"He's going to be in the show, too," Alex replied. "He's going to be stage manager."

I pulled on my white Camp Spirit Moon shorts and T-shirt and headed to the mess hall for dinner.

I saw a group of girls come out of the cabins on the other side. I searched for Lucy, but didn't see her.

I was feeling pretty good.

Not thinking about the strange things I'd seen.

Not thinking about the blue puddles of slime. The mysterious black fog.

Not thinking about the ghost story that Elvis said was true.

Not thinking about Lucy sticking her hand into the fire and pulling out my flaming hot dog.

Not thinking about Joey floating above his bed. Or Sam jamming a thick pole through his foot.

And not bleeding. Not crying out.

So totally calm about it. As if he couldn't feel it, couldn't feel any pain.

I was starving. Looking forward to dinner. Not thinking about any of these puzzling things.

Feeling really good.

But then Joey ruined my good mood at dinner. And forced all the scary thoughts back into my mind.

The food had just been served. Chicken in some kind of creamy sauce, spinach, and lumpy mashed potatoes.

I didn't care *what* it was. I was so hungry, I could eat anything!

But before I had a chance to eat, Joey called out to me from across the table. "Hey, Harry — look!"

I glanced up from my plate.

He picked up his fork — and jammed it deep into his neck!

14

"Ohhh." I let out a groan. My fork fell from my hand and clattered to the floor.

Joey grinned at me. The fork bobbed up and down, stuck in his neck.

I felt sick. My heart started to pound.

He pulled the fork out with a hard tug. His grin didn't fade. "*You* try it!" he called.

"Joey — stop it!" Elvis cried from across the table.

"Yeah. Give us a break," Sam agreed.

I stared at Joey's neck. No cut. No fork marks. No blood.

"How — how did you *do* that?" I finally stammered.

Joey's grin grew wider. "It's just a trick," he replied.

I glimpsed Alex at the end of the table. Had he seen Joey's "trick"?

Yes. Alex looked green. His mouth had dropped open in horror.

"Here. I'll show you how to do it," Joey offered.

He raised the fork again — but stopped when he saw Uncle Marv leaning over his shoulder.

"What's going on, Joey?" Uncle Marv demanded sharply.

Joey lowered the fork to the table. "Just kidding around," he replied, avoiding the camp director's hard stare.

"Well, let's eat our dinner, guys," Uncle Marv said sternly. "Without kidding around." His stubby fingers tightened over Joey's shoulders. "We have a night soccer game, you know. Boys against the girls."

Uncle Marv loosened his grip on Jocy's shoulders and moved on to the next table. A food fight had broken out there. And the mashed potatoes were flying.

Joey mumbled something under his breath. I couldn't hear him over all the noise.

I turned to see how Alex was doing at the end of the table. He had his fork in his hand, but he wasn't eating. He was staring hard at Joey. My brother had a very thoughtful expression on his face.

I knew he was wondering exactly the same thing I was.

What is going on here?

Joey said the fork-stabbing was just a trick. But how did he do it? Why didn't it hurt? Why didn't he bleed?

181

"Night soccer games are cool!" Elvis declared. He was stuffing chicken into his mouth. The cream sauce ran down his chin.

"Especially boys against the girls," Sam agreed. "We'll *kill* them! They're pitiful."

I glanced at the girls' table across the room. They were chattering noisily. Probably about the soccer game.

I saw Lucy in the shadows near the wall. She didn't seem to be talking to anyone. She had a solemn expression on her face.

Did she keep looking over at me?

I couldn't really tell.

I ate my dinner. But my appetite had disappeared.

"How did you do that fork thing?" I asked Joey.

"I told you. It's just a trick," he replied. He turned away from me to talk to Sam.

Dessert was little squares of red, yellow, and green Jell-O. It was okay. But it needed some whipped cream.

As I was finishing my dessert, I heard some squeals from the front of the big room. I turned toward the cries — and saw a bat swooping wildly back and forth over the mess hall.

Some of the younger kids were screaming. But everyone stayed calm at my table.

The bat fluttered noisily, swooping and diving, darting from one end of the hall to the other.

Uncle Marv followed it with a broom. And after

only a minute or two, he gently pinned the bat to the wall with the straw broom head.

Then he lifted the bat off the wall, carrying it in one hand.

It was so tiny! No bigger than a mouse.

He carried it out the door and let it go.

Everyone cheered.

"That happens all the time," Sam said to me. "It's because there aren't any screens on the mess hall doors."

"And the woods are full of bats," Joey added. "Killer bats that land in your hair and suck the blood out of your head."

Sam laughed. "Yeah. Right." He grinned at me. "That's what happened to Joey. That's why he acts so weird now."

I laughed along with everyone else.

But I wondered if Sam was really joking.

I mean, Joey *did* act weird.

"Soccer field, everyone!" Uncle Marv boomed from the mess hall door. "Check with the sports counselors. Alissa and Mark will set up the teams."

Chairs scraped over the stone floor as everyone jumped up.

I saw Lucy waving to me. But Sam and Joey pulled me away.

Into a cool, cloudy night. The full moon hidden behind low clouds. The grass already wet with a heavy dew.

The counselors divided up the teams. Alex and I were on the second team. That meant we didn't play the first period. Our job was to stand on the sidelines and cheer on the boys' first team.

Two floodlights on tall poles sent down wide triangles of white light over the field. It wasn't really enough light. Long shadows spread over the field.

But that was part of the fun.

Alex stood close beside me as the game began. The girls' team scored a goal in less than a minute.

Girls on the sidelines went wild.

The players on the boys' team stood around, scratching their heads and muttering unhappily.

"Lucky break! Lucky break!" yelled Mark, a tall, lanky boys' counselor. "Go get them, guys!"

The game started up again.

The light from the floodlights appeared to dim. I raised my eyes to the sky — and saw fog rolling in.

Another swirling fog.

Mark jogged past us, looking like a big stork. "Going to be another foggy night," he said to Alex and me. "Night games are more fun in the fog." He shouted instructions to the boys' team.

The thick fog swept over us quickly, driven by a gusting wind.

Alex huddled close to me. I turned and caught his worried expression.

"Did you see what Joey did at dinner?" he asked softly.

I nodded. "He said it was a trick."

Alex thought about that for a moment. "Harry," he said, keeping his eyes on the game. "Don't you think some of these kids are a little weird?"

"Yeah. A little," I replied. I thought about the tent pole going through Sam's foot.

"Something happened at the waterfront," Alex continued. "I can't stop thinking about it."

I watched the game, squinting into the drifting fog. It was getting hard to see the players.

Cheers rang out from the girls' side. I guessed they had scored another goal. Layers of heavy fog blocked my view.

I shivered. "What happened?" I asked my brother.

"I had free swim. After tryouts for the show," he said. "There was my group and a couple of girls' groups. Younger girls, mostly."

"The lake is nice," I commented. "It's so clear and clean. And not too cold."

"Yeah. It's good," Alex agreed. He frowned. "But something strange happened. I mean — I *think* it was strange."

He took a deep breath. I could see he was really upset.

"Let's go, guys! Go, go, go!" Mark shouted to the team.

185

The glow from the floodlights twisted and bent in the fog, sending strange shadows over the playing field. The fog was so thick now, I had trouble telling the players from the shadows.

"I was floating on top of the water," Alex continued, wrapping his arms around his chest. "Sort of taking it easy. Moving slowly. Stroke . . . stroke . . . very slow.

"It was free swim. So we could do what we wanted. Some of the guys were having a back-floating race near the shore. But I floated out by myself.

"The water was so clear. I put my face in the water, and I stared down to the bottom. And — and I saw something down there."

He swallowed hard.

"What was it? What did you see?" I asked.

"A girl," Alex replied with a shudder. "One of the girls from the younger group. I don't know her name. She has short, curly black hair."

"She was under the water?" I demanded. "You mean, swimming underwater?"

"No." Alex shook his head. "She wasn't swimming. She wasn't moving. She was *way* underwater. I mean, near the bottom of the lake."

"She dove down?" I asked.

Alex shrugged. "I got so scared!" he cried over the shouts of the two teams. "She wasn't moving. I didn't think she was breathing. Her arms floated up and down. And her eyes — her eyes stared out blankly into the water."

"She *drowned*?" I cried.

"That's what I thought," Alex said. "I panicked. I mean, I didn't know what to do. I couldn't think. I *didn't* think. I just dove down."

"You dove down to the bottom to get her?" I asked.

"Yeah. I didn't really know if I was too late. Or if I should get a counselor. Or what," Alex said, shuddering again.

"I swam down. I grabbed her arms. Then I gripped her under the shoulders. I pulled her up. She floated up easily. Like she was weightless or something.

"I pulled her up to the surface. Then I started to drag her to the shore. I was gasping for breath. Mostly from panic, I think. My chest felt about to burst. I was so scared.

"And then I heard laughing. She laughed at me. I was still holding her under the shoulders. She turned — and spit water in my face!"

"Oh, wow!" I gasped. "Wow, Alex. You mean she was okay?"

"Yeah," Alex replied, shaking his head. "She was perfectly okay. She was laughing at me. She thought it was really funny.

"I just stared at her. I couldn't believe it. I mean, she had been way down at the bottom. For a long, long time.

"I let go of her. She floated away from me, still laughing.

"I said, 'How did you do that?' That's what I asked her. I asked, 'How long can you hold your breath?'

"And that made her laugh even harder. 'How long?' I asked.

"And she said, 'A long, long time.'

"And then she swam back to the other girls."

"And what did *you* do?" I asked Alex.

"I had to get out of the water," he replied. "I was shaking all over. I couldn't stop shaking. I — I thought . . ." His voice trailed off.

"At least she was okay," he murmured after a while. "But don't you think that was weird, Harry? And then at dinner, when Joey stuck that fork in his neck — "

"It's weird, Alex," I said softly. "But it may just be jokes."

"Jokes?" he asked. His dark eyes stared hard into mine.

"Kids always play jokes on new campers," I told him. "It's a camp tradition. You know. Terrify the new kids. It's probably just jokes. That's all."

He chewed his bottom lip, thinking about it. Even though he was standing so close to me, the swirling black fog made him appear far away.

I turned back to the game. The boys were moving across the grass toward the goal. Passing the ball, kicking it from player to player. They looked unreal, moving in and out of the swirling shadows.

Jokes, I thought.

All jokes.

I squinted into the fog. And saw something that *couldn't* be a joke.

A boy kicked the ball to the net. The girls' goalie moved to block the shot.

She wasn't fast enough. Or she stumbled.

The ball hit her smack in the forehead.

It made a sickening *thud*.

The ball bounced onto the ground.

And her head bounced beside it.

15

I gasped. And started to run.

Through the thick wisps of black fog.

The swirling, dark mist seemed to float up from the ground and sweep down from the trees. It felt cold and wet on my face as I hurtled toward the girl.

Squinting into the heavy darkness, I could see her sprawled on her stomach on the ground.

And her head . . .

Her head . . .

I bent down and grabbed it. I don't know what I was thinking.

Did I plan to plop it back on her shoulders?

In a total panic, trembling with horror, I bent into the swirling mist — and picked up the head with both hands.

It felt surprisingly hard. *Inhumanly* hard.

I raised it. Raised it close to my face.

And saw that I held a soccer ball.

Not a head. Not a girl's head.

I heard a groan. And gazed down to see the girl climb to her knees. She muttered something under her breath and shook her head.

Her head. The head on her shoulders.

She stood and frowned at me.

I stared at her face, her head. My whole body was still shaking.

"Your head — " I choked out.

She tossed back her straight blond hair. Brushed dirt off her white shorts. Then she reached for the ball.

"Harry — you're not on the first team!" I heard a boy call.

"Get off the field!" another boy demanded.

I turned and saw that the players had all gathered around.

"But I saw her head fall off!" I blurted out.

I instantly regretted it. I *knew* I shouldn't have said it.

Everyone laughed. They tossed back their heads and laughed at me. Someone slapped me on the back.

Their grinning, laughing faces floated all around me. For a moment, it looked to me as if *all* their heads had come off. I was surrounded by laughing heads, bobbing in the eerie, shadowy light from the floodlights.

The girl raised her hands to the sides of her head and tugged up. "See, Harry?" she cried. "See? It's still glued on!"

"Someone better check Harry's head!" a boy cried.

Everyone laughed some more.

A kid came up, grabbed my head, and tugged it.

"Ow!" I screamed.

More wild laughter.

I tossed the goalie the soccer ball. Then I slunk off the field.

What is *wrong* with me? I wondered. Why am I so messed up?

Why do I keep seeing things?

Am I just nervous because I'm in a new camp? Or am I totally losing it?

I trudged to the sidelines and kept walking. I didn't know where I was going. I just knew I wanted to get away from the laughing kids, away from the soccer game.

The heavy fog had settled over the field. I glanced back. I could hear the players' shouts and cheers. But I could barely see them.

I turned and started toward the row of cabins. The dew on the tall grass tickled my legs as I walked.

I was halfway to the cabins when I realized I was being followed.

16

I spun around.

A face floated out of the darkness.

"Alex!" I cried. In all the excitement over the soccer ball and the goalie's head, I had forgotten all about him.

He stepped close to me, so close I could see beads of sweat on his upper lip. "I saw it, too," Alex whispered.

"Huh?" I gasped. I didn't understand. "You saw *what*?"

"The girl's head," Alex said sharply. He turned back to the soccer field. To see if anyone had followed him, I guess.

Then he turned back to me and tugged my T-shirt sleeve. "I saw her head fall off, too. I saw it bounce on the ground."

I swallowed hard. "You did? Really?"

He nodded. "I thought I was going to puke. It — it was so gross."

"But — it didn't fall off!" I cried. "Didn't you

see? When I ran onto the field? I picked up the ball. Not her head."

"But I *saw* it, Harry," Alex insisted. "At first I thought it was just the fog. You know. My eyes playing tricks on me because of the heavy fog. But — "

"It had to be the fog," I replied quietly. "That girl — she was perfectly okay."

"But if we both saw it . . ." Alex started. He stopped and sighed. "This camp — it's so weird."

"That's for sure," I agreed.

Alex shoved his hands into the pockets of his shorts. He shook his head unhappily. "Elvis says the ghost stories are true," he said.

I put my hands on Alex's shoulders. I could feel him trembling. We don't believe in ghosts — remember?" I told him. "Remember?"

He nodded slowly.

The first howl made us both jump.

I turned to the woods. Another eerie howl rose up from the same spot.

Not an animal howl. Not an animal cry at all.

A long, mournful howl. A *human* howl.

"*Owwoooooooooooooooo.*"

Another deeper cry made me gasp.

Alex grabbed my arm. His hand felt cold as ice.

"What *is* that?" he choked out.

I opened my mouth to reply — but another mournful howl interrupted.

"*Owwoooooooooooooo.*"

194

I heard two creatures howling. Maybe three. Maybe more.

The eerie wails floated up from behind the trees. Until it sounded as if the whole woods were howling.

Inhuman howls. *Ghostly* howls.

"We're surrounded, Harry," Alex whispered, still gripping my arm. "Whatever it is, it's got us surrounded."

17

"*Owwooooooo.*"

The frightening wails rose up from the trees.

"Run!" I whispered to Alex. "To the main lodge. Maybe we can find Uncle Marv. Maybe — "

Heading into the fog, we started running toward the lodge.

But the howls followed us. And grew louder.

I heard the heavy thud of footsteps behind us, tromping over the grass.

We can't escape, I realized.

Alex and I both turned at the same time.

And saw Elvis, Sam, and Joey — grinning as they ran after us.

Sam cupped his hands around his mouth and let out a long, ghostly howl. Laughing, Elvis and Joey tossed back their heads and howled too.

"You jerks!" I screamed, swinging a fist at them.

I could feel the blood rushing to my face.

I felt ready to explode. I wanted to punch those three clowns. And kick them. And pound their grinning faces.

"Gotcha!" Elvis cried. "Gotcha!" He turned to Sam and Joey. "Look at them! They're shaking! Oh, wow! They're shaking!"

Sam and Joey laughed gleefully. "Did you think there were wolves in the woods?" Sam asked.

"Or ghosts? Did you think we were ghosts?" Joey demanded.

"Shut up," I replied.

Alex didn't say a word. He lowered his eyes to the ground. I could see that he was as embarrassed as I was.

"Owwoooooo!" Elvis uttered another high-pitched howl. He threw his arms around my brother's waist and wrestled him to the ground.

"Get off! Get off!" Alex cried angrily.

The two of them wrestled around in the wet grass.

"Did I scare you?" Elvis demanded breathlessly. "Admit it, Alex. You thought it was a ghost, right? Right?"

Alex refused to reply. He let out a groan and heaved Elvis off him. They wrestled some more.

Sam and Joey stepped up beside me, grinning. Very pleased with themselves.

"You guys aren't funny," I grumbled. "That was so babyish. Really."

Joey slapped Sam a high five. "Babyish?" he cried. "If it was so babyish, why did you fall for it?"

I opened my mouth to reply — but only a choking sound came out.

Why *did* I fall for it? I asked myself.

Why did I let myself get scared by three guys standing behind trees and making howling sounds?

Normally, I would have laughed at such a dumb joke.

As the five of us walked to the cabin, I thought hard about it. The campers and counselors had all been trying to scare Alex and me since we arrived, I realized. Even Uncle Marv had tried to scare us with his creepy stories.

They must have a tradition of trying to scare new campers at Camp Spirit Moon, I decided.

And it works. It really has scared Alex and me. It has made us tense. Jumpy. Ready to leap out of our skins at the slightest noise.

We stepped into the cabin. I clicked the light on.

Elvis, Sam, and Joey were still laughing, still enjoying their joke.

Alex and I have got to get it together, I decided.

We've got to shove all the stupid stuff about ghosts out of our heads.

We don't believe in ghosts, I told myself.

We don't believe in ghosts. We don't believe in ghosts.

I repeated that sentence over and over. Like a chant.

Alex and I don't believe in ghosts. We've never believed in ghosts.

Never. Never.

One night later . . . after a short hike through the woods — I *did* believe in ghosts!

18

Alex and I took a lot of teasing the next day.

Coming out of the mess hall after breakfast, someone tossed a soccer ball at me and screamed, "My head! Give me back my head!"

We had instructional swim in the morning. Joey and Sam and some of the other guys started howling like ghosts. Everyone thought it was a riot.

I saw Lucy hanging out on the shore with some girls from her cabin. The other girls were laughing at the ghostly howls. Lucy was the only one who didn't laugh.

In fact, she had a solemn expression on her face. A thoughtful expression.

Several times, I caught her staring at me.

She's probably thinking about what a total baby I am, I told myself unhappily. I'll bet she feels sorry for me. Because I acted like such a jerk in front of everyone on the soccer field last night.

After instructional swim, I dried myself off.

Then I wrapped the towel around myself and walked over to Lucy at the little boat dock.

The other girls had wandered away. Lucy stood in her white shorts and T-shirt. She had one foot on a plastic canoe, making it bob up and down in the shallow water.

"Hi," I said. I suddenly realized I didn't know what to say.

"Hi," she replied.

She didn't smile. Her dark eyes locked on mine.

To my surprise, she turned quickly — and ran off.

"Hey — !" I called. I started to run after her. But stopped when my legs got tangled in my towel. "Hey — what's your problem?"

She vanished behind the Arts and Crafts cabin. She never looked back.

I *know* what her problem is, I told myself sadly. She doesn't want to be seen talking to a total nutcase. To someone who thinks that a girl's head can roll off. And who thinks there are howling ghosts lurking in the woods.

I wrapped the towel around me. Sam and Joey and some other guys were staring at me from the shore. I could see by the grins on their faces that they had seen Lucy run away from me.

"Maybe it's your breath!' Joey teased.

They all fell on the ground, howling.

*   *   *

After lunch, we had letter-writing time. The counselors made sure we all stayed in our bunks and wrote letters home to our parents.

It was a camp rule that we had to write home once a week. "So your parents won't worry about you," Uncle Marv announced at lunch. "We want them to know that you're having the best summer of your lives — right?"

"Yohhhhhhhhhh, Spirits!" everyone cheered.

I wasn't exactly having the best summer of my life.

In fact, so far, this was one of the worst.

But I decided not to write that in my letter home.

I climbed up to my top bunk and started to think about my letter to Mom and Dad.

Please come and get me, I thought I might write.

Everyone is weird here. Alex and I are both scared out of our wits.

No. No way. I couldn't write that.

I leaned over the side of the mattress and peered down at my brother. He was sitting on his bunk, crouched over his letter. I could see him scribbling away.

"What are you writing?" I called down.

"I'm telling them about the Camp Spirit Moon talent show," he replied. "How I'm going to be the star. And how I'm going to be in the musical next week."

"Nice," I muttered.

I decided I'd tell my parents only good things, too. Why worry them? Why make them think that I'm losing it?

If Alex isn't writing about all the weird things, I won't either, I decided.

I leaned over my sheet of paper and started my letter:

Dear Mom and Dad,

Camp Spirit Moon is a lot more exciting than I ever dreamed. . . .

"Tonight's after-dinner activity is a night hike," Uncle Marv announced.

A cheer shook the wooden rafters of the huge mess hall.

"Where are we going to hike?" someone called out.

Uncle Marv grinned. "Deep, deep into the woods."

Of course, that answer reminded everyone of Uncle Marv's ghost story. Some kids cheered. Others laughed.

Alex and I exchanged glances.

But the hike turned out to be fun. A full moon made the woods glow. We followed a path that curved around the lake.

Everyone seemed in a good mood. We sang the camp song so many times, I almost learned the words!

About halfway around the lake, two deer stepped out onto the path. A mother and her doe.

The little one was so cute. It looked just like Bambi.

The two deer stared at us. They turned up their noses, as if to say, "What are *you* doing in *our* woods?"

Then they calmly loped into the trees.

The path headed through a small, round clearing. As we stepped out of the trees, the ground appeared to light up. The moonlight poured down so brightly, I felt as if I could see every bush, every weed, every blade of grass.

It was really awesome.

I started to relax. Sam, Joey, and I walked along singing, making up funny words to songs we knew. We sang "On Top of Spaghetti" about twenty times — until kids *begged* us to stop singing it!

Why have I been so crazy? I asked myself.

I've made some cool new friends here at Camp Spirit Moon. I'm having an excellent time.

I felt great until we returned to camp.

The black fog had started to roll in. It greeted us, wrapping its cold, wet mists around us, darkening the sky, the ground, the whole camp.

"Lights Out in ten minutes," Uncle Marv announced.

Kids scampered to their cabins.

But two strong arms held me from behind. Held me back.

"Hey — !" I cried out. I felt myself being pulled into the trees.

"Ssshhhhh," someone whispered in my ear.

I spun around to find Lucy holding onto me. "What are you doing?" I whispered. "We have to go to our bunks. We have to get ready for — "

"Ssshhhhhh," she hissed again in my ear.

Her dark eyes searched my face. Were those tears staining her pale cheeks?

Clouds of fog rolled around us.

She loosened her grip on my arms. But her eyes stayed on mine. "Harry, you've got to help me," she whispered.

I swallowed hard. "Lucy, what's wrong?"

"I think you know," she said softly. "It's all true. What you think. It's true."

I didn't understand. I stared back at her with my mouth open.

"We're ghosts, Harry," Lucy told me. "We're all ghosts at this camp."

"But, Lucy — " I started.

"Yes." She nodded sadly. "Yes. Yes. Yes. I'm a ghost too."

19

The trees disappeared behind the fog. The moon-light made Lucy's eyes sparkle like dark jewels. But the light faded from her eyes as the fog covered the moon.

I didn't blink. I didn't move. I suddenly felt as wooden as the trees hiding behind the swirling fog.

"You — you're joking, right?" I stammered. "This is one of those great Camp Spirit Moon jokes?"

But I knew the answer.

I could read the answer in her dark eyes. In her trembling mouth. In her pale, pale skin.

"I'm a ghost," she repeated sadly. "The stories — they're true, Harry."

But I don't believe in ghosts!

That's what I almost blurted out.

But how could I not believe in ghosts when one stood right in front of me, staring into my face?

How could I not believe in Lucy?

"I believe you," I whispered.

She sighed. She turned her face away.

"How did it happen?" I asked.

"Just as Uncle Marv told in the story," she replied. "We were sitting around the campfire. All of us. Just like the other night. The fog rolled in. Such a dark, heavy fog."

She sighed again. Even in the darkness, I could see the tears glistening in her eyes.

"When the fog finally floated away," Lucy continued, "we were all dead. All ghosts. We've been out here ever since. I can't explain any more. I don't know any more."

"But when did it happen?" I demanded. "How long . . . how long have you been a ghost, Lucy?"

She shrugged. "I don't know. I've lost track of time. There *is* no time when you're a ghost. There's just one day and then the next. And then the next. Forever, I guess."

I stared at her without speaking.

Chill after chill swept down my back. My whole body was shaking. I didn't even try to stop it.

I reached out and grabbed her hand.

I guess I wanted to see if she was real or not. One last test to see if she was pulling a joke.

"Oh!" I dropped her hand as its icy cold shot through me. So cold. Her hand — as cold as the black fog.

"You believe me now?" she asked softly. Once again her dark eyes studied my face.

I nodded. "I — I believe you," I stammered. "I believe you, Lucy."

She didn't reply.

I could still feel the cold of her hand on my fingers.

"The blue puddles," I murmured. "The sticky blue puddles on the cabin floor. Do you know what they are?"

"Yes," she replied. "Those puddles are drops of protoplasm."

"Huh? Protoplasm?"

She nodded. "The puddles are made when we materialize. When we make ourselves visible."

She twisted her face into a sorrowful frown. "It takes so much strength to make ourselves visible. So much energy. The protoplasm puddles are made when we use that energy."

I didn't really understand.

But I knew when I stepped in them that the slimy blue puddles were something strange. Something inhuman.

Traces of ghosts.

"And the things Alex and I saw?" I demanded. "Kids floating above their bunks? Their eyes glowing like spotlights? Kids stabbing themselves and not bleeding? Not crying out in pain?"

"Some of the kids tried to scare you," Lucy confessed. "They only wanted a little fun, Harry.

It isn't fun being a ghost. Believe me. It isn't fun spending day after day after day out here, knowing you aren't real anymore. Knowing you will never grow. Knowing you will never change." She uttered a loud sob from deep in her chest. "Knowing you will never have a *life!*"

"I — I'm so sorry," I stammered.

Her expression changed.

Her eyes narrowed. Her mouth twisted into an unpleasant sneer.

I took a step back, suddenly afraid.

"Help me, Harry," Lucy whispered. "I can't stand it anymore. You've got to help me get away from here."

"Get away?" I cried, taking another step back. "How?"

"You've got to let me possess your mind," Lucy insisted. "You've got to let me take over your body!"

20

"No!" I gasped.

Panic shot through my body. I felt every muscle tense. The blood throbbed at my temples.

"I need to take over your mind, Harry," Lucy repeated, stepping toward me. "Please. Please help me."

"No!" I uttered again.

I wanted to turn and run. But I couldn't move. My legs felt like Jell-O. My whole body shook.

I don't believe in ghosts.

That thought flashed into my mind.

But it wasn't true anymore.

I stood at the edge of the woods — staring at Lucy. Staring at Lucy's ghost.

The fog swept around us.

Again, I tried to run. But my legs wouldn't cooperate.

"Wh-what do you want to do to me?" I finally choked out. "Why do you have to take over my mind?"

"It's my only way to escape," Lucy replied. Her eyes locked on mine. "My only way."

"Why don't you just run away?" I demanded.

She sighed. "If I try to leave the camp by myself, I'll disappear. If I try to leave the others, I'll fade away. I'll join the mist, be part of the fog."

"I — I don't understand," I stammered.

I took a step back. The fog seemed to tighten around me, cold and wet.

Lucy stood two feet in front of me. But I could barely see her. She seemed to shimmer in and out with the fog.

"I need help." Her voice floated softly. I had to struggle to hear her. "The only way a ghost can escape is to take over the mind of a living person."

"But — that's *impossible!*" I screeched.

What a dumb thing to say, I scolded myself. *Seeing a ghost* is impossible! *Everything* happening to me is impossible.

But it's happening.

"I need to possess the mind and body of a living boy or girl," Lucy explained. "I need to take over your body, Harry. I need you to take me away from here."

"No!" I screamed again. "I can't! I mean . . ." My heart thudded so hard, I could barely speak.

"I can't let you take over my mind," I finally managed to say. "If you do that, I won't be *me* anymore."

I started to back away.

211

I have to get to the cabin, I decided. I have to get Alex. We have to run away from this camp. As fast as we can.

"Don't be scared," Lucy pleaded. She followed me. The fog circled us, as if holding us inside.

"Don't be scared," Lucy said. "As soon as we are far away from here, I'll get out. I'll leave your mind. I'll leave your body. I promise, Harry. As soon as we escape this camp, I'll go away. You will be yourself again. You will be perfectly okay."

I stopped backing up. My whole body trembled. The fog washed its cold mist over me.

"Please, Harry," Lucy begged. "Please. I promise you'll be okay. I promise."

I squinted at her through the rising mists.

Should I do it?

Should I let Lucy take over my mind?

Will she give it back?

Can I believe her?

21

Lucy floated in front of me. Her dark eyes pleaded with me. "Please," she whispered.

"No. I'm sorry. I can't." The words escaped my lips almost before I thought them. "I can't, Lucy."

She shut her eyes. I could see the muscles in her jaw tighten as she gritted her teeth.

"I'm sorry," I repeated, backing up.

"I'm sorry too," she said coldly. Her eyes narrowed. Her lips formed a sneer. "I'm really sorry, Harry. But you don't have a choice. You *have* to help me!"

"No! No way!"

I turned and tried to run.

But something held me back. The fog. It tightened around me.

The thick, wet mist. A choking mist. It drew around me, pushing me, holding me in place.

I tried to scream for help. But the fog muffled my cry.

Lucy vanished behind the black fog.

And then I felt something cold on the top of my head.

My hair tingled.

I reached up with both hands. And felt ice. As if a frost had settled over my hair.

"No!" I screamed. "Lucy — no!"

The cold sank down. My scalp itched. My face froze.

I rubbed my cheeks.

Numb.

Cold and numb.

"Lucy — please!" I begged.

I could feel her — so light, so cold — settling into my body. Sinking into my brain.

I could feel her. And I could feel myself slipping away.

Slipping . . . slipping . . .

As if drifting into a deep sleep.

The cold spreading over me. Sweeping down my neck. Down my chest.

"Nooooo!" I uttered a long howl of protest.

I shut my eyes tight. I knew I had to concentrate. I had to think hard. I had to keep awake. I couldn't let myself fade away.

I couldn't let her take over.

I couldn't let her shove my mind aside. And take control. Take control of my body.

I set my jaw hard. And kept my eyes shut. And tightened every muscle.

No! I thought. *No — you can't do this to me, Lucy!*

You can't take my mind!

You can't take over. You can't — because I won't let you!

The cold settled over me. My skin tingled. I felt numb all over.

And so sleepy . . . so sleepy . . .

22

"Nooooo!" I tossed back my head in another long howl.

If I can keep screaming, I can keep awake, I told myself.

And I can fight Lucy off. I can force her away.

"Noooooooo!" I wailed into the spinning, whirling fog.

"Nooooooooo!"

And I felt the cold start to lift.

"Noooooo!"

I squeezed my arms. Rubbed my cheeks. And knew the feeling was returning.

"Noooooo!"

I suddenly felt lighter. And totally alert.

I did it! I realized. I fought her off!

But how long did I have before she tried to take over again?

I took a deep breath. Then another.

I'm breathing, I told myself. I'm me — and I'm breathing.

I felt stronger now. I lowered my head and darted into the fog.

My sneakers pounded the ground. I made my way to the cabin.

The lights were out. The other guys were in their bunks.

I burst inside and let the screen door slam behind me.

"What's up?" Sam demanded.

I didn't answer him. I ran across the room. Grabbed my brother. Shook him hard. "Come on. Hurry," I ordered.

"Huh?" Alex squinted up at me sleepily.

I didn't say another word. I tossed him his shorts and his sneakers.

I heard the other guys stirring. Joey sat up in his bed. "Harry — where *were* you?" he asked.

"Lights Out was ten minutes ago," Sam said. "You're going to get us all in trouble."

I ignored them. "Alex — hurry!" I whispered.

As soon as he had his sneakers tied, I grabbed his arm and tugged him to the door. "Harry — what's wrong?" he asked.

"Where are you two going?" I heard Joey call.

I pulled Alex outside. The screen door slammed behind us.

"Run!" I cried. "I'll explain later. We have to get out of here — now!"

"But, Harry — "

I pulled Alex over the grass. The fog had parted

enough to let a trail of moonlight slip through. We followed the trail to the woods.

Our sneakers slipped and slid over the wet grass. The only other sound was the chirp of crickets and the rush of wind rattling the pine trees.

After a minute or two, Alex wanted to stop to catch his breath.

"No," I insisted. "Keep moving. They'll follow us. They'll find us."

"Where are we going?" Alex demanded.

"Deep into the woods," I told him. "As far away from that camp as we can."

"But I can't keep running, Harry," Alex cried. "My side hurts and — "

"They're all ghosts!" I blurted out. "Alex — I know you won't believe me — but you've got to try. The kids. The counselors. Uncle Marv. They're all ghosts!"

Alex's expression grew solemn. "I know," he replied in a tiny voice.

"Huh? How do you know?" I demanded.

We squeezed between two tangled tree trunks. Over the chirp of crickets, I could hear the lake washing over the shore just beyond some tall shrubs.

We're still too close to the camp, I told myself.

I pulled my brother in the other direction. Away from the lake. Pushing aside tall weeds and shrubs, we made our own path, deeper into the woods.

"Alex — how do you know?" I repeated.

"Elvis told me," he replied, wiping sweat off his forehead with his arm.

We ducked under a tall thorn bush. Thorns scraped the top of my head. I ignored the pain and kept moving.

"Elvis said the ghost story about the fog was true," Alex continued. "I thought he was just trying to scare me. But then he — he — " Alex's voice trailed off.

We ran into a small clearing. Moonlight made the grass glow like silver. My eyes flashed in one direction, then the other. I couldn't decide which way to run.

I swatted a mosquito off my arm. "What did Elvis do?" I asked Alex.

Alex raked back his dark hair. "He tried to take over my mind," he told me in a trembling voice. "He floated into the fog. And then I started to feel really cold."

Twigs snapped. Dry leaves crackled.

Footsteps?

I shoved Alex back into the trees. Out of the clearing.

We pressed against a wide tree trunk and listened.

Silence now.

"Maybe it was a squirrel, or a chipmunk, or something," Alex whispered.

"Maybe," I replied, listening hard.

Moonlight trickled through the treetops. It made shadows dance over the smooth clearing.

"We have to keep going," I said. "We're still too close to the camp. If the ghosts follow us . . ."

I didn't finish my thought. I didn't want to *think* about what would happen if the ghosts followed us. If they caught us . . .

"Which way is the highway?" Alex asked, his eyes searching the trees. "It isn't too far from the camp — right? If we can get to the highway, someone will give us a ride."

"Good idea," I said. Why hadn't I thought of that?

Now here we were, in the middle of the woods. Far from the highway.

I didn't even know which direction to go to find it.

"It must be back that way," Alex suggested, pointing.

"No. That's the way back to the camp," I argued.

Alex started to reply — but a loud thumping sound made him stop. "Did you hear that?" he whispered.

I did.

And then I heard it again.

A loud thump. Very close by.

"Is it an animal?" I cried softly.

"I — I don't think so," Alex stammered.

KA-THUMP.

Louder.

Is it a ghost? I wondered.

Has one of them found us?

"Quick — this way!" I urged. I grabbed Alex by the wrist and tugged him hard.

We had to get away from whatever was making that frightening noise.

KA-THUMP.

Louder.

"We're going the wrong way!" I cried.

We spun around and darted back into the clearing.

KA-THUMP.

"Which way?" Alex screeched. "Which way? It — it's *everywhere!*"

KA-THUMP.

And then — from somewhere just ahead of us — a deep, booming voice growled, *"WHY ARE YOU STANDING ON MY HEART?"*

23

The ground tumbled and shook.

Alex and I both let out terrified cries.

But our cries were drowned out by a rumbling sound that quickly rose to a roar.

The ground gave way beneath us.

We both raised our arms high as we toppled over.

I landed on my hands and knees. Alex fell onto his back. The ground trembled and tossed, tumbling us around.

"It — it's the *monster!*" Alex shrieked.

But that's impossible! I thought, struggling to my feet.

That monster is from a story. A dumb camp ghost story.

It can't be here in the woods.

I helped pull Alex up. But the ground shook again, and we both fell to our knees.

KA-THUMP. KA-THUMP.

"It can't be real!" I cried. "It can't — "

My mouth dropped open in horror as a huge, hairy head raised itself in front of us. Its eyes glowed as red as flames — round, terrifying, glowing eyes set deep in an ugly, growling face. The creature glared furiously at us.

"Th-the monster!" Alex stuttered.

We were both on our knees, bouncing helplessly on the rolling, tossing ground.

Was it the ground? Or the monster's chest?

The creature opened an enormous cavern of a mouth. It flashed rows and rows of jagged yellow teeth.

Slowly it raised its head, moving closer. Closer.

Opening its hairy jaws wide. Preparing to swallow us as we frantically struggled to scramble away.

"Harry — ! Harry — !" Alex shrieked my name. "It's going to eat us! It's going to swallow us whole!"

And then — in a flash — I had an idea.

24

The huge monster uttered a low growl.

Its hairy mouth opened wider. An enormous purple tongue rolled out. I gasped when I saw that the tongue was covered in prickly burrs.

"Look out, Alex!" I cried.

Too late.

The ground tossed, bouncing us both into the air. We landed with a hard *plop* on the tongue.

"Owwww!" we both howled. It felt like a cactus!

Slowly, the prickly purple tongue began to slide, carrying us into the creature's open mouth.

"We don't believe in monsters," I told Alex.

I had to shout over the bellowing of the hungry monster. The tongue carried us closer. Closer to the rows of jagged yellow teeth.

"We don't believe in this monster!" I shouted. "It is just made up. Part of a story. If we don't believe in it, it can't exist!"

Alex's whole body shook. He hunched over,

making himself into a tight ball. "It looks pretty real!" he choked out.

The tongue dragged us closer. I could smell the monster's foul breath. I could see black stains on its jagged teeth.

"Concentrate," I instructed my brother. "We don't believe in you. We don't believe in you."

Alex and I began chanting those words, over and over.

"We don't believe in you. We don't believe in you."

The purple tongue carried us into the huge mouth. I tried to grab onto the teeth. But they were too slippery.

My hands slid off. I felt myself being swallowed.

Down, down. Into sour darkness.

"We don't believe in you. We don't believe in you." Alex and I continued to chant.

But our voices were muffled as we slid down the creature's throbbing throat.

"Harry — it *swallowed* us!" Alex wailed.

"Keep chanting," I ordered him. "If we don't believe in it, it *can't* exist!"

"We don't believe in you. We don't believe in you."

A glob of thick saliva rolled over me. I gagged as it clung to my clothes, my skin — hot and sticky.

The walls of the throat throbbed harder.

Pulling us down. Down.

Down into the vast, churning gurgling pit of a stomach below.

"Ohhhh." Alex let out a long, defeated sigh. He sank to his knees. He was covered in thick saliva too.

"Keep chanting! It's got to work! It's got to!" I screamed.

"We don't believe in you. We don't believe in you."

"We don't believe in you!"

Alex and I both opened our mouths in screams of horror as we began to fall.

Falling, falling, into the churning stomach below.

25

I shut my eyes.

And waited for the splash. Waited for the crash.

Waited to hit the stomach floor.

Waited.

When I opened my eyes, I was standing on the ground. Standing next to Alex in a grassy clearing.

The pine trees shivered in the breeze. A full moon poked out from behind wispy clouds.

"Hey — !" I cried. I was so happy to hear my own voice!

So happy to see the sky. The ground. So happy to breathe the cool air.

Alex started spinning. Spinning like a top. Laughing at the top of his lungs. "We didn't believe in you!" he cried gleefully. "We didn't believe in you — and it *worked!*"

We were both so thrilled. So excited that the monster had vanished.

Poof! A puff of imagination.

I started to spin with Alex. Spinning and laughing.

We stopped when we realized we were no longer alone.

I let out a startled cry when I saw the faces all around us. The pale, pale faces with their glowing eyes.

I recognized Sam, and Joe, and Lucy, and Elvis.

I moved close to Alex as the campers — the ghost campers — moved to form a circle around us. To trap us.

Uncle Marv moved into the circle. His tiny eyes glowed red as fire. He narrowed them angrily at Alex and me.

"Capture them!" he bellowed. "Take them back to camp. No one ever escapes Camp Spirit Moon."

Several counselors moved quickly to grab us.

We couldn't move. There was nowhere to run.

"What are you going to *do* to us?" I cried.

26

"We need living kids," Uncle Marv boomed. "We cannot allow living kids to escape. Unless they carry one of us with them."

"Noooo!" Alex wailed. "You can't take over my mind! You can't! I won't let you!"

The ghostly circle tightened. The ghost campers moved in on us.

I tried to stop my legs from shaking. Tried to slow my pounding heart.

"Alex — we don't believe in *them*, either," I whispered.

He stared at me, confused for a moment. Then he understood.

We made the monster vanish by not believing in him. We could do the same thing to the ghost campers.

"Grab them. Take them back to camp," Uncle Marv ordered the counselors.

"We don't believe in you. We don't believe in you," Alex and I started to chant.

"We don't believe in you. We don't believe in you."

I stared hard at the circle of ghostly faces. Waited for them to disappear.

I chanted with my brother. Chanted faster. Chanted louder.

"We don't believe in you. We don't believe in you."

I shut my eyes. Shut them tight.

And when I opened them . . .

The ghosts were still there.

"You can't make us disappear, Harry," Lucy said, stepping into the circle. She narrowed her eyes at me. They glittered cold and silvery in the moonlight.

"You made the monster disappear because it wasn't real, just one of our ghost tricks," Lucy explained. "We made you see it. But we're all real! All of us! And we're not going to vanish in a puff of smoke."

"We're not going away," Elvis added, moving close to my brother. "In fact, we're coming closer. A lot closer."

"I'm taking over your mind," Lucy whispered to me. "I'm going to escape Camp Spirit Moon inside your mind and body."

"Nooo! No — please!" I protested.

I tried to back up. But the other ghost campers had me trapped.

"You can't! I won't let you!" I shrieked to Lucy, frozen in terror.

"Go away!" Alex shouted at Elvis.

The woods darkened as clouds swept over the moon. All around me, the ghostly eyes appeared to glow brighter.

I saw Elvis reach for my brother.

And then my view was blocked by Lucy. She floated up. Up off the ground. Up over me.

"No! Stay away! Stay away!" I screamed.

But I felt my hair tingle.

I felt the cold sweep down over me. Down, down.

I felt Lucy's ghostly cold. Felt her slipping into my mind.

Slipping down, down. Taking over.

And I knew I couldn't escape.

27

"Get away, Lucy. I'm going first!" I heard a voice shout.

"No way!" a boy cried. "Move out of the way. Uncle Marv said I could be first!"

I could feel the cold sweep up from my body. I opened my eyes — and saw Lucy back on the ground.

Other kids tugged her away.

"Let go of me!" Lucy screamed, pulling back. "I saw him first!"

"Finders keepers!" another ghostly girl cried.

They are fighting over me, I realized.

They pulled Lucy away. And now they're fighting to see who will take over my mind.

"Hey — let go!" I heard a ghostly girl cry. I saw her wrestling with another girl.

The ghosts were wrestling and fighting, shoving and clawing at each other. I saw the counselors join the fight.

"Stop this! Stop this!" Uncle Marv bellowed.

He tried to pull the fighting campers apart.

But they ignored him and continued to battle.

And as I stared in horror, they began to spin around me. Faster and faster. A ghostly circle of wrestling, fighting, shrieking campers. Boys and girls, counselors and Uncle Marv, spinning, struggling, clawing.

Faster. Faster.

They spun around and around my brother and me.

Until they became a swirl of white light.

And then the light faded. Faded to gray smoke.

Wisps of smoke that floated to the trees. And disappeared in the trembling branches.

Alex and I stood watching until the last wisp of smoke had floated away.

"They're gone," I choked out. "They fought each other. And they're gone. All of them."

I shook my head. I drew in a deep breath of fresh air.

My heart was still pounding. My whole body trembled.

But I was okay. Alex and I were okay.

"Are they really gone?" Alex asked in a tiny voice.

"Yes. Let's go," I said, taking his arm. "Come on. Hurry. Let's get away from here."

He followed me eagerly. "Where are we going?"

"To the highway," I said. "We'll walk past the camp to the highway. And we'll stop the first car that comes by. We'll get to a phone. We'll call Mom and Dad."

I slapped my brother on the back. "We'll be okay, Alex!" I cried happily. "We'll be home before you know it!"

We walked quickly through the woods. Pushing bushes and weeds out of the way. Making our own path.

As we made our way to the highway, Alex started to hum a song to himself.

"Whoa!" I cried. "Alex, what's wrong?"

"Huh?" He stared at me in surprise.

I stopped and held him in place. "Sing that again," I ordered.

He sang a little more.

Horrible! His singing was horrible. Totally off-key and sour.

I stared hard into my brother's eyes. "Elvis — is that *you* in there?" I cried.

Elvis's voice came out of Alex's mouth. "Please, Harry, don't tell," he begged. "I *swear* I'll never sing again — if you promise not to tell!"

Goosebumps®

WELCOME TO
CAMP NIGHTMARE

I stared out the dusty window as the camp bus bounced over the narrow, winding road. I could see sloping red hills in the distance beneath a bright yellow sky.

Stumpy white trees lined the road like fence posts. We were way out in the wilderness. We hadn't passed a house or a farm for nearly an hour.

The bus seats were made of hard blue plastic. When the bus hit a bump, we all bounced up off our seats. Everyone laughed and shouted. The driver kept growling at us, yelling for us to pipe down.

There were twenty-two kids going to camp on the bus. I was sitting in the back row on the aisle, so I could count them all.

There were eighteen boys and only four girls. I guessed that the boys were all going to Camp Nightmoon, which is where I was going. The girls were going to a girls' camp nearby.

The girls sat together in the front rows and

talked quietly to each other. Every once in a while, they'd glance back quickly to check out the boys.

The boys were a lot louder than the girls, cracking jokes, laughing, making funny noises, shouting out dumb things. It was a long bus ride, but we were having a good time.

The boy next to me was named Mike. He had the window seat. Mike looked a little like a bulldog. He was kind of chubby, with a round face and pudgy arms and legs. He had short, spiky black hair, which he scratched a lot. He was wearing baggy brown shorts and a sleeveless green T-shirt.

We had been sitting together the whole trip, but Mike didn't say much. I figured he was shy, or maybe very nervous. He told me this was his first time at sleepaway camp.

It was my first time, too. And I have to admit that, as the bus took me farther and farther from my home, I was already starting to miss my mom and dad just a little.

I'm twelve, but I've never really stayed away from home before. Even though the long bus ride was fun, I had this sad kind of feeling. And I think Mike was feeling the same way.

He pressed his chubby face against the window glass and stared out at the red hills rolling by in the distance.

"Are you okay, Mike?" I asked.

"Yeah. Sure, Billy," he replied quickly without turning around.

I thought about my mom and dad. Back at the bus station, they had seemed so serious. I guess they were nervous, too, about me going off to camp for the first time.

"We'll write every day," Dad said.

"Do your best," Mom said, hugging me harder than usual.

What a weird thing to say. Why didn't she say, "Have a good time"? Why did she say, "Do your best"?

As you can tell, I'm a bit of a worrier.

The only other boys I'd met so far were the two in the seat in front of us. One was named Colin. He had long brown hair down to his collar, and he wore silver sunglasses so you couldn't see his eyes. He acted kind of tough, and he wore a red bandanna on his forehead. He kept tying and untying the bandanna.

Sitting next to him in the seat on the aisle was a big, loud kid named Jay. Jay talked a lot about sports and kept bragging about what a good athlete he was. He liked showing off his big, muscular arms, especially when one of the girls turned around to check us out.

Jay teased Colin a lot and kept wrestling with him, gripping Colin's head in a headlock and messing up Colin's bandanna. You know. Just kidding around.

Jay had wild, bushy red hair that looked as if it had never been brushed. He had big blue eyes. He never stopped grinning and horsing around. He spent the whole trip telling gross jokes and shouting things at the girls.

"Hey — what's your name?" Jay called to a blonde-haired girl who sat at the front by the window.

She ignored him for a long time. But the fourth time Jay called out the question, she turned around, her green eyes flashing. "Dawn," she replied. Then she pointed to the red-haired girl next to her. "And this is my friend Dori."

"Hey — that's amazing! My name is Dawn, too!" Jay joked.

A lot of the guys laughed, but Dawn didn't crack a smile. "Nice to meet you, Dawn," she called back to him. Then she turned back to the front.

The bus bounced over a hole in the road, and we all bounced with it.

"Hey, look, Billy," Mike said suddenly, pointing out the window.

Mike hadn't said anything for a long time. I leaned toward the window, trying to see what he was pointing at.

"I think I saw a prairie cat," he said, still staring hard.

"Huh? Really?" I saw a clump of low, white trees and a lot of jagged, red rocks. But I couldn't see any prairie cats.

"It went behind those rocks," Mike said, still pointing. Then he turned toward me. "Have you seen any towns or anything?"

I shook my head. "Just desert."

"But isn't the camp supposed to be near a town?" Mike looked worried.

"I don't think so," I told him. "My dad told me that Camp Nightmoon is past the desert, way out in the woods."

Mike thought about this for a while, frowning. "Well, what if we want to call home or something?" he asked.

"They probably have phones at the camp," I told him.

I glanced up in time to see Jay toss something up toward the girls at the front. It looked like a green ball. It hit Dawn on the back of the head and stuck in her blonde hair.

"Hey!" Dawn cried out angrily. She pulled the sticky, green ball from her hair. "What *is* this?" She turned to glare at Jay.

Jay giggled his high-pitched giggle. "I don't know. I found it stuck under the seat!" he called to her.

Dawn scowled at him and heaved the green ball back. It missed Jay and hit the rear window, where it stuck with a loud *plop*.

Everyone laughed. Dawn and her friend Dori made faces at Jay.

Colin fiddled with his red bandanna. Jay

241

slumped down low and raised his knees against the seat in front of him.

A few rows ahead of me, two grinning boys were singing a song we all knew, but with really gross words replacing the original words.

A few other kids began to sing along.

Suddenly, without warning, the bus squealed to a stop, the tires skidding loudly over the road.

We all cried out in surprise. I bounced off my seat, and my chest hit the seat in front of me.

"Ugh!" That hurt.

As I slid back in the seat, my heart still pounding, the bus driver stood up and turned to us, leaning heavily into the aisle.

"Ohh!" Several loud gasps filled the small bus as we saw the driver's face.

His head was enormous and pink, topped with a mop of wild, bright blue hair that stood straight up. He had long, pointed ears. His huge red eyeballs bulged out from their dark sockets, bouncing in front of his snoutlike nose. Sharp white fangs drooped from his gaping mouth. A green liquid oozed over his heavy black lips.

As we goggled in silent horror, the driver tilted back his monstrous head and uttered an animal roar.

2

The driver roared so loud, the bus windows rattled.

Several kids shrieked in fright.

Mike and I both ducked down low, hiding behind the seat in front of us.

"He's turned into a *monster*!" Mike whispered, his eyes wide with fear.

Then we heard laughter at the front of the bus.

I raised myself up in time to see the bus driver reach one hand up to his bright blue hair. He tugged — and his face slid right off!

"Ohhh!" Several kids shrieked in horror.

But we quickly realized that the face dangling from the driver's hand was a mask. He had been wearing a rubber monster mask.

His real face was perfectly normal, I saw with relief. He had pale skin, short, thinning black hair, and tiny blue eyes. He laughed, shaking his head, enjoying his joke.

"This fools 'em every time!" he declared, holding up the ugly mask.

A few kids laughed along with him. But most of us were too surprised and confused to think it was funny.

Suddenly, his expression changed. "Everybody out!" he ordered gruffly.

He pulled a lever and the door slid open with a *whoosh*.

"Where are we?" someone called out.

But the driver ignored the question. He tossed the mask onto the driver's seat. Then, lowering his head so he wouldn't bump the roof, he quickly made his way out the door.

I leaned across Mike and stared out the window, but I couldn't see much. Just mile after mile of flat, yellow ground, broken occasionally by clumps of red rock. It looked like a desert.

"Why are we getting out here?" Mike asked, turning to me. I could see he was really worried.

"Maybe this is the camp," I joked. Mike didn't think that was funny.

We were all confused as we pushed and shoved our way off the bus. Mike and I were the last ones off since we were sitting in the back.

As I stepped onto the hard ground, I shielded my eyes against the bright sunlight, high in the afternoon sky. We were in a flat, open area. The bus was parked beside a concrete platform, about the size of a tennis court.

"It must be some kind of bus station or something," I told Mike. "You know. A drop-off point."

He had his hands shoved into the pockets of his shorts. He kicked at the dirt, but didn't say anything.

On the other side of the platform, Jay was in a shoving match with a boy I hadn't met yet. Colin was leaning against the side of the bus, being cool. The four girls were standing in a circle near the front of the platform, talking quietly about something.

I watched the driver walk over to the side of the bus and pull open the luggage compartment. He began pulling out bags and camp trunks and carrying them to the concrete platform.

A couple of guys had sat down on the edge of the platform to watch the driver work. On the other side of the platform, Jay and some other guys were having a contest, tossing little red pebbles as far as they could.

Mike, his hands still buried in his pockets, stepped up behind the sweating bus driver. "Hey, where are we? Why are we stopping here?" Mike asked him nervously.

The driver slid a heavy black trunk from the back of the luggage compartment. He completely ignored Mike's questions. Mike asked them again. And again the driver pretended Mike wasn't there.

Mike made his way back to where I was standing, walking slowly, dragging his shoes across the hard ground. He looked really worried.

I was confused, but I wasn't worried. I mean, the bus driver was calmly going about his business, unloading the bus. He knew what he was doing.

"Why won't he answer me? Why won't he tell us anything?" Mike demanded.

I felt bad that Mike was so nervous. But I didn't want to hear any more of his questions. He was starting to make me nervous, too.

I wandered away from him, making my way along the side of the platform to where the four girls were standing. Across the platform, Jay and his buddies were still having their stone-throwing contest.

Dawn smiled at me as I came closer. Then she glanced quickly away. She's really pretty, I thought. Her blonde hair gleamed in the bright sunlight.

"Are you from Center City?" her friend Dori asked, squinting at me, her freckled face twisted against the sun.

"No," I told her. "I'm from Midlands. It's north of Center City. Near Outreach Bay."

"I *know* where Midlands is!" Dori snapped snottily. The other three girls laughed.

I could feel myself blushing.

"What's your name?" Dawn asked, staring at me with her green eyes.

"Billy," I told her.

"My bird's name is Billy!" she exclaimed, and the girls all laughed again.

"Where are you girls going?" I asked quickly, eager to change the subject. "I mean, what camp?"

"Camp Nightmoon. There's one for boys and one for girls," Dori answered. "This is an all-Camp Nightmoon bus."

"Is your camp near ours?" I asked. I didn't even know there was a Camp Nightmoon for girls.

Dori shrugged. "We don't know," Dawn replied. "This is our first year."

"All of us," Dori added.

"Me, too," I told them. "I wonder why we stopped here."

The girls all shrugged.

I saw that Mike was lingering behind me, looking even more scared. I turned and made my way back to him.

"Look. The driver is finished carrying out our stuff," he said, pointing.

I turned in time to see the driver slam the luggage compartment door shut.

"What's happening?" Mike cried. "Is someone picking us up here? Why did he unload all our stuff?"

"I'll go find out," I said quietly. I started to jog over to the driver. He was standing in front of the open bus door, mopping his perspiring forehead with the short sleeve of his tan driver's uniform.

He saw me coming — and quickly climbed into the bus. He slid into the driver's seat, pulling a green sun visor down over his forehead as I stepped up to the door.

"Is someone coming for us?" I called in to him.

To my surprise, he pulled the lever, and the bus door slammed shut in my face.

The engine started up with a roar and a burst of gray exhaust fumes.

"Hey — !" I screamed and pounded angrily on the glass door.

I had to leap back as the bus squealed away, its tires spinning noisily on the hard dirt. "Hey!" I shouted. "You don't have to run me over!"

I stared angrily as the bus bounced onto the road and roared away. Then I turned back to Mike. He was standing beside the four girls. They were all looking upset now.

"He — he left," Mike stammered as I approached them. "He just *left* us here in the middle of nowhere."

We gazed down the road at the bus until it disappeared over the darkening horizon. We all grew very quiet.

A few seconds later, we heard the frightening animal cries.

Very close. And getting closer.

3

"Wh-what's that?" Mike stammered.

We turned in the direction of the shrill cries.

They seemed to be coming from across the platform. At first, I thought that Jay and Colin and their friends were playing a joke on us, making the animal cries to frighten us.

But then I saw the scared, wide-eyed expressions on their faces. Jay, Colin, and the others had frozen in place. They weren't making the noises.

The cries grew louder. Closer.

Shrill warnings.

And, then, staring into the distance beyond the platform, I saw them. Small, dark creatures, keeping low, rolling rapidly along the flat ground, tossing their heads back and uttering excited shrieks as they came toward us.

"What are they?" Mike cried, moving close to me.

"Are they prairie wolves?" Dori asked in a trembling voice.

"I hope not!" one of the other girls called out.

We all climbed onto the concrete platform and were huddled behind our trunks and bags.

The animal cries grew louder as the creatures drew near. I could see dozens of them. They scurried toward us over the flat ground as if being blown by the wind.

"Help! Somebody *help* us!" I heard Mike scream.

Next to me, Jay still had two of the red rocks from his rock-throwing competition in his hand. "Pick up rocks!" he was shouting frantically. "Maybe we can scare them away!"

The creatures stopped a few yards from the concrete platform and raised themselves up menacingly on their hind feet.

Huddled between Mike and Jay, I could see them clearly now. They were wolves or wildcats of some sort. Standing upright, they were nearly three feet tall.

They had slender, almost scrawny bodies, covered with spotty red-brown fur. Their paws had long, silvery nails growing out of them. Their heads were nearly as slender as their bodies. Tiny red weasel eyes stared hungrily at us. Their long mouths snapped open and shut, revealing double rows of silvery, daggerlike teeth.

"No! No! Help!" Mike dropped to his knees. His

entire body convulsed in a shudder of terror.

Some of the kids were crying. Others gaped at the advancing creatures in stunned silence.

I was too scared to cry out or move or do *anything*.

I stared at the row of creatures, my heart thudding, my mouth as dry as cotton.

The creatures grew silent. Standing a few feet from the platform, they eyed us, snapping their jaws loudly, hungrily. White froth began to drip from their mouths.

"They — they're going to attack!" a boy yelled.

"They look hungry!" I heard one of the girls say.

The white froth poured thickly over their pointed teeth. They continued to snap their jaws. It sounded like a dozen steel traps being snapped shut.

Suddenly, one of them leapt onto the edge of the platform.

"No!" several kids cried out in unison.

We huddled closer together, trying to stay behind the pile of trunks and bags.

Another creature climbed onto the platform. Then three more.

I took a step back.

I saw Jay pull back his arm and heave a red rock at one of the frothing creatures. The rock hit the platform with a *crack* and bounced away.

The creatures were not frightened. They arched their backs, preparing to attack.

They began to make a high-pitched chattering sound.

And moved nearer. Nearer.

Jay threw another rock.

This one hit one of the advancing creatures on the side. It uttered a shrill *eek* of surprise. But it kept moving steadily forward, its red eyes trained on Jay, its jaws snapping hungrily.

"Go away!" Dori cried in a trembling voice. "Go home! Go away! Go *away!*"

But her shouts had no effect.

The creatures advanced.

"Run!" I urged "Run!"

"We can't outrun them!" someone shouted.

The shrill chittering grew louder. Deafening. Until it seemed as if we were surrounded by a wall of sound.

The ugly creatures lowered themselves to pounce.

"Run!" I repeated. "Come on — run!"

My legs wouldn't cooperate. They felt rubbery and weak.

Trying to back away from the attacking creatures, I toppled over backwards off the platform.

I saw flashing stars as the back of my head hit the hard ground.

They're going to get me, I realized.

I can't get away.

4

I heard the sirenlike attack cry.

I heard the scrape of the creatures' long toenails over the concrete platform.

I heard the screams and cries of the frightened campers.

Then, as I struggled frantically to pull myself up, I heard the deafening roar.

At first I thought it was an explosion.

I thought the platform had blown up.

But then I turned and saw the rifle.

Another explosion of gunfire. White smoke filled the air.

The creatures spun around and darted away, silent now, their scraggly fur scraping the ground as they kept low, their tails between their furry legs.

"Ha-ha! Look at 'em run!" The man kept the rifle poised on his shoulder as he watched the creatures retreat.

Behind him stood a long green bus.

I pulled myself up and brushed myself off.

Everyone was laughing now, jumping up and down joyfully, celebrating the narrow escape.

I was still too shaken up to celebrate.

"They're running like jackrabbits!" the man declared in a booming voice. He lowered the rifle.

It took me a while to realize he had come out of the camp bus to rescue us. We didn't hear or see the bus pull up because of the attack cries of the animals.

"Are you okay, Mike?" I asked, walking over to my frightened-looking new friend.

"I guess," he replied uncertainly. "I guess I'm okay now."

Dawn slapped me on the back, grinning. "We're okay!" she cried. "We're all okay!"

We gathered in front of the man with the rifle.

He was big and red-faced, mostly bald except for a fringe of curly yellow hair around his head. He had a blond mustache under an enormous beak of a nose, and tiny black bird eyes beneath bushy blond eyebrows.

"Hi, guys! I'm Uncle Al. I'm your friendly camp director. I hope you enjoyed that welcome to Camp Nightmoon!" he boomed in a deep voice.

I heard muttered replies.

He leaned the rifle against the bus and took a few steps toward us, studying our faces. He was wearing white shorts and a bright green camp T-shirt that stretched over his big belly. Two

254

young guys, also in green and white, stepped out of the bus, serious expressions on their faces.

"Let's load up," Uncle Al instructed them in his deep voice.

He didn't apologize for being late.

He didn't explain about the weird animals. And he didn't ask if we were okay after that scare.

The two counselors began dragging the camp trunks and shoving them into the luggage compartment on the bus.

"Looks like a good group this year," Uncle Al shouted. "We'll drop you girls off first across the river. Then we'll get you boys settled in."

"What *were* those awful animals?" Dori called to Uncle Al.

He didn't seem to hear her.

We began climbing onto the bus. I looked for Mike and found him near the end of the line. His face was pale, and he still looked really shaken. "I — I was really scared," he admitted.

"But we're okay," I reassured him. "Now we can relax and have fun."

"I'm so hungry," Mike complained. "I haven't eaten all day."

One of the counselors overheard him. "You won't be hungry when you taste the camp food," he told Mike.

We piled into the bus. I sat next to Mike. I could hear the poor guy's stomach growling. I suddenly realized I was starving, too. And I was really eager to see what Camp Nightmoon looked like. I hoped it wouldn't be a long bus ride to get there.

"How far away is our camp?" I called to Uncle Al, who had slid into the driver's seat.

He didn't seem to hear me.

"Hey, Mike, we're on our way!" I said happily as the bus pulled onto the road.

Mike forced a smile. "I'm so glad to get *away* from there!"

To my surprise, the bus ride took less than five minutes.

We all muttered our shock at what a short trip it was. Why hadn't the first bus taken us all the way?

A big wooden sign proclaiming CAMP NIGHT-MOON came into view, and Uncle Al turned the bus onto a gravel road that led through a patch of short trees into the camp.

We followed the narrow, winding road across a small, brown river. Several small cabins came into view. "Girls' camp," Uncle Al announced. The bus stopped to let the four girls off. Dawn waved to me as she climbed down.

A few minutes later, we pulled into the boys' camp. Through the bus window I could see a row of small, white cabins. On top of a gently sloping hill stood a large, white-shingled building, probably a meeting lodge or mess hall.

At the edge of a field, three counselors, all dressed in white shorts and green T-shirts, were working to start a fire in a large stone barbecue pit.

"Hey, we're going to have a cookout!" I exclaimed to Mike. I was starting to feel really excited.

Mike smiled, too. He was practically drooling at the thought of food!

The bus came to an abrupt stop at the end of the row of small bunks. Uncle Al pulled himself up quickly from the driver's seat and turned to us. "Welcome to beautiful Camp Nightmoon!" he bellowed. "Step down and line up for your bunk assignments. Once you get unpacked and have dinner, I'll see you at the campfire."

We pushed our way noisily out of the bus. I saw Jay enthusiastically slapping another boy on the back. I think we were all feeling a lot better, forgetting about our close call.

I stepped down and took a deep breath. The cool air smelled really sweet and fresh. I saw a long row of short evergreen trees behind the white lodge on the hill.

As I took my place in line, I searched for the waterfront. I could hear the soft rush of the river behind a thick row of evergreens, but I couldn't see it.

Mike, Jay, Colin, and I were assigned to the

same bunk. It was Bunk 4. I thought the bunk should have a more interesting name. But it just had a number. Bunk 4.

It was really small, with a low ceiling and windows on two sides. It was just big enough for six campers. There were bunk beds against three walls and tall shelves on the fourth wall, with a little square of space in the middle.

There was no bathroom. I guessed it was in another building.

As the four of us entered the bunk, we saw that one of the beds had already been claimed. It had been carefully made, the green blanket tucked in neatly, some sports magazines and a tape player resting on top.

"That must belong to our counselor," Jay said, inspecting the tape player.

"Hope we don't have to wear those ugly green T-shirts," Colin said, grinning. He was still wearing his silver sunglasses, even though the sun was nearly down and it was just about as dark as night in the cabin.

Jay claimed a top bunk, and Colin took the bed beneath his.

"Can I have a lower one?" Mike asked me. "I roll around a lot at night. I'm afraid I might fall out of a top one."

"Yeah. Sure. No problem," I replied. I wanted the top bunk anyway. It would be a lot more fun.

"Hope you guys don't snore," Colin said.

"We're not going to sleep in here anyway," Jay said. "We're going to party all night!" He playfully slapped Mike on the back, so hard that Mike went sprawling into the dresser.

"Hey!" Mike whined. "That hurt!"

"Sorry. Guess I don't know my own strength," Jay replied, grinning at Colin.

The cabin door opened, and a red-headed guy with dark freckles all over his face walked in, carrying a big gray plastic bag. He was tall and very skinny and was wearing white shorts and a green camp T-shirt.

"Hey, guys," he said, and dropped the large bag on the cabin floor with a groan. He checked us out, then pointed to the bag. "There's your bed stuff," he said. "Make your beds. Try to make them as neat as mine." He pointed to the bunk against the window with the tape player on it.

"Are you our counselor?" I asked.

He nodded. "Yeah. I'm the lucky one." He turned and started to walk out.

"What's your name?" Jay called after him.

"Larry," he said, pushing open the cabin door. "Your trunks will be here in a few minutes," he told us. "You can fight it out over drawer space. Two of the drawers are stuck shut."

He started out the door, then turned back to us. "Keep away from my stuff." The door slammed hard behind him.

Peering out the window, I watched him lope

259

away, taking long, fast strides, bobbing his head as he walked.

"Great guy," Colin muttered sarcastically.

"Real friendly," Jay added, shaking his head.

Then we dived into the plastic bag and pulled out sheets and wool blankets. Jay and Colin got into a wrestling match over a blanket they claimed was softer than the others.

I tossed a sheet onto my mattress and started to climb up to tuck it in.

I was halfway up the ladder when I heard Mike scream.

5

Mike was right beneath me, making his bed. He screamed so loud, I cried out and nearly fell off the ladder.

I leapt off the ladder, my heart pounding, and stepped beside him.

Staring straight ahead, his mouth wide open in horror, Mike backed away from his bed.

"Mike — what's wrong?" I asked. "What *is* it?"

"S-snakes!" Mike stammered, staring straight ahead at his unmade bed as he backed away.

"Huh?" I followed his gaze. It was too dark to see anything.

Colin laughed. "Not *that* old joke!" he cried.

"Larry put rubber snakes in your bed," Jay said, grinning as he stepped up beside us.

"They're not rubber! They're real!" Mike insisted, his voice trembling.

Jay laughed and shook his head. "I can't believe you fell for that old gag." He took a few steps toward the bed — then stopped. "Hey — !"

I moved close, and the two snakes came into focus. Raising themselves from the shadows, they arched their slender heads, pulling back as if preparing to attack.

"They're real!" Jay cried, turning back to Colin. "Two of them!"

"Probably not poisonous," Colin said, venturing closer.

The two let out angry hisses, raising themselves high off the bed. They were very long and skinny. Their heads were wider than their bodies. Their tongues flicked from side to side as they arched themselves menacingly.

"I'm scared of snakes," Mike uttered in a soft voice.

"They're probably scared of you!" Jay joked, slapping Mike on the back.

Mike winced. He was in no mood for Jay's horse-play. "We've got to get Larry or somebody," Mike said.

"No way!" Jay insisted. "You can handle 'em, Mike. There's only two of them!"

Jay gave Mike a playful shove toward the bed. He only meant to give him a scare.

But Mike stumbled — and fell onto the bed.

The snakes darted in unison.

I saw one of them clamp its teeth into Mike's hand.

Mike raised himself to his feet. He didn't react

at first. Then he uttered a high-pitched shriek.

Two drops of blood appeared on the back of his right hand. He stared down at them, then grabbed the hand.

"It *bit* me!" he shrieked.

"Oh, no!" I cried.

"Did it puncture the skin?" Colin asked. "Is it bleeding?"

Jay rushed forward and grabbed Mike's shoulder. "Hey, man — I'm really sorry," he said. "I didn't mean to — "

Mike groaned in pain. "It — really hurts," he whispered. He was breathing really hard, his chest heaving, making weird noises as he breathed.

The snakes, coiled in the middle of his lower bunk, began to hiss again.

"You'd better hurry to the nurse," Jay said, his hand still on Mike's shoulder. "I'll come with you."

"N-no," Mike stammered. His face was as pale as a ghost. He held his hand tightly. "I'll go find her!" He burst out of the cabin, running at full speed. The door slammed behind him.

"Hey — I didn't mean to push him, you know," Jay explained to us. I could see he was really upset. "I was just joking, just trying to scare him a little. I didn't mean for him to fall or anything. . . ." His voice trailed off.

"What are we going to do about *them*?" I asked, pointing at the two coiled snakes.

"I'll get Larry," Colin offered. He started toward the door.

"No, wait." I called him back. "Look. They're sitting on Mike's sheet, right?"

Jay and Colin followed my gaze to the bed. The snakes arched themselves high, preparing to bite again.

"So?" Jay asked, scratching his disheveled hair.

"So we can wrap them up in the sheet and carry them outside," I said.

Jay stared at me. "Wish I'd thought of that. Let's do it, man!"

"You'll get bit," Colin warned.

I stared at the snakes. They seemed to be studying me, too. "They can't bite us through the sheet," I said.

"They can try!" Colin exclaimed, hanging back.

"If we're fast enough," I said, taking a cautious step toward the bed, "we can wrap them up before they know what's happening."

The snakes hissed out a warning, drawing themselves higher.

"How did they get in here, anyway?" Colin asked.

"Maybe the camp is *crawling* with snakes," Jay said, grinning. "Maybe you've got some in *your* bed, too, Colin!" He laughed.

"Let's get serious here," I said sternly, my eyes locked on the coiled snakes. "Are we going to try this or not?"

"Yeah. Let's do it," Jay answered. "I mean, I owe it to Mike."

Colin remained silent.

"I'll bet I could grab one by the tail and swing him out through the window," Jay said. "You could grab the tail end of the other one and — "

"Let's try my plan first," I suggested quietly.

We crept over to the snakes, sneaking up on them. It was kind of silly since they were staring right at us.

I pointed to one end of the sheet, which was folded up onto the bed. "Grab it there," I instructed Jay. "Then pull it up."

He hesitated. "What if I miss? Or you miss?"

"Then we're in trouble," I replied grimly. My eyes on the snakes, I reached my hand forward to the other corner of the sheet. "Ready? On three," I whispered.

My heart was in my mouth. I could barely choke out, "One, two, three."

At the count of three, we both grabbed for the ends of the sheet.

"Pull!" I cried in a shrill voice I couldn't believe was coming from me.

We pulled up the sheet and brought the ends together, making a bundle.

At the bottom of the bundle, the snakes wriggled frantically. I heard their jaws snap. They wriggled so hard, the bottom of the bundle swung back and forth.

"They don't like this," Jay said as we hurried to the door, carrying our wriggling, swaying bundle between us, trying to keep our bodies as far away from it as possible.

I pushed open the door with my shoulder, and we ran out onto the grass.

"Now what?" Jay asked.

"Keep going," I replied. I could see one of the snakes poking its head out. "Hurry!"

We ran past the cabins toward a small clump of shrubs. Beyond the shrubs stood a patch of low trees. When we reached the trees, we swung the bundle back, then heaved the whole sheet into the trees.

It opened as it fell to the ground. The two snakes slithered out instantly and pulled themselves to shelter under the trees.

Jay and I let out loud sighs of relief. We stood there for a moment, hunched over, hands on our knees, trying to catch our breath.

Crouching down, I looked for the snakes. But they had slithered deep into the safety of the evergreens.

I stood up. "I guess we should take back Mike's sheet," I said.

"He probably won't want to sleep on it," Jay

said. But he reached down and pulled it up from the grass. He balled it up and tossed it to me. "It's probably dripping with snake venom," he said, making a disgusted face.

When we got back to the cabin, Colin had made his bed and was busily unpacking the contents of his trunk, shoving everything into the top dresser drawer. He turned as we entered. "How'd it go?" he asked casually.

"Horrible," Jay replied quickly, his expression grim. "We both got bit. Twice."

"You're a terrible liar!" Colin told him, laughing. "You shouldn't even try."

Jay laughed, too.

Colin turned to me. "You're a hero," he said.

"Thanks for all your help," Jay told him sarcastically.

Colin started to reply. But the cabin door opened, and Larry poked his freckled face in. "How's it going?" he asked. "You're not finished yet?"

"We had a little problem," Jay told him.

"Where's the fourth guy? The chubby one?" Larry asked, lowering his head so he wouldn't bump it on the doorframe as he stepped inside.

"Mike got bit. By a snake," I told him.

"There were two snakes in his bed," Jay added.

Larry's expression didn't change. He didn't seem at all surprised. "So where did Mike go?" he asked casually, swatting a mosquito on his arm.

267

"His hand was bleeding. He went to the nurse to get it taken care of," I told him.

"Huh?" Larry's mouth dropped open.

"He went to find the nurse," I repeated.

Larry tossed back his head and started to laugh. "Nurse?" he cried, laughing hard. *"What* nurse?!"

6

The door opened and Mike returned, still holding his wounded hand. His face was pale, his expression frightened. "They said there was no nurse," he told me.

Then he saw Larry perched on top of his bunk. "Larry — my hand," Mike said. He held the hand up so the counselor could see it. It was stained with bright red blood.

Larry lowered himself to the floor. "I think I have some bandages," he told Mike. He pulled out a slender black case from beneath his bunk and began to search through it.

Mike stood beside him, holding up his hand. Drops of blood splashed on the cabin floor. "They said the camp doesn't have a nurse," Mike repeated.

Larry shook his head. "If you get hurt in *this* camp," he told Mike seriously, "you're on your own."

"I think my hand is swelling a little," Mike said.

Larry handed him a roll of bandages. "The washroom is at the end of this row of cabins," he told Mike, closing the case and shoving it back under the bed. "Go wash the hand and bandage it. Hurry. It's almost dinnertime."

Holding the bandages tightly in his good hand, Mike hurried off to follow Larry's instructions.

"By the way, how'd you guys get the snakes out of here?" Larry asked, glancing around the cabin.

"We carried them out in Mike's sheet," Jay told him. He pointed at me. "It was Billy's idea."

Larry stared hard at me. "Hey, I'm impressed, Billy," he said. "That was pretty brave, man."

"Maybe I inherited something from my parents," I told him. "They're scientists. Explorers, kind of. They go off for months at a time, exploring the wildest places."

"Well, Camp Nightmoon is pretty wild," Larry said. "And you guys had better be careful. I'm warning you." His expression turned serious. "There's no nurse at Camp Nightmoon. Uncle Al doesn't believe in coddling you guys."

The hot dogs were all charred black, but we were so hungry, we didn't care. I shoved three of them down in less than five minutes. I don't think I'd ever been so hungry in all my life.

The campfire was in a flat clearing surrounded by a circle of round, white stones. Behind us, the large, white-shingled lodge loomed over the sloping hill. Ahead of us a thick line of evergreen trees formed a fence that hid the river from view.

Through a small gap in the trees, I could see a flickering campfire in the distance on the other side of the river. I wondered if that was the campfire of the girls' camp.

I thought about Dawn and Dori. I wondered if the two camps ever got together, if I'd ever see them again.

Dinner around the big campfire seemed to put everyone in a good mood. Jay was the only one sitting near me who complained about the hot dogs being burned. But I think he put away four or five of them anyway!

Mike had trouble eating because of his bandaged hand. When he dropped his first hot dog, I thought he was going to burst into tears. By the end of dinner, he was in a much better mood. His wounded hand had swelled up just a little. But he said it didn't hurt as much as before.

The counselors were easy to spot. They all wore identical white shorts and green T-shirts. There were eight or ten of them, all young guys probably sixteen or seventeen. They ate together quietly, away from us campers. I kept looking at Larry, but he never once turned around to look at any of us.

I was thinking about Larry, trying to figure out if he was shy or if he just didn't like us campers

271

very much. Suddenly, Uncle Al climbed to his feet and motioned with both hands for us all to be quiet.

"I want to welcome you boys to Camp Nightmoon," he began. "I hope you're all unpacked and comfortable in your bunks. I know that most of you are first-time campers."

He was speaking quickly, without any pauses between sentences, as if he was running through this for the thousandth time and wanted to get it over with.

"I'd like to tell you some of our basic rules," he continued. "First, lights out is at nine sharp."

A lot of guys groaned.

"You might think you can ignore this rule," Uncle Al continued, paying no attention to their reaction. "You might think you can sneak out of your cabins to meet or take a walk by the river. But I'm warning you now that we don't allow it, and we have very good ways of making sure this rule is obeyed."

He paused to clear his throat.

Some boys were giggling about something. Across from me, Jay burped loudly, which caused more giggles.

Uncle Al didn't seem to hear any of this. "On the other side of the river is the girls' camp," he continued loudly, motioning to the trees. "You might be able to see their campfire. Well, I want to make it clear that swimming or rowing over to the girls' camp is strictly forbidden."

Several boys groaned loudly. This made everyone laugh. Even some of the counselors laughed. Uncle Al remained grim-faced.

"The woods around Camp Nightmoon are filled with grizzlies and tree bears," Uncle Al continued. "They come to the river to bathe and to drink. And they're usually hungry."

This caused another big reaction from all of us sitting around the fading campfire. Someone made a loud growling sound. Another kid screamed. Then everyone laughed.

"You won't be laughing if a bear claws your head off," Uncle Al said sternly.

He turned to the group of counselors outside our circle. "Larry, Kurt, come over here," he ordered.

The two counselors climbed obediently to their feet and made their way to the center of the circle beside Uncle Al.

"I want you two to demonstrate to the new campers the procedure to follow when — er, I mean, *if* you are attacked by a grizzly bear."

Immediately, the two counselors dropped to the ground on their stomachs. They lay flat and covered the backs of their heads with their hands.

"That's right. I hope you're all paying close attention," the camp director thundered at us.

"Cover your neck and head. Try your best not to move." He motioned to the two counselors. "Thanks, guys. You can get up."

"Have there ever been any bear attacks here?" I called out, cupping my hands so Uncle Al could hear me.

He turned in my direction. "Two last summer," he replied.

Several boys gasped.

"It wasn't pretty," Uncle Al continued. "It's hard to remain still when a huge bear is pawing you and drooling all over you. But if you move . . ." His voice trailed off, leaving the rest to our imaginations, I guess.

I felt a cold shiver run down my back. I didn't want to think about bears and bear attacks.

What kind of camp did Mom and Dad send me to? I found myself wondering. I couldn't wait to call them and tell them about all that had happened already.

Uncle Al waited for everyone to get silent, then pointed off to the side. "Do you see that cabin over there?" he asked.

In the dim evening light, I could make out a cabin standing halfway up the hill toward the lodge. It appeared a little larger than the other cabins. It seemed to be built on a slant, sort of tipping on its side, as if the wind had tried to blow it over.

"I want you to make sure you see that cabin,"

Uncle Al warned, his voice thundering out above the crackling of the purple fire. "That is known as the Forbidden Bunk. We don't talk about that bunk — and we don't go near it."

I felt another cold shiver as I stared through the gray evening light at the shadowy, tilted cabin. I felt a sharp sting on the back of my neck and slapped a mosquito, too late to keep it from biting me.

"I'm going to repeat what I just said," Uncle Al shouted, still pointing to the dark cabin on the hill. "That is known as the Forbidden Bunk. It has been closed and boarded up for many years. No one is to go near that cabin. *No one.*"

This started everyone talking and laughing. Nervous laughter, I think.

"Why is the Forbidden Bunk forbidden?" someone called out.

"We never talk about it," Uncle Al replied sharply.

Jay leaned over and whispered in my ear, "Let's go check it out."

I laughed. Then I turned back to Jay uncertainly. "You're kidding — right?"

He grinned in reply and didn't say anything.

I turned back toward the fire. Uncle Al was wishing us all a good stay and saying how much he was looking forward to camp this year. "And one more rule — " he called out. "You must write to your parents every day. Every day! We want them to know what a great time you're having at Camp Nightmoon."

I saw Mike holding his wounded hand gingerly. "It's starting to throb," he told me, sounding very frightened.

"Maybe Larry has something to put on it," I said. "Let's go ask him."

Uncle Al dismissed us. We all climbed to our feet, stretching and yawning, and started to make our way in small groups back to the bunks.

Mike and I lingered behind, hoping to talk to Larry. We saw him talking to the other counselors. He was at least a head taller than all of them.

"Hey, Larry — " Mike called.

But by the time we pushed our way through the groups of kids heading the other way, Larry had disappeared.

"Maybe he's going to our bunk to make sure we obey lights out," I suggested.

"Let's go see," Mike replied anxiously.

We walked quickly past the dying campfire. It had stopped crackling but still glowed a deep purple-red. Then we headed along the curve of the hill toward Bunk 4.

"My hand really hurts," Mike groaned, holding it tenderly in front of him. "I'm not just complaining. It's throbbing and it's swelling up. And I'm starting to have chills."

"Larry will know what to do," I replied, trying to sound reassuring.

"I hope so," Mike said shakily.

We both stopped when we heard the howls.

Hideous howls. Like an animal in pain. But too human to be from an animal.

Long, shrill howls that cut through the air and echoed down the hill.

Mike uttered a quiet gasp. He turned to me. Even in the darkness, I could see the fright on his face.

"Those cries," he whispered. "They're coming from . . . the Forbidden Bunk!"

7

A few minutes later, Mike and I trudged into the cabin. Jay and Colin were sitting tensely on their beds. "Where's Larry?" Mike asked, fear creeping into his voice.

"Not here," Colin replied.

"Where *is* he?" Mike demanded shrilly. "I've got to find him. My *hand*!"

"He should be here soon," Jay offered.

I could still hear the strange howls through the open window. "Do you hear that?" I asked, walking over to the window and listening hard.

"Probably a prairie cat," Colin said.

"Prairie cats don't howl," Mike told him. "Prairie cats screech, but they don't howl."

"How do you know?" Colin asked, walking over to Larry's bunk and sitting down on the bottom bed.

"We studied them in school," Mike replied.

Another howl made us all stop and listen.

"It sounds like a man," Jay offered, his eyes

lighting up excitedly. "A man who's been locked up in the Forbidden Bunk for years and years."

Mike swallowed hard. "Do you really think so?"

Jay and Colin laughed.

"What should I do about my hand?" Mike asked, holding it up. It was definitely swollen.

"Go wash it again," I told him. "And put a fresh bandage on it." I peered out the window into the darkness. "Maybe Larry will show up soon. He probably knows where to get something to put on it."

"I can't believe there's no nurse," Mike whined. "Why would my parents send me to a camp where there's no nurse or infirmary or anything?"

"Uncle Al doesn't like to coddle us," Colin said, repeating Larry's words.

Jay stood up and broke into an imitation of Uncle Al. "Stay away from the Forbidden Bunk!" he cried in a booming deep voice. He sounded a lot like him. "We don't talk about it and we don't ever go near it!"

We all laughed at Jay's impression. Even Mike.

"We should go there tonight!" Colin said enthusiastically. "We should check it out immediately!"

We heard another long, sorrowful howl roll down the hill from the direction of the Forbidden Bunk.

"I — I don't think we should," Mike said softly, examining his hand. He started to the door. "I'm going to go wash this." The door slammed behind him.

"He's scared," Jay scoffed.

"I'm a little scared, too," I admitted. "I mean, those awful howls . . ."

Jay and Colin both laughed. "Every camp has something like the Forbidden Bunk. The camp director makes it up," Colin said.

"Yeah," Jay agreed. "Camp directors love scaring kids. It's the only fun they have."

He puffed out his chest and imitated Uncle Al again. "Don't go out after lights out or you'll never be seen again!" he thundered, then burst out laughing.

"There's nothing in that Forbidden Bunk," Colin said, shaking his head. "It's probably completely empty. It's all just a joke. You know. Like camp ghost stories. Every camp has its own ghost story."

"How do you know?" I asked, dropping down onto Mike's bed. "Have you been to camp before?"

"No," Colin replied. "But I have friends who told me about *their* camp." He reached up and pulled off his silver sunglasses for the first time. He had bright sky-blue eyes, like big blue marbles.

We suddenly heard the sound of a bugle, repeating a slow, sad-sounding tune.

"That must be the signal for lights out," I said, yawning. I started to pull off my shoes. I was too tired to change or wash up. I planned to sleep in my clothes.

"Let's sneak out and explore the Forbidden Bunk," Jay urged. "Come on. We can be the first ones to do it!"

I yawned again. "I'm really too tired," I told them.

"Me, too," Colin said. He turned to Jay. "How about tomorrow night?"

Jay's face fell in disappointment.

"Tomorrow," Colin insisted, kicking his shoes into the corner and starting to pull off his socks.

"I wouldn't do it if I were you!"

The voice startled all three of us. We turned to the window where Larry's head suddenly appeared from out of the darkness. He grinned in at us. "I'd listen to Uncle Al if I were you," he said.

How long had he been out there listening to us? I wondered. Was he deliberately *spying* on us?

The door opened. Larry lowered his head as he loped in. His grin had faded. "Uncle Al wasn't kidding around," he said seriously.

"Yeah. Sure," Colin replied sarcastically. He climbed up to his bed and slid beneath the wool blanket.

"I guess the camp ghost will get us if we go out after lights out," Jay joked, tossing a towel across the room.

"No. No ghost," Larry said softly. "But Sabre

will." He pulled out his drawer and began searching for something inside it.

"Huh? Who's Sabre?" I asked, suddenly wide awake.

"Sabre is an *it*," Larry answered mysteriously.

"Sabre is a red-eyed monster who eats a camper every night," Colin sneered. He stared down at me. "There *is* no Sabre. Larry's just giving us another phony camp story."

Larry stopped searching his drawer and gazed up at Colin. "No, I'm not," he insisted in a low voice. "I'm trying to save you guys some trouble. I'm not trying to scare you."

"Then what is Sabre?" I asked impatiently.

Larry pulled a sweater from the drawer, then pushed the drawer shut. "You don't want to find out," he replied.

"Come on. Tell us what it is," I begged.

"He isn't going to," Colin said.

"I'll tell you guys only one thing. Sabre will rip your heart out," Larry said flatly.

Jay snickered. "Yeah. Sure."

"I'm serious!" Larry snapped. "I'm not kidding, you guys!" He pulled the sweater over his head. "You don't believe me? Go out one night. Go out and meet Sabre." He struggled to get his arm into the sweater sleeve. "But before you do," he warned, "leave me a note with your address so I'll know where to send your stuff."

282

8

We had fun the next morning.

We all woke up really early. The sun was just rising over the horizon to the south, and the air was still cool and damp. I could hear birds chirping.

The sound reminded me of home. As I lowered myself to the floor and stretched, I thought of my mom and dad and wished I could call them and tell them about the camp. But it was only the second day. I'd be too embarrassed to call them on the second day.

I was definitely homesick. But luckily there wasn't any time to feel sad. After we pulled on fresh clothes, we hurried up to the lodge on the hill, which served as a meeting hall, theater, and mess hall.

Long tables and benches were set up in straight rows in the center of the enormous room. The floorboards and walls were all dark redwood. Redwood ceiling beams crisscrossed high above our heads. There were very few windows, so it felt as if we were in an enormous, dark cave.

The clatter of dishes and cups and silverware was deafening. Our shouts and laughter rang off the high ceiling, echoed off the hardwood walls. Mike shouted something to me from across the table, but I couldn't hear him because of the racket.

Some guys complained about the food, but I thought it was okay. We had scrambled egg squares, bacon strips, fried potatoes, and toast, with tall cups of juice. I never eat a breakfast that big at home. But I found that I was really starved, and I gobbled it up.

After breakfast we lined up outside the lodge to form different activity groups. The sun had climbed high in the sky. It was going to be really hot. Our excited voices echoed off the sloping hill. We were all laughing and talking, feeling good.

Larry and two other counselors, clipboards in hand, stood in front of us, shielding their eyes from the bright sun as they divided us into groups. The first group of about ten boys headed off to the river for a morning swim.

Some people have all the luck, I thought. I was eager to get to the waterfront and see what the river was like.

As I waited for my name to be called, I spotted a pay phone on the wall of the lodge. My parents flashed into my mind again. Maybe I *will* call them later, I decided. I was so eager to describe the camp to them and tell them about my new friends.

"Okay, guys. Follow me to the ball field," Larry instructed us. "We're going to play our first game of scratchball."

About twelve of us, including everyone from my bunk, followed Larry down the hill toward the flat grassy area that formed the playing field.

I jogged to catch up to Larry, who always seemed to walk at top speed, stretching out his long legs as if he were in a terrible hurry. "Are we going to swim after this?" I asked.

Without slowing his pace, he glanced at his clip-board. "Yeah. I guess," he replied. "You guys'll need a swim. We're going to work up a sweat."

"You ever play scratchball before?" Jay asked me as we hurried to keep up with Larry.

"Yeah. Sure," I replied. "We play it a lot in school."

Larry stopped at the far corner of the wide, green field, where the bases and batter's square had already been set up. He made us line up and divided us into two teams.

Scratchball is an easy game to learn. The batter throws the ball in the air as high and as far as he can. Then he has to run the bases before someone on the other team catches the ball, tags him with it, or throws him out.

Larry started calling out names, dividing us into teams. But when he called out Mike's name,

285

Mike stepped up to Larry, holding his bandaged hand tenderly. "I — I don't think I can play, Larry," Mike stammered.

"Come on, Mike. Don't whine," Larry snapped.

"But it really hurts," Mike insisted. "It's throbbing like crazy, Larry. The pain is shooting all the way up and down my side. And, look" — he raised the hand to Larry's face — "It's all swelled up!"

Larry pushed the arm away gently with his clipboard. "Go sit in the shade," he told Mike.

"Shouldn't I get some medicine or something to put on it?" Mike asked shrilly. I could see the poor guy was really in bad shape.

"Just sit over there by that tree," Larry ordered, pointing to a clump of short, leafy trees at the edge of the field. "We'll talk about it later."

Larry turned away from Mike and blew a whistle to start the game. "I'll take Mike's place on the Blue team," he announced, jogging onto the field.

I forgot about Mike as soon as the game got underway. We were having a lot of fun. Most of the guys were pretty good scratchball players, and we played much faster than my friends do back home at the playground.

My first time up at the batter's square, I heaved the ball really high. But it dropped right into a fielder's hands, and I was out. My second time up, I made it to three bases before I was tagged out.

Larry was a great player. When he came up to the batter's square, he tossed the ball harder than I ever saw anyone toss it. It sailed over the fielders' heads and, as they chased after it, Larry rounded all the bases, his long legs stretching out gracefully as he ran.

By the fourth inning, our team, the Blue team, was ahead twelve to six. We had all played hard and were really hot and sweaty. I was looking forward to that swim at the waterfront.

Colin was on the Red team. I noticed that he was the only player who wasn't enjoying the game. He had been tagged out twice, and he'd missed an easy catch in the field.

I realized that Colin wasn't very athletic. He had long, skinny arms without any muscles, and he also ran awkwardly.

In the third inning Colin got into an argument with a player on my team about whether a toss had been foul or not. A few minutes later, Colin argued angrily with Larry about a ball that he claimed should have been out.

He and Larry shouted at each other for a few minutes. It was no big deal, a typical sports argument. Larry finally ordered Colin to shut up and get back to the outfield. Colin grudgingly obeyed, and the game continued.

I didn't think about it again. I mean, that kind of arguing happens all the time in ball games. And there are guys who enjoy the arguments as much as the game.

But then, in the next inning, something strange happened that gave me a really bad feeling and made me stop and wonder just what was going on.

Colin's team came to bat. Colin stepped up to the batter's square and prepared to toss the ball.

Larry was playing the outfield. I was standing nearby, also in the field.

Colin tossed the ball high, but not very far.

Larry and I both came running in to get it.

Larry got there first. He picked up the small, hard ball on the first bounce, drew back his arm — and then I saw his expression change.

I saw his features tighten in anger. I saw his eyes narrow, his copper-colored eyebrows lower in concentration.

With a loud grunt of effort, Larry heaved the ball as hard as he could.

It struck Colin in the back of the head, making a loud *crack* sound as it hit.

Colin's silver sunglasses went flying in the air.

Colin stopped short and uttered a short, high-pitched cry. His arms flew up as if he'd been shot. Then his knees buckled.

He collapsed in a heap, facedown on the grass. He didn't move.

The ball rolled away over the grass.

I cried out in shock.

Then I saw Larry's expression change again. His eyes opened wide in disbelief. His mouth dropped open in horror.

"No!" he cried. "It slipped! I didn't mean to throw it at him!"

I knew Larry was lying. I had seen the anger on his face before he threw the ball.

I sank down to my knees on the ground as Larry went running toward Colin. I felt dizzy and upset and confused. I had this sick feeling in my stomach.

"The ball slipped!" Larry was yelling. "It just slipped."

Liar, I thought. Liar. Liar. Liar.

I forced myself up on my feet and hurried to join the circle of guys around Colin. When I got there, Larry was kneeling over Colin, raising Colin's head off the ground gently with both hands.

Colin's eyes were open wide. He stared up at Larry groggily, and uttered low moans.

"Give him room," Larry was shouting. "Give him room." He gazed down at Colin. "The ball slipped. I'm real sorry. The ball slipped."

Colin moaned. His eyes rolled around in his head. Larry pulled off Colin's red bandanna and mopped Colin's forehead with it.

Colin moaned again. His eyes closed.

"Help me carry him to the lodge," Larry instructed two guys from the Red team. "The rest of you guys get changed for your swim. The waterfront counselor will be waiting for you."

I watched as Larry and the two guys hoisted Colin up and started to carry him toward the lodge. Larry gripped him under the shoulders. The two boys awkwardly took hold of his legs.

The sick feeling in my stomach hadn't gone away. I kept picturing the intense expression of anger on Larry's face as he heaved the ball at the back of Colin's head.

I knew it had been deliberate.

I started to follow them. I don't know why. I guess I was so upset, I wasn't thinking clearly.

They were nearly to the bottom of the hill when I saw Mike catch up to them. He ran alongside Larry, holding his swollen hand.

"Can I come, too?" Mike pleaded. "Someone has to look at my hand. It's really bad, Larry. Please — can I come, too?"

"Yeah. You'd better," I heard Larry reply curtly.

Good, I thought. Finally someone was going to pay some attention to Mike's snakebite wound.

Ignoring the sweat pouring down my forehead, I watched them make their way up the hill to the lodge.

This shouldn't have happened, I thought, suddenly feeling a chill despite the hot sun.

Something is wrong. Something is terribly wrong here.

How was I to know that the horrors were just beginning?

9

Later that afternoon, Jay and I were writing our letters to our parents. I was feeling pretty upset about things. I kept seeing the angry expression on Larry's face as he heaved the ball at the back of Colin's head.

I wrote about it in my letter, and I also told my mom and dad about how there was no nurse here, and about the Forbidden Bunk.

Jay stopped writing and looked up at me from his bunk. He was really sunburned. His cheeks and forehead were bright red.

He scratched his red hair. "We're dropping like flies," he said, gesturing around the nearly empty cabin.

"Yeah," I agreed wistfully. "I hope Colin and Mike are okay." And then I blurted out, "Larry deliberately hit Colin."

"Huh?" Jay stopped scratching his hair and lowered his hand to the bunk. "He *what*?"

"He deliberately threw at Colin's head. I *saw*

him," I said, my voice shaky. I wasn't going to tell anyone, but now I was glad I did. It made me feel a little bit better to get it out.

But then I saw that Jay didn't believe me. "That's impossible," he said quietly. "Larry's our counselor. His hand slipped. That's all."

I started to argue when the cabin door opened and Colin entered, with Larry at his side.

"Colin! How *are* you?" I cried. Jay and I both jumped up.

"Not bad," Colin replied. He forced a thin smile. I couldn't see his eyes. They were hidden once again behind his silver sunglasses.

"He's still a little wobbly, but he's okay," Larry said cheerfully, holding Colin's arm.

"I'm sort of seeing double," Colin admitted. "I mean, this cabin looks really crowded to me. There are two of each of you."

Jay and I uttered short, uncomfortable laughs.

Larry helped Colin over to the lower bunk where Jay had been sitting. "He'll be just fine in a day or two," Larry told us.

"Yeah. The headache is a little better already," Colin said, gently rubbing the back of his head, then lying down on top of the bedcovers.

"Did you see a doctor?" I asked.

"Huh-uh. Just Uncle Al," Colin replied. "He looked it over and said I'd be fine."

I cast a suspicious glance at Larry, but he turned his back on us and crouched down to search for something in the duffel bag he kept under his bed.

"Where's Mike? Is he okay?" Jay asked Larry.

"Uh-huh," Larry answered without turning around. "He's fine."

"But where is he?" I demanded.

Larry shrugged. "Still at the lodge, I guess. I don't really know."

"But is he coming back?" I insisted.

Larry shoved the bag under his bed and stood up. "Have you guys finished your letters?" he asked. "Hurry and get changed for dinner. You can mail your letters at the lodge."

He started to the door. "Hey, don't forget tonight is Tent Night. You guys are sleeping in a tent tonight."

We all groaned. "But, Larry, it's too cold out!" Jay protested.

Larry ignored him and turned away.

"Hey, Larry, do you have anything I can put on this sunburn?" Jay called after him.

"No," Larry replied and disappeared out the door.

Jay and I helped Colin up to the lodge. He was still seeing double, and his headache was pretty bad.

The three of us sat at the end of the long table nearest the window. A strong breeze blew cool air over the table, which felt good on our sunburned skin.

We had some kind of meat with potatoes and gravy for dinner. It wasn't great, but I was so hungry, it didn't matter. Colin didn't have much appetite. He picked at the edges of his gray meat.

The mess hall was as noisy as ever. Kids were laughing and shouting to friends across the long tables. At one table, the guys were throwing breadsticks back and forth like javelins.

As usual, the counselors, dressed in their green and white, ate together at a table in the far corner and ignored us campers completely.

The rumor spread that we were going to learn all of the camp songs after dinner. Guys were groaning and complaining about that.

About halfway through dinner, Jay and the boy across the table, a kid named Roger, started horsing around, trying to wrestle a breadstick from each other. Jay pulled hard and won the breadstick — and spilled his entire cup of grape juice on my tan shorts.

"Hey!" I jumped up angrily, staring down as the purple stain spread across the front of my shorts.

"Billy had an accident!" Roger cried out. And everyone laughed.

"Yeah. He purpled in his pants!" Jay added.

Everyone thought that was hilarious. Someone

threw a breadstick at me. It bounced off my chest and landed on my dinner plate. More laughter.

The food fight lasted only a few minutes. Then two of the counselors broke it up. I decided I'd better run back to the bunk and change my shorts. As I hurried out, I could hear Jay and Roger calling out jokes about me.

I ran full-speed down the hill toward the bunks. I wanted to get back up to the mess hall in time for dessert.

Pushing open the bunk door with my shoulder, I darted across the small room to the dresser and pulled open my drawer.

"Huh?"

To my surprise, I stared into an empty drawer. It had been completely cleaned out.

"What's going on here?" I asked aloud. "Where's my stuff?"

Confused, I took a step back — and realized I had opened the wrong drawer. This wasn't my drawer.

It was Mike's.

I stared for a long while into the empty drawer.

Mike's clothes had all been removed. I turned and looked for his trunk, which had been stacked on its side behind our bunk.

Mike's trunk was gone, too.

Mike wasn't coming back.

* * *

I was so upset, I ran back to the mess hall without changing my shorts.

Panting loudly, I made my way to the counselors' table and came up behind Larry. He was talking to the counselor next to him, a fat guy with long, scraggly blond hair. "Larry — Mike's gone!" I cried breathlessly.

Larry didn't turn around. He kept talking to the other counselor as if I weren't there.

I grabbed Larry's shoulder. "Larry — listen!" I cried. "Mike — he's gone!"

Larry turned around slowly, his expression annoyed. "Go back to your table, Billy," he snapped. "This table is for counselors only."

"But what about Mike?" I insisted shrilly. "His stuff is gone. What happened to him? Is he okay?"

"How should I know?" Larry replied impatiently.

"Did they send him home?" I asked, refusing to back away until I had some kind of an answer.

"Yeah. Maybe." Larry shrugged and lowered his gaze. "You spilled something on your shorts."

My heart was pounding so hard, I could feel the blood pulsing at my temples. "You really don't know what happened to Mike?" I asked, feeling defeated.

Larry shook his head. "I'm sure he's fine," he replied, turning back to his pals.

"He probably went for a swim," the scraggly-haired guy next to him snickered.

Larry and some of the other counselors laughed, too.

I didn't think it was funny. I felt pretty sick. And a little frightened.

Don't the counselors at this camp care what happens to us? I asked myself glumly.

I made my way back to the table. They were passing out chocolate pudding for dessert, but I wasn't hungry.

I told Colin, and Jay, and Roger about Mike's dresser drawer being cleaned out, and about how Larry pretended he didn't know anything about it. They didn't get as upset about it as I was.

"Uncle Al probably had to send Mike home because of his hand," Colin said quietly, spooning up his pudding. "It was pretty swollen."

"But why wouldn't Larry tell me the truth?" I asked, my stomach still feeling as if I had eaten a giant rock for dinner. "Why did he say he didn't know what happened to Mike?"

"Counselors don't like to talk about bad stuff," Jay said, slapping the top of his pudding with his spoon. "It might give us poor little kids nightmares." He filled his spoon with pudding, tilted it back, and flung a dark gob of pudding onto Roger's forehead.

"Jay — you're dead meat now!" Roger cried, plunging his spoon into the chocolate goo. He shot a gob of it onto the front of Jay's sleeveless T-shirt.

That started a pudding war that spread down the long table.

There was no more talk about Mike.

After dinner, Uncle Al talked about Tent Night and what a great time we were going to have sleeping in tents tonight. "Just be very quiet so the bears can't find you!" he joked. Some joke.

Then he and the counselors taught us the camp songs. Uncle Al made us sing them over and over until we learned them.

I didn't feel much like singing. But Jay and Roger began making up really gross words to the songs. And pretty soon, a whole bunch of us joined in, singing our own versions of the songs as loudly as we could.

Later, we were all making our way down the hill toward our tents. It was a cool, clear night. A wash of pale stars covered the purple-black sky.

I helped Colin down the hill. He was still seeing double and feeling a little weak.

Jay and Roger walked a few steps ahead of us, shoving each other with their shoulders, first to the left, then to the right.

Suddenly, Jay turned back to Colin and me. "Tonight's the night," he whispered, a devilish grin spreading across his face.

"Huh? Tonight's *what* night?" I demanded.

"Ssshhh." He raised a finger to his lips. "When everyone's asleep, Roger and I are going to go check out the Forbidden Bunk." He turned to Colin. "You with us?"

Colin shook his head sadly. "I don't think I can, Jay."

Walking backwards in front of us, Jay locked his eyes on mine. "How about you, Billy? You coming?"

10

"I — I think I'll stay with Colin," I told him.

I heard Roger mutter something about me being a chicken. Jay looked disappointed. "You're going to miss out," he said.

"That's okay. I'm kind of tired," I said. It was true. I felt so weary after this long day, every muscle ached. Even my hair hurt!

Jay and Roger made whispered plans all the way back to the tent.

At the bottom of the hill, I stopped and gazed up at the Forbidden Bunk. It appeared to lean toward me in the pale starlight. I listened for the familiar howls that seemed to come from inside it. But tonight there was only a heavy silence.

The large plastic tents were lined up in the bunk area. I crawled into ours and lay down on top of my sleeping bag. The ground was really hard. I could see this was going to be a long night.

Jay and Colin were messing around with their

sleeping bags at the back of the tent. "It seems weird without Mike here," I said, feeling a sudden chill.

"Now you'll have more room to put your stuff," Jay replied casually. He sat hunched against the tent wall, his expression tense, his eyes on the darkness outside the tent door, which was left open a few inches.

Larry was nowhere in sight. Colin sat quietly. He still wasn't feeling right.

I shifted my weight and stretched out, trying to find a comfortable position. I really wanted to go to sleep. But I knew I wouldn't be able to sleep until after Jay and Roger returned from their adventure.

Time moved slowly. It was cold outside, and the air was heavy and wet inside the tent.

I stared up at the dark plastic tent walls. A bug crawled across my forehead. I squashed it with my hand.

I could hear Jay and Colin whispering behind me, but I couldn't make out their words. Jay snickered nervously.

I must have dozed off. An insistent whispering sound woke me up. It took me a while to realize it was someone whispering outside the tent.

I lifted my head and saw Roger's face peering in. I sat up, alert.

"Wish us luck," Jay whispered.

"Good luck," I whispered back, my voice clogged from sleep.

In the darkness I saw Jay's large, shadowy form crawl quickly to the tent door. He pushed it open, revealing a square of purple sky, then vanished into the darkness.

I shivered. "Let's sneak back to the bunk," I whispered to Colin. "It's too cold out here. And the ground feels like solid rock."

Colin agreed. We both scrambled out of the tent and made our way silently to our nice, warm bunk. Inside, we headed to the window to try to see Jay and Roger.

"They're going to get caught," I whispered. "I just know it."

"They won't get caught," Colin disagreed. "But they won't see anything, either. There's nothing to see up there. It's just a stupid cabin."

Poking my head out the window, I could hear Jay and Roger giggling quietly out somewhere in the dark. The camp was so silent, so eerily silent. I could hear their whispers, their legs brushing through the tall grass.

"They'd better be quiet," Colin muttered, leaning against the window frame. "They're making too much noise."

"They must be up to the hill by now," I whispered. I stuck my head out as far as I could, but I couldn't see them.

Colin started to reply, but the first scream made him stop.

It was a scream of horror that cut through the silent air.

"Oh!" I cried out and pulled my head in.

"Was that Jay or Roger?" Colin asked, his voice trembling.

The second scream was more terrifying than the first.

Before it died down, I heard animal snarls. Loud and angry. Like an eruption of thunder.

Then I heard Jay's desperate plea: "Help us! Please — somebody help us!"

My heart thudding in my chest, I lurched to the cabin door and pulled it open. The hideous screams still ringing in my ears, I plunged out into the darkness, the dew-covered ground soaking my bare feet.

"Jay — where are you?" I heard myself calling, but I didn't recognize my shrill, frightened voice.

And then I saw a dark form running toward me, running bent over, arms outstretched.

"Jay!" I cried. "What — *is* it? What *happened*?"

He ran up to me, still bent forward, his face twisted in horror, his eyes wide and unblinking. His bushy hair appeared to stand straight up.

"It — it got Roger," he moaned, his chest heaving as he struggled to straighten up.

"What did?" I demanded.

"What was it?" Colin asked, right behind me.

"I — I don't know!" Jay stammered, shutting his eyes tight. "It — it tore Roger to pieces."

Jay uttered a loud sob. Then he opened his eyes and spun around in terror. "Here it comes!" he shrieked. "Now it's coming after *us*!"

11

In the pale starlight, I saw Jay's eyes roll up in his head. His knees collapsed, and he began to slump to the ground.

I grabbed him before he fell and dragged him into the cabin. Colin slammed the door behind us.

Once inside, Jay recovered slowly. The three of us froze in place and listened hard. I was still holding onto Jay's heaving shoulders. He was as pale as a bedsheet, and his breath came out in short, frightened moans.

We listened.

Silence.

The air hung hot and still.

Nothing moved.

No footsteps. No animal approaching.

Just Jay's frightened moans and the pounding of my heart.

And then, somewhere far in the distance, I heard the howl. Soft and low at first, then rising on the wind. A howl that chilled my blood and made me cry out.

"It's Sabre!"

"Don't let it get me!" Jay shrieked, covering his face with his hands. He dropped to his knees on the cabin floor. "Don't let it get me!"

I raised my eyes to Colin, who was huddled against the wall, away from the window. "We have to get Larry," I managed to choke out. "We have to get help."

"But how?" Colin demanded in a trembling voice.

"Don't let it get me!" Jay repeated, crumpled on the floor.

"It isn't coming here," I told him, trying to sound certain, trying to sound soothing. "We're okay inside the bunk, Jay. It isn't coming here."

"But it got Roger and — " Jay started. His entire body convulsed in a shudder of terror.

Thinking about Roger, I felt a stab of fear in my chest.

Was it really true? Was it true that Roger had been attacked by some kind of creature? That he'd been slashed to pieces?

I'd heard the screams from the hillside. Two bloodcurdling screams.

They'd been so loud, so horrifying. Hadn't anyone else in camp heard them, too? Hadn't any other kids heard Roger's cries? Hadn't any counselors heard?

I froze in place and listened.

Silence. The whisper of the breeze rustling the tree leaves.

No voices. No cries of alarm. No hurried footsteps.

I turned back toward the others. Colin had helped Jay to his bunk. "Where can Larry be?" Colin asked. His eyes, for once not hidden behind the silver sunglasses, showed real fear.

"Where can *everyone* be?" I asked, crossing my arms over my chest and starting to pace back and forth in the small space between the beds. "There isn't a sound out there."

I saw Jay's eyes go wide with horror. He was staring at the open window. "The creature — " he cried. "Here it comes! It's coming through the window!"

12

All three of us gaped in horror at the open window.

But no creature jumped in.

As I stared, frozen in the center of the cabin, I could see only darkness and a fringe of pale stars.

Outside in the trees, crickets started up a shrill clatter. There was no other sound.

Poor Jay was so frightened and upset, he was seeing things.

Somehow Colin and I got him a little calmed down. We made him take off his sneakers and lie down on the lower bed. And we covered him up with three blankets to help him to stop trembling.

Colin and I wanted to run for help. But we were too frightened to go outside.

The three of us were up all night. Larry never showed up.

Except for the crickets and the brush of the wind through the trees, the camp was silent.

I think I must have finally dozed off just before

dawn. I had strange nightmares about fires and people trying to run away.

I was awakened by Colin shaking me hard. "Breakfast," he said hoarsely. "Hurry. We're late."

I sat up groggily. "Where's Larry?"

"He never showed," Colin replied, motioning to Larry's unused bunk.

"We've got to find him! We've got to tell him what happened!" Jay cried, hurrying to the cabin door with his sneakers untied.

Colin and I stumbled after him, both of us only half-awake. It was a cool, gray morning. The sun was trying hard to poke through high white clouds.

The three of us stopped halfway up the hill to the mess hall. Reluctantly, our eyes searched the ground around the Forbidden Bunk.

I don't know what I expected to see. But there was no sign of Roger.

No sign of any struggle. No dried blood on the ground. The tall grass wasn't bent or matted down.

"Weird," I heard Jay mutter, shaking his head. "That's weird."

I tugged his arm to get him moving, and we hurried the rest of the way up to the lodge.

The mess hall was as noisy as ever. Kids were laughing and shouting to each other. It all seemed perfectly normal. I guessed that no one had made an announcement about Roger yet.

Some kids called to Colin and me. But we ignored them and searched for Roger, moving quickly through the aisles between the tables.

No sign of him.

I had a heavy, queasy feeling in my stomach as we hurried to the counselors' table in the corner.

Larry glanced up from a big plate of scrambled eggs and bacon as the three of us advanced on him.

"What happened to Roger?"

"Is he okay?"

"Where were you last night?"

"Roger and I were attacked."

"We were afraid to go find you."

All three of us bombarded Larry at once.

His face was filled with confusion, and he raised both hands to silence us. "Whoa," he said. "Take a breath, guys. What are you talking about?"

"About Roger!" Jay screamed, his face turning bright red. "The creature — it jumped on him. And — and — "

Larry glanced at the other counselors at the table, who looked as confused as he did. "Creature? What creature?" Larry demanded.

"It attacked Roger!" Jay screamed. "It was coming after me and — "

Larry stared up at Jay. "Someone was attacked? I don't think so, Jay." He turned to the counselor next to him, a pudgy boy named Derek.

"Did you hear anything in your area?"

Derek shook his head.

"Isn't Roger in your group?" Larry asked Derek.

Derek shook his head. "Not in *my* group."

"But Roger — !" Jay insisted.

"We didn't get any report about any attack," Larry said, interrupting. "If a camper was attacked by a bear or something, we'd hear about it."

"And we'd hear the noise," Derek offered. "You know. Screams or something."

"I heard screams," I told them.

"We both heard screams," Colin added quickly. "And Jay came running back, crying for help."

"Well, why didn't anyone else hear it?" Larry demanded, turning his gaze on Jay. His expression changed. "Where did this happen? When?" he asked suspiciously.

Jay's face darkened to a deeper red. "After lights out," he admitted. "Roger and I went up to the Forbidden Bunk, and — "

"Are you sure it wasn't a bear?" Derek interrupted. "Some bears were spotted downriver yesterday afternoon."

"It was a *creature*!" Jay screamed angrily.

"You shouldn't have been out," Larry said, shaking his head.

"Why won't you listen to me?" Jay screamed.

"Roger was attacked. This big thing jumped on him and — "

"We would've heard something," Derek said calmly, glancing at Larry.

"Yeah," Larry agreed. "The counselors were all up here at the lodge. We would've heard any screams."

"But, Larry — you've got to check it out!" I cried. "Jay isn't making it up. It really happened!"

"Okay, okay," Larry replied, raising his hands as if surrendering. "I'll go ask Uncle Al about it, okay?"

"Hurry," Jay insisted. "Please!"

"I'll ask Uncle Al after breakfast," Larry said, turning back to his eggs and bacon. "I'll see you guys at morning swim later. I'll report what Uncle Al says."

"But, Larry — " Jay pleaded.

"I'll ask Uncle Al," Larry said firmly. "If anything happened last night, he'll know about it." He raised a strip of bacon to his mouth and chewed on it. "I think you just had a bad nightmare or something," he continued, eyeing Jay suspiciously. "But I'll let you know what Uncle Al says."

"It wasn't a nightmare!" Jay cried shrilly. Larry turned his back on us and continued eating his breakfast. "Don't you *care*?" Jay screamed at him. "Don't you *care* what happens to us?"

I saw that a lot of kids had stopped eating their breakfast to gawk at us. I pulled Jay away, and tried to get him to go to our table. But he insisted on searching the entire mess hall again. "I know Roger *isn't* here," he insisted. "He — he *can't* be!"

For the second time, the three of us made our way up and down the aisles between the tables, studying every face.

One thing was for sure: Roger was nowhere to be seen.

The sun burned through the high clouds just as we reached the waterfront for morning swim. The air was still cool. The thick, leafy shrubs along the riverbank glistened wetly in the white glare of sunlight.

I dropped my towel under a bush and turned to the gently flowing green water. "I'll bet it's cold this morning," I said to Colin, who was re-tying the string on his swim trunks.

"I just want to go back to the bunk and go to sleep," Colin said, plucking at a knot. He wasn't seeing double any longer, but he was tired from being up all night.

Several guys were already wading into the river. They were complaining about the cold water, splashing each other, shoving each other forward.

"Where's Larry?" Jay demanded breathlessly,

314

pushing his way through the clump of shrubs to get to us. His auburn hair was a mess, half of it standing straight up on the side of his head. His eyes were red-rimmed and bloodshot.

"Where's Larry? He promised he'd be here," Jay said, frantically searching the waterfront.

"Here I am." The three of us spun around as Larry appeared from the bushes behind us. He was wearing baggy green Camp Nightmoon swim trunks.

"Well?" Jay demanded. "What did Uncle Al say? About Roger?"

Larry's expression was serious. His eyes locked on Jay's. "Uncle Al and I went all around the Forbidden Bunk," he told Jay. "There wasn't any attack there. There couldn't have been."

"But it — it got Roger," Jay cried shrilly. "It slashed him. I saw it!"

Larry shook his head, his eyes still burning into Jay's. "That's the other thing," he said softly. "Uncle Al and I went up to the office and checked the records, Jay. And there *is* no camper here this year named Roger. Not a first name or a middle name. No Roger. No Roger at all."

13

Jay's mouth dropped open and he uttered a low gasp.

The three of us stared in disbelief at Larry, letting this startling news sink in.

"Someone's made a mistake," Jay said finally, his voice trembling with emotion. "We searched the mess hall for him, Larry. And he's gone. Roger isn't here."

"He never *was* here," Larry said without any emotion at all.

"I — I just don't believe this!" Jay cried.

"How about a swim, guys," Larry said, motioning to the water.

"Well, what do *you* think?" I demanded of Larry. I couldn't believe he was being so calm about this. "What do *you* think happened last night?"

Larry shrugged. "I don't know what to think," he replied, his eyes on a cluster of swimmers farthest from the shore. "Maybe you guys are trying to pull a weird joke on me."

"Huh? Is *that* what you think?" Jay cried. "That it's a *joke*?!"

Larry shrugged again. "Swim time, guys. Get some exercise, okay?"

Jay started to say more, but Larry quickly turned and went running into the green water. He took four or five running steps off the shore, then dove, pulling himself quickly through the water, taking long, steady strokes.

"I'm not going in," Jay insisted angrily. "I'm going back to the bunk." His face was bright red. His chin was trembling. I could see that he was about to cry. He turned and began running through the bushes, dragging his towel along the ground.

"Hey, wait up!" Colin went running after him.

I stood there trying to decide what to do. I didn't want to follow Jay to the bunk. There wasn't anything I could do to help him.

Maybe a cold swim will make me feel better, I thought.

Maybe *nothing* will make me feel better, I told myself glumly.

I stared out at the other guys in the water. Larry and another counselor were setting up a race. I could hear them discussing what kind of stroke should be used.

They all seem to be having a great time, I thought, watching them line up.

So why aren't I?

Why have I been so frightened and unhappy since I arrived here? Why don't the other campers see how weird and frightening this place is?

I shook my head, unable to answer my questions.

I need a swim, I decided.

I took a step toward the water.

But someone reached out from the bushes and grabbed me roughly from behind.

I started to scream out in protest.

But my attacker quickly clamped a hand over my mouth to silence me.

14

I tried to pull away, but I'd been caught off guard.

As the hands tugged me, I lost my balance and I was pulled back into the bushes.

Is this a joke? What's going on? I wondered.

Suddenly, as I tried to tug myself free, the hands let go.

I went sailing headfirst into a clump of fat green leaves.

It took me a long moment to pull myself up. Then I spun around to face my attacker.

"Dawn!" I cried.

"Ssshhhh!" She leapt forward and clamped a hand over my mouth again. "Duck down," she whispered urgently. "They'll see you."

I obediently ducked behind the low bush. She let go of me again and moved back. She was wearing a blue, one-piece bathing suit. It was wet. Her blonde hair was also wet, dripping down onto her bare shoulders.

"Dawn — what are you *doing* here?" I whispered, settling onto my knees.

Before Dawn could reply, another figure in a bathing suit moved quickly from the bushes, crouching low. It was Dawn's friend Dori.

"We swam over. Early this morning," Dori whispered, nervously pushing at her curly red hair. "We waited here. In the bushes."

"But it's not allowed," I said, unable to hide my confusion. "If you're caught — "

"We had to talk to you," Dawn interrupted, raising her head to peek over the top of the bushes, then quickly ducking back down.

"We decided to risk it," Dori added.

"What — what's wrong?" I stammered. A red-and-black bug crawled up my shoulder. I brushed it away.

"The girls' camp. It's a nightmare," Dori whispered.

"Everyone calls it Camp *Nightmare* instead of Camp Nightmoon," Dawn added. "Strange things have been happening."

"Huh?" I gaped at her. Not far from us in the water, I could hear the shouts and splashes of the swim race beginning. "What kinds of strange things?"

"Scary things," Dori replied, her expression solemn.

"Girls have disappeared," Dawn told me. "Just vanished from sight."

"And no one seems to care," Dori added in a trembling whisper.

"I don't believe it!" I uttered. "The same thing has happened here. At the boys' camp." I swallowed hard. "Remember Mike?"

Both girls nodded.

"Mike disappeared," I told them. "They removed his stuff, and he just disappeared."

"It's unbelievable," Dori said. "Three girls are gone from our camp."

"They announced that one was attacked by a bear," Dawn whispered.

"What about the other two?" I asked.

"Just gone," Dawn replied, the words catching in her throat.

I could hear whistles blowing in the water. The race had ended. Another one was being organized.

The sun disappeared once again behind high white clouds. Shadows lengthened and grew darker.

I told them quickly about Roger and Jay and the attack at the Forbidden Bunk. They listened in open-mouthed silence. "Just like at our camp," Dawn said.

"We have to do something," Dori said heatedly.

"We have to get together. The boys and the girls," Dawn whispered, peering once again over the tops of the leaves. "We have to make a plan."

"You mean to escape?" I asked, not really understanding.

The two girls nodded. "We can't stay here," Dawn said grimly. "Every day another girl disappears. And the counselors act as if nothing is happening."

"I think they *want* us to get killed or something," Dori added with emotion.

"Have you written to your parents?" I asked.

"We write every day," Dori replied. "But we haven't heard from them."

I suddenly realized that I hadn't received any mail from my parents, either. They had both promised to write every day. But I had been at camp for nearly a week, and I hadn't received a single piece of mail.

"Visitors Day is next week," I said. "Our parents will be here. We can tell them everything."

"It may be too late," Dawn said grimly.

"Everyone is so scared!" Dori declared. "I haven't slept in two nights. I hear these horrible screams outside every night."

Another whistle blew, closer to shore. I could hear the swimmers returning. Morning swim was ending.

"I — I don't know what to say," I told them. "You've got to be careful. Don't get caught."

"We'll swim back to the girls' camp when everyone has left," Dawn said. "But we have to meet again, Billy. We have to get more guys together. You know. Maybe if we all get organized . . ." Her voice trailed off.

"There's something bad going on at this camp," Dori said with a shiver, narrowing her eyes. "Something evil."

"I — I know," I agreed. I could hear boys' voices now. Close by. Just on the other side of the leafy bushes. "I've got to go."

"We'll try to meet here again the day after tomorrow," Dawn whispered. "Be careful, Billy."

"*You* be careful," I whispered. "Don't get caught."

They slipped back, deeper in the bushes.

Crouching low, I made my way away from the shore. When I was past the clump of bushes, I stood up and began to run. I couldn't wait to tell Colin and Jay about what the girls had said.

I felt frightened and excited at the same time. I thought maybe it would make Jay feel a little better to know that the same kinds of horrible things were happening across the river at the girls' camp.

Halfway to the bunks, I had an idea. I stopped and turned toward the lodge.

I suddenly remembered seeing a pay phone on the wall on the side of the building. Someone had told me that phone was the only one campers were allowed to use.

I'll call Mom and Dad, I decided.

Why hadn't I thought of it before?

I can call my parents, I realized, and tell them everything. I could ask them to come and get me.

And they could get Jay, Colin, Dawn, and Dori, too.

Behind me, I saw my group heading toward the scratchball field, their swimming towels slung over their shoulders. I wondered if anyone had noticed that I was missing.

Jay and Colin were missing, too, I told myself. Larry and the others probably think I'm with them.

I watched them trooping across the tall grass in twos and threes. Then I turned and started jogging up the hill toward the lodge.

The idea of calling home had cheered me up already.

I was so eager to hear my parents' voices, so eager to tell them the strange things that were happening here.

Would they believe me?

Of *course* they would. My parents always believed me. Because they trusted me.

As I ran up the hill, the dark pay phone came into view on the white lodge wall. I started to run at full speed. I wanted to *fly* to the phone.

I hope Mom and Dad are home, I thought.

They've *got* to be home.

I was panting loudly as I reached the wall. I lowered my hands to my knees and crouched there for a moment, waiting to catch my breath.

Then I reached up to take the receiver down.

And gasped.

The pay phone was plastic. Just a stage prop. A phony.

It was a thin sheet of molded plastic held to the wall by a nail, made to look just like a telephone.

It wasn't real. It was a fake.

They don't want us to call out, I thought with a sudden chill.

My heart thudding, my head spinning in bitter disappointment, I turned away from the wall — and bumped right into Uncle Al.

15

"Billy — what are you doing up here?" Uncle Al asked. He was wearing baggy green camp shorts and a sleeveless white T-shirt that revealed his meaty pink arms. He carried a brown clipboard filled with papers. "Where are you supposed to be?"

"I . . . uh . . . wanted to make a phone call," I stammered, taking a step back. "I wanted to call my parents."

He eyed me suspiciously and fingered his yellow mustache. "Really?"

"Yeah. Just to say hi," I told him. "But the phone — "

Uncle Al followed my gaze to the plastic phone. He chuckled. "Someone put that up as a joke," he said, grinning at me. "Did it fool you?"

"Yeah," I admitted, feeling my face grow hot. I raised my eyes to his. "Where is the real phone?"

His grin faded. His expression turned serious.

326

"No phone," he replied sharply. "Campers aren't allowed to call out. It's a rule, Billy."

"Oh." I didn't know what to say.

"Are you really homesick?" Uncle Al asked softly.

I nodded.

"Well, go write your mom and dad a long letter," he said. "It'll make you feel a lot better."

"Okay," I said. I didn't think it *would* make me feel better. But I wanted to get away from Uncle Al.

He raised his clipboard and gazed at it. "Where are you supposed to be now?" he asked.

"Scratchball, I think," I replied. "I didn't feel too well, see. So I — "

"And when is your canoe trip?" he asked, not listening to me. He flipped through the sheets of paper on the clipboard, glancing over them quickly.

"Canoe trip?" I hadn't heard about any canoe trip.

"Tomorrow," he said, answering his own question. "Your group goes tomorrow. Are you excited?" He lowered his eyes to mine.

"I — I didn't really know about it," I confessed.

"Lots of fun!" he exclaimed enthusiastically. "The river doesn't look like much up here. But it gets pretty exciting a few miles down. You'll find yourself in some good rapids."

327

He squeezed my shoulder briefly. "You'll enjoy it," he said, grinning. "Everyone always enjoys the canoe ride."

"Great," I said. I tried to sound a little excited, but my voice came out flat and uncertain.

Uncle Al gave me a wave with his clipboard and headed around toward the front of the lodge, taking long strides. I stood watching him till he disappeared around the corner of the building. Then I made my way down the hill to the bunk.

I found Colin and Jay on the grass at the side of the cabin. Colin had his shirt off and was sprawled on his back, his hands behind his head. Jay sat cross-legged beside him, nervously pulling up long, slender strands of grass, then tossing them down.

"Come inside," I told them, glancing around to make sure no one else could hear.

They followed me into the cabin. I closed the door.

"What's up?" Colin asked, dropping onto a lower bunk. He picked up his red bandanna and twisted it in his hands.

I told them about Dawn and Dori and what they had reported about the girls' camp.

Colin and Jay both reacted with shock.

"They really swam over here and waited for you?" Jay asked.

I nodded. "They think we have to get organized or escape or something," I said.

"They could get in big trouble if they get caught," Jay said thoughtfully.

"We're all in big trouble," I told him. "We have to get *out!*"

"Visitors Day is next week," Colin muttered.

"I'm going to write to my parents right now," I said, pulling out the case from under my bunk where I kept my paper and pens. "I'm going to tell them I *have* to come home on Visitors Day."

"I guess I will, too," Jay said, tapping his fingers nervously against the bunk frame.

"Me, too," Colin agreed. "It's just too . . . weird here!"

I pulled out a couple of sheets of paper and sat down on the bed to write. "Dawn and Dori were really scared," I told them.

"So am I," Jay admitted.

I started to write my letter. I wrote *Dear Mom and Dad, HELP!*, then stopped. I raised my eyes across the cabin to Jay and Colin. "Do you guys know about the canoe trip tomorrow?" I asked.

They stared back at me, their expressions surprised.

"Whoa!" Colin declared. "A three-mile hike this afternoon, and a canoe trip tomorrow?"

It was my turn to be surprised. "Hike? What hike?"

"Aren't you coming on it?" Jay asked.

"You know that really tall counselor? Frank? The one who wears the yellow cap?" Colin asked.

"He told Jay and me we're going on a three-mile hike after lunch."

"No one told me," I replied, chewing on the end of my pen.

"Maybe you're not in the hike group," Jay said.

"You'd better ask Frank at lunch," Colin suggested. "Maybe he couldn't find you. Maybe you're supposed to come, too."

I groaned. "Who wants to go on a three-mile hike in this heat?"

Colin and Jay both shrugged.

"Frank said we'd really like it," Colin told me, knotting and unknotting the red bandanna.

"I just want to get out of here," I said, returning to my letter.

I wrote quickly, intensely. I wanted to tell my parents all the frightening, strange things that had happened. I wanted to make them see why I couldn't stay at Camp Nightmoon.

I had written nearly a page and a half, and I was up to the part where Jay and Roger went out to explore the Forbidden Bunk, when Larry burst in. "You guys taking the day off?" he asked, his eyes going from one of us to the other. "You on vacation or something?"

"Just hanging out," Jay replied.

I folded up my letter and started to tuck it under my pillow. I didn't want Larry to see it. I realized I didn't trust Larry at all. I had no reason to.

"What are *you* doing, Billy?" he asked suspiciously, his eyes stopping on the letter I was shoving under the pillow.

"Just writing home," I replied softly.

"You homesick or something?" he asked, a grin spreading across his face.

"Maybe," I muttered.

"Well, it's lunchtime, guys," he announced. "Let's hustle, okay?"

We all climbed out of our bunks.

"Jay and Colin are going on a hike with Frank this afternoon, I heard," Larry said. "Lucky guys." He turned and started out the door.

"Larry!" I called to him. "Hey, Larry — what about me? Am I supposed to go on the hike, too?"

"Not today," he called back.

"But why not?" I said.

But Larry disappeared out the door.

I turned back to my two bunk mates. "Lucky guys!" I teased them.

They both growled back at me in reply. Then we headed up the hill to lunch.

They served pizza for lunch, which is usually my favorite. But today, the pizza was cold and tasted like cardboard, and the cheese stuck to the roof of my mouth.

I wasn't really hungry.

I kept thinking about Dawn and Dori, how frightened they were, how desperate. I wondered when I'd see them again. I wondered if they would

331

swim over and hide at the boys' camp again before Visitors Day.

After lunch, Frank came by our table to pick up Jay and Colin. I asked him if I was supposed to come, too.

"You weren't on the list, Billy," he said, scratching at a mosquito bite on his neck. "I can only take two at a time, you know? The trail gets a little dangerous."

"Dangerous?" Jay asked, climbing up from the table.

Frank grinned at him. "You're a big strong guy," he told Jay. "You'll do okay."

I watched Frank lead Colin and Jay out of the mess hall. Our table was empty now, except for a couple of blond-haired guys I didn't know who were arm-wrestling down at the end near the wall.

I pushed my tray away and stood up. I wanted to go back to the bunk and finish the letter to my parents. But as I took a few steps toward the door, I felt a hand on my shoulder.

I turned to see Larry grinning down at me. "Tennis tournament," he said.

"Huh?" I reacted with surprise.

"Billy, you're representing Bunk 4 in the tennis tournament," Larry said. "Didn't you see the lineup? It was posted on the announcements board."

"But I'm a terrible tennis player!" I protested.

"We're counting on you," Larry replied. "Get a

racquet and get your bod to the courts!"

I spent the afternoon playing tennis. I beat a little kid in straight sets. I had the feeling he had never held a tennis racquet before. Then I lost a long, hard-fought match to one of the blond-haired boys who'd been arm-wrestling at lunch.

I was drowning in sweat, and every muscle in my body ached when the match was over. I headed to the waterfront for a refreshing swim.

Then I returned to the bunk, changed into jeans and a green-and-white Camp Nightmoon T-shirt, and finished my letter to my parents.

It was nearly dinnertime. Jay and Colin weren't back from their hike yet. I decided to go up to the lodge and mail my letter. As I headed up the hill, I saw clusters of kids hurrying to their bunks to change for dinner. But no sign of my two bunk mates.

Holding the letter tightly, I headed around to the back of the lodge building where the camp office was located. The door was wide open, so I walked in. A young woman was usually behind the counter to answer questions and to take the letters to be mailed.

"Anyone here?" I called, leaning over the counter and peering into the tiny back room, which was dark.

No reply.

"Hi. Anyone here?" I repeated, clutching the envelope.

333

No. The office was empty.

Disappointed, I started to leave. Then I glimpsed the large burlap bag on the floor just inside the tiny back room.

The mailbag!

I decided to put my letter in the bag with the others to be mailed. I slipped around the counter and into the back room and crouched down to put my envelope into the bag.

To my surprise, the mailbag was stuffed full with letters. As I pulled the bag open and started to shove my letter inside, a bunch of letters fell out onto the floor.

I started to scoop them up when a letter caught my eye.

It was one of mine. Addressed to my parents.

One I had written yesterday.

"Weird," I muttered aloud.

Bending over the bag, I reached in and pulled out a big handful of letters. I sifted through them quickly. I found a letter Colin had written.

I pulled out another pile.

And my eyes fell upon two other letters I had written nearly a week ago when I first arrived in camp.

I stared at them, feeling a cold chill run down my back.

All of our letters, all of the letters we had written since the first day of camp, were here. In this mailbag.

None of them had been mailed.

We couldn't call home.

And we couldn't *write* home.

Frantically, my hands trembling, I began shoving the envelopes back into the mailbag.

What is going on here? I wondered. *What is going on?*

16

By the time I got into the mess hall, Uncle Al was finishing the evening announcements. I slid into my seat, hoping I hadn't missed anything important.

I expected to see Jay and Colin across the table from me. But their places on the bench were empty.

That's strange, I thought, still shaken from my discovery about the mailbag. They should be back by now.

I wanted to tell them about the mail. I wanted to share the news that our parents weren't getting any of the letters we wrote.

And we weren't getting any of theirs.

The camp had to be keeping our mail from us, I suddenly realized.

Colin and Jay — where are you?

The fried chicken was greasy, and the potatoes were lumpy and tasted like paste. As I forced the food down, I kept turning to glance at the mess hall door, expecting to see my two bunk mates.

But they didn't show up.

A heavy feeling of dread formed in my stomach. Through the mess hall window, I could see that it was already dark outside.

Where could they be?

A three-mile hike and back shouldn't take this many hours.

I pulled myself up and made my way to the counselors' table in the corner. Larry was having a loud argument about sports with two of the other counselors. They were shouting and gesturing with their hands.

Frank's chair was empty.

"Larry, did Frank get back?" I interrupted their discussion.

Larry turned, a startled expression on his face. "Frank?" He motioned to the empty chair at the table. "Guess not."

"He took Jay and Colin on the hike," I said. "Shouldn't they be back by now?"

Larry shrugged. "Beats me." He returned to his argument, leaving me standing there staring at Frank's empty chair.

After the trays had been cleared, we pushed the tables and benches against the wall and had indoor relay races. Everyone seemed to be having a great time. The shouts and cheers echoed off the high-raftered ceiling.

I was too worried about Jay and Colin to enjoy the games.

Maybe they decided to camp out overnight, I told myself.

But I had seen them leave, and I knew they hadn't taken any tents or sleeping bags or other overnight supplies.

So where *were* they?

The games ended a little before lights out. As I followed the crowd to the door, Larry appeared beside me. "We're leaving early tomorrow," he said. "First thing."

"Huh?" I didn't understand what he meant.

"The canoe trip. I'm the canoe counselor. I'll be taking you guys," he explained, seeing my confusion.

"Oh. Okay," I replied without enthusiasm. I was so worried about Jay and Colin, I'd nearly forgotten about the canoe trip.

"Right after breakfast," Larry said. "Wear a bathing suit. Bring a change of clothes. Meet me at the waterfront." He hurried back to help the other counselors pull the tables into place.

"After breakfast," I muttered. I wondered if Jay and Colin were also coming on the canoe trip. I had forgotten to ask Larry.

I headed quickly down the dark hill. The dew had already fallen, and the tall grass was slippery and wet. Halfway down, I could see the dark outline of the Forbidden Bunk, hunched forward as if preparing to strike.

Forcing myself to look away, I jogged the rest of the way to Bunk 4.

To my surprise, I could see through the window that someone was moving around inside.

Colin and Jay are back! I thought.

Eagerly, I pushed open the door and burst inside. "Hey — where've you guys been?" I cried.

I stopped short. And gasped.

Two strangers stared back at me.

One was sitting on the edge of Colin's top bunk, pulling off his sneakers. The other was leaning over the dresser, pulling a T-shirt from one of the drawers.

"Hi. You in here?" the boy at the dresser stood up straight, his eyes studying me. He had very short black hair, and a gold stud in one ear.

I swallowed hard. "Am I in the wrong bunk? Is this Bunk 4?"

They both stared at me, confused.

I saw that the other boy, the one in Colin's bunk, also had black hair, but his was long and scraggly and fell over his forehead. "Yeah. This is Bunk 4," he said.

"We're new," the short-haired boy added. "I'm Tommy, and he's Chris. We just started today."

"Hi," I said uncertainly. "My name's Billy." My heart was pounding like a tom-tom in my chest. "Where's Colin and Jay?"

"Who?" Chris asked. "They told us this bunk was mostly empty."

"Well, Colin and Jay — " I started.

"We just arrived. We don't know anyone," Tommy interrupted. He pushed the drawer shut.

"But that's Jay's drawer," I said, bewildered, pointing. "What did you do with Jay's stuff?"

Tommy gazed back at me in surprise. "The drawer was empty," he replied.

"Almost all the drawers were empty," Chris added, tossing his sneakers down to the floor. "Except for the bottom two drawers."

"That's my stuff," I said, my head spinning. "But Colin and Jay — their stuff was here," I insisted.

"The whole cabin was empty," Tommy said. "Maybe your friends got moved."

"Maybe," I said weakly. I sat down on the lower bunk beneath my bed. My legs felt shaky. A million thoughts were whirring through my mind, all of them frightening.

"This is weird," I said aloud.

"It's not a bad bunk," Chris said, pulling down his blanket and settling in. "Kind of cozy."

"How long you staying at camp?" Tommy asked, pulling on an oversized white T-shirt. "All summer?"

"No!" I exclaimed with a shudder. "I'm not staying!" I sputtered. "I mean — I mean . . . I'm

340

leaving. On . . . uh . . . I'm leaving on Visitors Day next week."

Chris flashed Tommy a surprised glance. "Huh? When are you leaving?" he asked again.

"On Visitors Day," I repeated. "When my parents come up for Visitors Day."

"But didn't you hear Uncle Al's announcement before dinner?" Tommy asked, staring hard at me. "Visitors Day has been canceled!"

17

I drifted in and out of a troubled sleep that night. Even with the blanket pulled up to my chin, I felt chilled and afraid.

It felt so weird to have two strange guys in the bunk, sleeping where Jay and Colin slept. I was worried about my missing friends.

What had happened to them? Why hadn't they come back?

As I tossed restlessly in my top bunk, I heard howls off in the distance. Animal cries, probably coming from the Forbidden Bunk. Long, frightening howls carried by the wind into our open bunk window.

At one point, I thought I heard kids screaming. I sat up straight, suddenly alert, and listened.

Had I dreamed the frightful shrieks? I was so scared and confused, it was impossible to tell what was real and what was a nightmare.

It took hours to fall back to sleep.

I awoke to a gray, overcast morning, the air

heavy and cold. Pulling on swim trunks and a T-shirt, I raced to the lodge to find Larry. I had to find out what had happened to Jay and Colin.

I searched everywhere for him without success. Larry wasn't at breakfast. None of the other counselors admitted to knowing anything. Frank, the counselor who had taken my two friends on the hike, was also not there.

I finally found Larry at the waterfront, preparing a long metal canoe for our river trip. "Larry — where are they?" I cried out breathlessly.

He gazed up at me, holding an armload of canoe paddles. His expression turned to bewilderment. "Huh? Chris and Tommy? They'll be here soon."

"No!" I cried, grabbing his arm. "Jay and Colin! Where are they? What happened to them, Larry? You've *got* to tell me!"

I gripped his arm tightly. I was gasping for breath. I could feel the blood pulsing at my temples. "You've got to tell me!" I repeated shrilly.

He pulled away from me and let the paddles fall beside the canoe. "I don't know anything about them," he replied quietly.

"But Larry!"

"Really, I don't," he insisted in the same quiet voice. His expression softened. He placed a hand on my trembling shoulder. "Tell you what, Billy," he said, staring hard into my eyes. "I'll ask Uncle Al about it after our trip, okay? I'll find out for you. When we get back."

I stared back at him, trying to decide if he was being honest.

I couldn't tell. His eyes were as calm and cold as marbles.

He leaned forward and pushed the canoe into the shallow river water. "Here. Take one of those life preservers," he said, pointing to a pile of blue rubber vests behind me. "Strap it on. Then get in."

I did as he instructed. I saw that I had no choice.

Chris and Tommy came running up to us a few seconds later. They obediently followed Larry's instructions and strapped on the life-preserver vests.

A few minutes later, the four of us were seated cross-legged inside the long, slender canoe, drifting slowly away from the shore.

The sky was still charcoal-gray, the sun hidden behind hovering, dark clouds. The canoe bumped over the choppy river waters. The current was stronger than I had realized. We began to pick up speed. The low trees and shrubs along the riverbank slid past rapidly.

Larry sat facing us in the front of the canoe. He demonstrated how to paddle as the river carried us away.

He watched us carefully, a tight frown on his face, as the three of us struggled to pick up the rhythm he was showing us. Then, when we finally seemed to catch on, Larry grinned and carefully turned around, gripping the sides of the canoe as he shifted his position.

"The sun is trying to come out," he said, his voice muffled in the strong breeze over the rippling water.

I glanced up. The sky looked darker than before.

He stayed with his back to us, facing forward, allowing the three of us to do the paddling. I had never paddled a canoe before. It was harder than I'd imagined. But as I fell into the rhythm of it with Tommy and Chris, I began to enjoy it.

Dark water smacked against the prow of the canoe, sending up splashes of white froth. The current grew stronger, and we picked up speed. The air was still cold, but the steady work of rowing warmed me. After a while, I realized I was sweating.

We rowed past tangles of yellow- and gray-trunked trees. The river suddenly divided in two, and we shifted our paddles to take the left branch. Larry began paddling again, working to keep us off the tall rocks that jutted between the river branches.

The canoe bobbed up and slapped down. Bobbed

up and slapped down. Cold water poured over the sides.

The sky darkened even more. I wondered if it was about to storm.

As the river widened, the current grew rapid and strong. I realized we didn't really need to paddle. The river current was doing most of the work.

The river sloped down. Wide swirls of frothing white water made the canoe leap and bounce.

"Here come the rapids!" Larry shouted, cupping his hands around his mouth so we could hear him. "Hang on! It gets pretty wild!"

I felt a tremor of fear as a wave of icy water splashed over me. The canoe rose up on a shelf of white water, then hit hard as it landed.

I could hear Tommy and Chris laughing excitedly behind me.

Another icy wave rolled over the canoe, startling me. I cried out and nearly let go of my paddle.

Tommy and Chris laughed again.

I took a deep breath and held on tightly to the paddle, struggling to keep up the rhythm.

"Hey, look!" Larry cried suddenly.

To my astonishment, he climbed to his feet. He leaned forward, pointing into the swirling, white water.

"Look at those fish!" he shouted.

As he leaned down, the canoe was jarred by a powerful rush of current. The canoe spun to the right.

I saw the startled look on Larry's face as he lost his balance. His arms shot forward, and he plunged headfirst into the tossing waters.

"Noooooo!" I screamed.

I glanced back at Tommy and Chris, who had stopped paddling and were staring into the swirling, dark waters, their expressions frozen in open-mouthed horror.

"Larry! Larry!" I was screaming the name over and over without realizing it.

The canoe continued to slide rapidly down the churning waters.

Larry didn't come up.

"Larry!"

Behind me, Tommy and Chris also called out his name, their voices shrill and frightened.

Where was he? Why didn't he swim to the surface?

The canoe was drifting farther and farther downriver.

"Larrrrrry!"

"We have to stop!" I screamed. "We have to slow down!"

"We can't!" Chris shouted back. "We don't know how!"

Still no sign of Larry. I realized he must be in trouble.

Without thinking, I tossed my paddle into the river, climbed to my feet, and plunged into the dark, swirling waters to save him.

18

I jumped without thinking and swallowed a mouthful of the brown water as I went down.

My heart thudded in my chest as I struggled frantically to the surface, sputtering and choking.

Gasping in a deep breath, I lowered my head and tried to swim against the current. My sneakers felt as if they weighed a thousand pounds.

I realized I should have pulled them off before I jumped.

The water heaved and tossed. I moved my arms in long, desperate strokes, pulling myself toward the spot where Larry had fallen. Glancing back, I saw the canoe, a dark blur growing smaller and smaller.

"Wait!" I wanted to shout to Tommy and Chris. "Wait for me to get Larry!"

But I knew that they didn't know how to slow the canoe. They were helpless as the current carried them away.

Where was Larry?

I sucked in another mouthful of air — and froze as I felt a sharp cramp in my right leg.

The pain shot up through my entire right side.

I slid under the water and waited for the pain to lessen.

The cramp seemed to tighten until I could barely move the leg. Water rushed over me. I struggled to pull myself up to the surface.

As I choked in more air, I stroked rapidly and hard, pulling myself up, ignoring the sharp pain in my leg.

Hey!

What was that object floating just ahead of me? A piece of driftwood being carried by the current?

Brown water washed over me, blinding me, tossing me back. Sputtering, I pulled myself back up.

Water rolled down my face. I struggled to see.

Larry!

He came floating right to me.

"Larry! Larry!" I managed to scream.

But he didn't answer me. I could see clearly now that he was floating face down.

The leg cramp miraculously vanished as I reached out with both arms and grabbed Larry's shoulders. I pulled his head up from the water, rolled him onto his back, and wrapped my arm around his neck. I was using the lifesaving technique my parents had taught me.

Turning downriver, I searched for the canoe. But the current had carried it out of sight.

I swallowed another mouthful of icy water. Choking, I held onto Larry. I kicked hard. My right leg still felt tight and weak, but at least the pain had gone. Kicking and pulling with my free hand, I dragged Larry toward the shore.

To my relief, the current helped. It seemed to pull in the same direction.

A few seconds later, I was close enough to shore to stand. Wearily, panting like a wild animal, I tottered to my feet and dragged Larry onto the wet mud of the shore.

Was he dead? Had he drowned before I reached him?

I stretched him out on his back and, still panting loudly, struggling to catch my breath, to stop my entire body from trembling, I leaned over him.

And he opened his eyes.

He stared up at me blankly, as if he didn't recognize me.

Finally, he whispered my name. "Billy," he choked out, "are we okay?"

Larry and I rested for a bit. Then we walked back to camp, following the river upstream.

We were soaked clear through and drenched with mud, but I didn't care. We were alive. We were okay. I had saved Larry's life.

We didn't talk much all the way back. It was taking every ounce of strength we had just to walk.

I asked Larry if he thought Tommy and Chris would be okay.

"Hope so," he muttered, breathing hard. "They'll probably ride to shore and walk back like us."

I took this opportunity to ask him again about Jay and Colin. I thought maybe Larry would tell me the truth since we were completely alone and since I had just saved his life.

But he insisted he didn't know anything about my two bunk mates. As we walked, he raised one hand and swore he didn't know anything at all.

"So many frightening things have happened," I muttered.

He nodded, keeping his eyes straight ahead. "It's been strange," he agreed.

I waited for him to say more. But he walked on in silence.

It took three hours to walk back. We hadn't traveled downriver as far as I had thought, but the muddy shore kept twisting and turning, making our journey longer.

As the camp came into view, my knees buckled and my legs nearly collapsed under me.

Breathing hard, drenched in perspiration, our

clothes still damp and covered in mud, we trudged wearily onto the waterfront.

"Hey — !" a voice called from the swim area. Uncle Al, dressed in baggy, green sweats, came hurrying across the dirt to us. "What happened?" he asked Larry.

"We had an accident!" I cried before Larry had a chance to reply.

"I fell in," Larry admitted, his face reddening beneath the splattered mud. "Billy jumped in and saved me. We walked back."

"But Tommy and Chris couldn't stop the canoe. They drifted away!" I cried.

"We both nearly drowned," Larry told the frowning camp director. "But, Billy — he saved my life."

"Can you send someone to find Tommy and Chris?" I asked, suddenly starting to shake all over, from exhaustion, I guess.

"The two boys floated on downriver?" Uncle Al asked, staring hard at Larry, scratching the back of his fringe of yellow hair.

Larry nodded.

"We have to find them!" I insisted, trembling harder.

Uncle Al continued to glare at Larry. "What about my canoe?" he demanded angrily. "That's our best canoe! How am I supposed to replace it?"

Larry shrugged unhappily.

"We'll have to go look for that canoe tomorrow," Uncle Al snapped.

He doesn't care about the two boys, I realized. *He doesn't care about them at all.*

"Go get into dry clothes," Uncle Al instructed Larry and me. He stormed off toward the lodge, shaking his head.

I turned and started to the cabin, feeling chilled, my entire body still trembling. I could feel a strong wave of anger sweep over me.

I had just saved Larry's life, but Uncle Al didn't care about that.

And he didn't care that two campers were lost on the river.

He didn't care that two campers and a counselor never returned from their hike.

He didn't care that boys were attacked by *creatures!*

He didn't care that kids disappeared and were never mentioned again.

He didn't care about any of us.

He only cared about his canoe.

My anger quickly turned to fear.

Of course, I had no way of knowing that the *scariest* part of my summer was still to come.

19

I was all alone in the bunk that night.

I pulled an extra blanket onto my bed and slid into a tight ball beneath the covers. I wondered if I'd be able to fall asleep. Or if my frightened, angry thoughts would keep me tossing and turning for another night.

But I was so weary and exhausted, even the eerie, mournful howls from the Forbidden Bunk couldn't keep me awake.

I fell into deep blackness and didn't wake up until I felt someone shaking my shoulders.

Startled alert, I sat straight up. "Larry!" I cried, my voice still clogged with sleep. "What's happening?"

I squinted across the room. Larry's bed was rumpled, the blanket balled up at the end. He had obviously come in late and slept in the bunk.

But Tommy's and Chris's beds were still untouched from the day before.

"Special hike," Larry said, walking over to his bunk. "Hurry. Get dressed."

"Huh?" I stretched and yawned. Outside the window, it was still gray. The sun hadn't risen. "What kind of hike?"

"Uncle Al called a special hike," Larry replied, his back to me. He grabbed the sheet and started to make his bed.

With a groan, I lowered myself to the cabin floor. It felt cold beneath my bare feet. "Don't we get to rest? I mean, after what happened yesterday?" I glanced once again at Tommy's and Chris's unused beds.

"It's not just us," Larry replied, smoothing the sheet. "It's the whole camp. Everyone's going. Uncle Al is leading it."

I pulled on a pair of jeans, stumbling across the cabin with one leg in. A sudden feeling of dread fell over me. "It wasn't scheduled," I said darkly. "Where is Uncle Al taking us?"

Larry didn't reply.

"Where?" I repeated shrilly.

He pretended he didn't hear me.

"Tommy and Chris — they didn't come back?" I asked glumly, pulling on my sneakers. Luckily, I had brought two pairs. My shoes from yesterday sat in the corner, still soaked through and mud-covered.

"They'll turn up," Larry replied finally. But he didn't sound as if he meant it.

I finished getting dressed, then ran up the hill to get breakfast. It was a warm, gray morning. It must have rained during the night. The tall grass glistened wetly.

Yawning and blinking against the harsh gray light, campers headed quietly up the hill. I saw that most of them had the same confused expression I had.

Why were we going on this unscheduled hike so early in the morning? How long was it going to be? Where were we going?

I hoped that Uncle Al or one of the counselors would explain everything to us at breakfast, but none of them appeared in the mess hall.

We ate quietly, without the usual joking around.

I found myself thinking about the terrifying canoe trip yesterday. I could almost taste the brackish brown water again. I saw Larry floating toward me, facedown, floating on the churning water like a clump of seaweed.

I pictured myself trying to get to him, struggling to swim, struggling to go against the current, to keep afloat in the swirls of white water.

And I saw the blur of the canoe as the strong river current carried it out of sight.

Suddenly Dawn and Dori burst into my thoughts. I wondered if they were okay. I wondered if they were going to try and meet me again by the waterfront.

357

Breakfast was French toast with syrup. It was usually my favorite. But this morning, I just poked at it with my fork.

"Line up outside!" a counselor cried from the doorway.

Chairs scraped loudly. We all obediently climbed to our feet and began making our way outside.

Where are they taking us?

Why doesn't anyone tell us what this is about?

The sky had brightened to pink, but the sun still hadn't risen over the horizon.

We formed a single line along the side wall of the lodge. I was near the end of the line toward the bottom of the hill.

Some kids were cracking jokes and playfully shoving each other. But most were standing quietly or leaning against the wall, waiting to see what was going to happen.

Once the line was formed, one of the counselors walked the length of it, pointing his finger and moving his lips in concentration as he counted us. He counted us twice to make sure he had the right number.

Then Uncle Al appeared at the front of the line. He wore a brown-and-green camouflage outfit, the kind soldiers wear in movies. He had on very black sunglasses, even though the sun wasn't up yet.

He didn't say a word. He signaled to Larry and

another counselor, who were both carrying very large, heavy-looking brown bags over their shoulders. Then Uncle Al strode quickly down the hill, his eyes hidden behind the dark glasses, his features set in a tight frown.

He stopped in front of the last camper. "This way!" he announced loudly, pointing toward the waterfront.

Those were his only words. "This way!"

And we began to follow, walking at a pretty fast clip. Our sneakers slid against the wet grass. A few kids were giggling about something behind me.

To my surprise, I realized I was now nearly at the front of the line. I was close enough to call out to Uncle Al. So I did. "Where are we going?" I shouted.

He quickened his pace and didn't reply.

"Uncle Al — is this a long hike?" I called.

He pretended he hadn't heard.

I decided to give up.

He led us toward the waterfront, then turned right. Thick clumps of trees stood a short way up ahead where the river narrowed.

Glancing back to the end of the line, I saw Larry and the other counselor, bags on their shoulders, hurrying to catch up to Uncle Al.

What is this about? I wondered.

And as I stared at the clumps of low, tangled

trees up ahead, a thought pushed its way into my head.

I can escape.

The thought was so frightening — but suddenly so real — it took a long time to form.

I can escape into these trees.

I can run away from Uncle Al and this frightening camp.

The idea was so exciting, I nearly stumbled over my own feet. I bumped into the kid ahead of me, a big bruiser of a guy named Tyler, and he turned and glared at me.

Whoa, I told myself, feeling my heart start to pound in my chest. Think about this. Think carefully. . . .

I kept my eyes locked on the woods. As we drew closer, I could see that the thick trees, so close together that their branches were all intertwined, seemed to stretch on forever.

They'd never find me in there, I told myself. It would be really easy to hide in those woods.

But then what?

I couldn't stay in the woods forever.

Then what?

Staring at the trees, I forced myself to concentrate, forced myself to think clearly.

I could follow the river. Yes. Stay on the shore. Follow the river. It was bound to come to a town eventually. It *had* to come to a town.

I'd walk to the first town. Then I'd call my parents.

I can do it, I thought, so excited I could barely stay in line.

I just have to run. Make a dash for it. When no one is looking. Into the woods. Deep into the woods.

We were at the edge of the trees now. The sun had pulled itself up, brightening the rose-colored morning sky. We stood in the shadows of the trees.

I can do it, I told myself.

Soon.

My heart thudded loudly. I was sweating even though the air was still cool.

Calm down, Billy, I warned myself. *Just calm down.*

Wait your chance.

Wait till the time is right.

Then leave Camp Nightmare behind. Forever.

Standing in the shade, I studied the trees. I spotted a narrow path into the woods a few yards up ahead.

I tried to calculate how long it would take me to reach the path. Probably ten seconds at most. And, then, in another five seconds, I could be into the protection of the trees.

I can do it, I thought.

I can be gone in less than ten seconds.

I took a deep breath. I braced myself. I tensed my leg muscles, preparing to run.

Then I glanced to the front of the line.

To my horror, Uncle Al was staring directly at me. And he held a rifle in his hands.

20

I cried out when I saw the rifle in his hands.

Had he read my thoughts? Did he know I was about to make a run for it?

A cold chill slid down my back as I gaped at the rifle. As I raised my eyes to Uncle Al's face, I realized he wasn't looking at me.

He had turned his attention to the two counselors. They had lowered the bags to the ground and were bending over them, trying to get them open.

"Why did we stop?" Tyler, the kid ahead of me, asked.

"Is the hike over?" another kid joked. A few kids laughed.

"Guess we can go back now," another kid said.

I stood watching in disbelief as Larry and the other counselor began unloading rifles from the two bags.

"Line up and get one," Uncle Al instructed us, tapping the handle of his own rifle against the ground. "One rifle per boy. Come on — hurry!"

No one moved. I think everyone thought Uncle Al was kidding or something.

"What's *wrong* with you boys? I said *hurry!*" he snapped angrily. He grabbed up an armload of rifles and began moving down the line, pushing one into each boy's hands.

He pushed a rifle against my chest so hard, I staggered back a few steps. I grabbed it by the barrel before it fell to the ground.

"What's going on?" Tyler asked me.

I shrugged, studying the rifle with horror. I'd never held any kind of real gun before. My parents were both opposed to firearms of all kinds.

A few minutes later, we were all lined up in the shadow of the trees, each holding a rifle. Uncle Al stood near the middle of the line and motioned us into a tight circle so we could hear him.

"What's going on? Is this target practice?" one boy asked.

Larry and the other counselor snickered at that. Uncle Al's features remained hard and serious.

"Listen up," he barked. "No more jokes. This is serious business."

The circle of campers tightened around him. We grew silent. A bird squawked noisily in a nearby tree. Somehow it reminded me of my plan to escape.

Was I about to be really sorry that I hadn't made a run for it?

"Two girls escaped from the girls' camp last night," Uncle Al announced in a flat, businesslike tone. "A blonde and a redhead."

Dawn and Dori! I exclaimed to myself. I'll bet it was them!

"I believe," Uncle Al continued, "that these are the same two girls who sneaked over to the boys' camp and hid near the waterfront a few days ago."

Yes! I thought happily. It *is* Dawn and Dori! They escaped!

I suddenly realized a broad smile had broken out on my face. I quickly forced it away before Uncle Al could see my happy reaction to the news.

"The two girls are in these woods, boys. They're nearby," Uncle Al continued. He raised his rifle. "Your guns are loaded. Aim carefully when you see them. They won't get away from us!"

21

"Huh?" I gasped in disbelief. "You mean we're supposed to *shoot* them?"

I glanced around the circle of campers. They all looked as dazed and confused as I did.

"Yeah. You're supposed to shoot them," Uncle Al replied coldly. "I *told* you — they're trying to escape."

"But we can't!" I cried.

"It's easy," Uncle Al said. He raised his rifle to his shoulder and pretended to fire it. "See? Nothing to it."

"But we can't kill people!" I insisted.

"Kill?" His expression changed behind the dark glasses. "I didn't say anything about killing, did I? These guns are loaded with tranquilizer darts. We just want to stop these girls — not hurt them."

Uncle Al took two steps toward me, the rifle still in his hands. He stood over me menacingly, lowering his face close to mine.

"You got a problem with that, Billy?" he demanded.

He was challenging me.

I saw the other boys back away.

The woods grew silent. Even the bird stopped squawking.

"You got a problem with that?" Uncle Al repeated, his face so close to mine, I could smell his sour breath.

Terrified, I took a step back, then another.

Why was he doing this to me? Why was he challenging me like this?

I took a deep breath and held it. Then I screamed as loudly as I could: "I — I won't do it!"

Without completely realizing what I was doing, I raised the rifle to my shoulder and aimed the barrel at Uncle Al's chest.

"You're gonna be sorry," Uncle Al growled in a low voice. He tore off the sunglasses and heaved them into the woods. Then he narrowed his eyes furiously at me. "Drop the rifle, Billy. I'm gonna make you sorry."

"No," I told him, standing my ground. "You're not. Camp is over. You're not going to do anything."

My legs were trembling so hard, I could barely stand.

But I wasn't going to go hunting Dawn and Dori. I wasn't going to do anything else Uncle Al said. Ever.

"Give me the rifle, Billy," he said in his low, menacing voice. He reached out a hand toward my gun. "Hand it over, boy."

"No!" I cried.

"Hand it over now," he ordered, his eyes narrowed, burning into mine. "Now!"

"No!" I cried.

He blinked once. Twice.

Then he leapt at me.

I took a step back with the rifle aimed at Uncle Al — and pulled the trigger.

22

The rifle emitted a soft *pop*.

Uncle Al tossed his head back and laughed. He let his rifle drop to the ground at his feet.

"Hey — !" I cried out, confused. I kept the rifle aimed at his chest.

"Congratulations, Billy," Uncle Al said, grinning warmly at me. "You passed." He stepped forward and reached out his hand to shake mine.

The other campers dropped their rifles. Glancing at them, I saw that they were all grinning, too. Larry, also grinning, flashed me a thumbs-up sign.

"What's going on?" I demanded suspiciously. I slowly lowered the rifle.

Uncle Al grabbed my hand and squeezed it hard. "Congratulations, Billy. I *knew* you'd pass."

"Huh? I don't understand!" I screamed, totally frustrated.

But instead of explaining anything to me, Uncle Al turned to the trees and shouted, "Okay, everyone! It's over! He passed! Come out and congratulate him!"

And as I stared in disbelief, my wide-open mouth hanging down around my knees, people began stepping out from behind the trees.

First came Dawn and Dori.

"You *were* hiding in the woods!" I cried.

They laughed in response. "Congratulations!" Dawn cried.

And then others came out, grinning and congratulating me. I screamed when I recognized Mike. He was okay!

Beside him were Jay and Roger!

Colin stepped out of the woods, followed by Tommy and Chris. All smiling and happy and okay.

"What — what's going *on* here?" I stammered. I was totally stunned. I felt dizzy.

I didn't get it. I really didn't get it.

And then my mom and dad stepped out from the trees. Mom rushed up and gave me a hug. Dad patted the top of my head. "I knew you'd pass, Billy," he said. I could see happy tears in his eyes.

Finally, I couldn't take it anymore. I pushed Mom gently away. "Passed *what*?" I demanded. "What *is* this? What's going on?"

Uncle Al put his arm around my shoulder and guided me away from the group of campers. Mom and Dad followed close behind.

"This isn't really a summer camp," Uncle Al explained, still grinning at me, his face bright pink. "It's a government-testing lab."

"Huh?" I swallowed hard.

"You know your parents are scientists, Billy," Uncle Al continued. "Well, they're about to leave on a very important expedition. And this time they wanted to take you along with them."

"How come you didn't tell me?" I asked my parents.

"We couldn't!" Mom exclaimed.

"According to government rules, Billy," Uncle Al continued, "children aren't allowed to go on official expeditions unless they pass certain tests. That's what you've been doing here. You've been taking tests."

"Tests to see what?" I demanded, still dazed.

"Well, we wanted to see if you could obey orders," Uncle Al explained. "You passed when you refused to go to the Forbidden Bunk." He held up two fingers. "Second, we had to test your bravery. You demonstrated that by rescuing Larry." He held up a third finger. "Third, we had to see if you knew when *not* to follow orders. You passed that test by refusing to hunt for Dawn and Dori."

"And everyone was in on it?" I asked. "All the campers? The counselors? Everyone? They were all actors?"

Uncle Al nodded. "They all work here at the testing lab." His expression turned serious. "You see, Billy, your parents want to take you to a very dangerous place, perhaps the most dangerous place in the known universe. So we had to make sure you can handle it."

The most dangerous place in the universe?

"Where?" I asked my parents. "Where are you taking me?"

"It's a very strange planet called Earth," Dad replied, glancing at Mom. "It's very far from here. But it could be exciting. The inhabitants there are weird and unpredictable, and no one has ever studied them."

Laughing, I stepped between my mom and dad and put my arms around them. "Earth?! It sounds pretty weird. But it could *never* be as dangerous or exciting as Camp Nightmoon!" I exclaimed.

"We'll see," Mom replied quietly. "We'll see."

About the Author

R. L. STINE is the author of the series *Fear Street, Nightmare Room, Give Yourself Goosebumps,* and the phenomenally successful *Goosebumps.* His thrilling teen titles have sold more than 250 million copies internationally — enough to earn him a spot in the *Guinness Book of World Records*! Mr. Stine lives in New York City with his wife, Jane, and his son, Matt.

If You Liked
The Campfire Collection, You'll Love

MONSTER BLOOD!

Goosebumps®

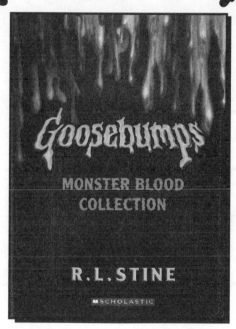

Three spooky tales about an innocent looking can marked "monster blood." When Evan buys it as a freaky gag, he discovers the can is anything but innocent—and the monster blood inside has a monstrous appetite to go along with its terrifying powers.

SCHOLASTIC, GOOSEBUMPS, and associated logos are trademarks and/or registered trademarks of Scholastic Inc.

■ SCHOLASTIC